Clues & Cruel Catastrophes

Cleverly Shores Small Town Cozy Mystery

Renee Lyles

CONTENTS

INTRODUCTION

Finding a dead woman that had drifted to shore right outside the diner, isn't how she anticipated her re-opening day.

When Holly Middleton's father passed away, the family's business died alongside him. The diner was very well loved by the community. Holly didn't realize how the closing of the diner would impact her, so she packed up her stuff in New York and was looking forward to her new start.

Once she was back in her hometown, she couldn't wait to re-open the diner again.

She soon realized someone was framing her for the murder of Annalisa Rice, owner of the rival diner in town. Sheriff Carlton, who didn't seem to like Holly much, jumped at the chance to arrest her.

Holly and Scarlet, her loose-lipped best friend, are unraveling the clues in order to prove her innocence. Small towns talk, and right now, the talk in town is not looking good for Holly's return.

Once the murder is solved, she can get back to building the diner of her dreams, but first she must uncover the secrets her father left behind.

It's a rat race against time to find out who the real killer is before Holly ends up in the grave next to Annalisa.

CHAPTER ONE

"Look who's back in town." The familiar light-breezy tone murmured behind Holly made her freeze in her stride that Sunday afternoon. It didn't take much for her to figure out who was behind her. Holly spent the past few years speaking to the woman nearly every day over the phone.

The cool afternoon sea-breeze ruffled Holly's hair as a small smile spread out on her lips. Holly heard the whoosh of ocean waves as it crashed into the shores a few feet away from them, and the sound smoothed over her. It released a euphoric feeling of serenity that she always enjoyed.

Perks of living in a beach town. Holly especially loved the view of the beach from her room upstairs, above the diner. She never grew tired of it.

"Scarlet," Holly greeted as she turned around and spread her arms wide for her best friend's hug.

"It's good to have you back," Scarlet murmured as they hugged tightly, both cradling each other close.

"It's good to be back," she moved away from her friend a little. She brushed off some strands of hair from her face and tucked them behind her ear. "I never thought I'd say this, but I missed Cleverly Shores. I missed you even more."

"Aww..." Both women chuckled as they hugged again, and Holly took the time to admire her friend once she stepped back.

"What has it been, five years? Not much has changed since you've been gone, trust me. Cleverly Shores is just as you remember it."

"All of it?" Holly lead Scarlet inside the diner she spent her entire morning cleaning. The place was a dusty mess. Every corner and floorboard needed cleaning. The windows were blackened by years of dirt. Holly had contemplated hiring a cleaning company at first, but then she decided to just get it done herself.

She had started out in the kitchen, then worked her way through the rest of the dining area, till she got to the front porch.

"Well maybe not all of it. There's been a few developments," Scarlet answered with a cheery laugh. "At least we've got a bigger park now. Oh right, and there's a bonfire this Wednesday night. You should come to that and meet up with some of the people in the community. It'll give you an opportunity to catch up with some people you haven't seen in years and let them know you are back to stay. I know it will be a good time."

Inside the diner now, Scarlet looked around. "You're working magic here already. This place has been out of business for a long time. It's hard to even remember what the recipes taste like."

"Well, not for long," Holly told her as she lifted a box of cleaning supplies from the ground and placed them on the table. "I'm back now! And I'm starting up Frijole's again. I should have it up and running in just a couple days. Thankfully, there's not much to fix up besides the broken pipes in the kitchen. The bonfire night sounds like the perfect chance to let the town know I'm back in business, don't you think? I'll definitely be there."

Scarlet nodded, "Well, if you need any help, I'm always a ring away. Frijole's has always been my favorite diner. Your dad's enchiladas can't be compared to any others, not even Double Flavors. Ever since your dad shut down the diner, Annalisa Rice's restaurant has become a franchise without competition."

The mention of Frijole's rich competition reminded Holly a little of the last time she was here in Cleverly Shores. She recalled the day like it just happened, even though it was five years ago. Annalisa wasted no time at all coming over and relished in the fact that the diner had to temporarily close due to some licensing issues.

"She still walks around town gloating to everyone about how successful her business is. Everyone knows her husband funded the entire thing from scratch, but who cares? She's the boss. Always has been."

Scarlet took off the shawl wrapped around her neck and eased herself down on one chair. Holly realized her friend was just as she remembered. Brown hair cropped to her shoulders just like Holly's, and a vibrant shade of brown eyes. Scarlet's ever standing grin spread out wider as she stared at Holly with excitement.

"Want to know something even better," Scarlet continued with her gossip. Holly noticed that her friend's penchant for gossip still remained the same. It lured a smile onto Holly's lips as she pulled out a chair for herself. "Annalisa got divorced. She cheated on Mr. Rice...Big scandal and he filed for a divorce. It was messy, trust me. The entire town knew about it."

"Wow, a lot really has happened," Holly whispered as she took all of Scarlet's info in all at once.

Holly's mind was still processing when she heard the nearby rev of a car's engine. She stood up, walked to the window, and stared outside to see a white Mercedes pull up in front of her property.

"Expecting someone?" Scarlet came over to stand by Holly's side and gasped once the car door opened and the driver stepped out. "Speak of the devil. Why is Annalisa visiting you?"

"To gloat?" Holly suggested and Scarlet scoffed in return. "Who knows? It's not like Annalisa's that unpredictable."

Holly's sentence was barely complete when the front door swung open. Her presence instantly filled the air with the thick citrusy scent of her perfume. The woman was just as Holly remembered her. Tall, with a model like slenderness, and platinum blonde hair she liked to wear cropped short to her neck. Her eyes are the same mariner blue. They have a chilled feel each time she stared at someone, and Holly was never able to be at ease around her, even in the past.

Holly muffled a sigh as she remembered sneaking into the Rice's beach mansion during the summers to spend time with their son Timothy. The fond memories of their short-lived romance warmed her heart for a few seconds. Immediately, she shrugged off the nostalgic feeling before it took over. Holly rarely ever thought of Timothy. Not after how she ended their romance and left Cleverly Shores without saying goodbye.

"Holly," Annalisa greeted with a cheery smile that didn't reach her eyes. "It's so good to see you again, dear. When I heard the rumors that you were back in town, I couldn't believe it."

"It's nice to see you too, Mrs. Rice. You look good as always."

"Thanks dear."

"Hello, Mrs. Rice," Scarlet greeted with a wave, but she barely spared her a glance and responded with a small nod.

Holly and Scarlet fell quiet as her piercing eyes scanned the entire dining area. She held a designer purse in her left hand, and her right hand sat on her hip with poise.

"This place is just as I remember it," she commented before her eyes settled on Holly again. "It's going to take a lot to bring this place back to life, and even with all the repairs you might have to do, it still won't be up to standard." She smiled as she looked right at Holly, "Cleverly Shores now has standardized restaurants thanks to Double Flavors."

"I heard," Holly responded while keeping her smile. "I'm sure you still serve the best enchiladas anyone in Cleverly Shores has ever tasted."

"Of course," she laughed, and the bubbling cheeriness spiked a little irritation in Holly.

Can the woman's pride get worse than this?

"Trust me dear, it really is the best. I wish you all the luck though. You'll need it to get this place going again."

"Thank you, Mrs. Rice."

She tilted one shoulder up in a carefree shrug, hummed once, then turned and walked out of the door. Once she was gone and out of sight, Holly and Scarlett exchanged knowing looks.

"Told you she was here to brag," Holly said to her friend as they both walked to the window to watch Annalisa drive off.

"You know what? We should visit Double Flavors tonight. Their enchiladas are really not that good." Scarlet frowned as she commented, then rolled her eyes. "Their pizza's the worst. Your crust wasn't that dry on your first try, trust me."

"I don't see Annalisa as competition," She told Scarlet before walking away from the window so she could continue her cleaning. "Besides, Cleverly Shores is big enough to have more than one good Mexican diner, don't you think?"

"Absolutely. That's a great way to think about it," Scarlet agreed just before a long howl speared into the air around them and stopped both of them in their tracks. Holly turned to Scarlet, "Did you hear that?"

"Sounds like a ..." Holly didn't complete her sentence before a tiny bark cut in again. This time, she walked out of the diner, and around the building to check for the noise.

There was a German short-haired pointer wandering around the back yard when Holly and Scarlet arrived. The dog froze for a second once she noticed them, then barked again before rushing towards Holly while wagging her tail.

"That's Mrs. Genesis's dog," Scarlet murmured once the dog neared them and Holly dropped to a squat to gently touch her head. "Mrs. Genesis, our English teacher in the sixth grade...she passed away a few months ago."

"Oh, that is sad," Holly sympathized while the dog kept wagging her tail. She continued to stroke her head a little, and sighed, "She's probably all alone. Did Mrs. Genesis live by herself?"

"Yeah, she did. And I know this dog meant a lot to her."

"Good dog." The dog started to jump a little, salivate, then jumped around some more. "I think I'm going to keep her. Sounds like we both could use the company."

"You think you can handle a dog on your own?"

"I had a puppy once, remember? They are like kids. All you need to give them is a little love and attention."

Holly ruffled the dog's head some more as she barked and lied on the sandy ground before rolling around in it. "See," she pointed out, "A little love and attention."

Scarlet still looked a bit skeptical. "If you say so," she agreed before folding her hands over her chest. "It's probably not a bad idea since you are all by yourself in the apartment."

Holly smirked at her friend and returned her attention to the playful dog. Scarlet was right, the last time she was in Cleverly Shores, she had her father. Now she was alone. Scarlet was the closest person she had to family, and this dog could be a good companion to have around.

"I'll call her Chile. It's got a nice ring to it."

CHAPTER TWO

Two days later, Holly and Scarlet delighted in a long stroll at the town's annual bonfire anniversary celebration. Holly was enjoying the cool breeze in the night's air while almost the entire town was gathered around the beach shore.

The wind tugged at Holly's clothes and hair. The briny sea air carried a whiff of burning wood chips from the nearby barbecue stand. The light music played in the well-lit beach area lightened up the mood, and the folks gathered around seemed to be having a good time.'

The serenity of the beach at night reminded Holly how much she missed strolling here in the evenings, and running in the mornings when the sun was just about to come out to play. Or when the air still carried a hint of rain from the previous night. Life in a big city was much more of a haze compared to a small town like Cleverly Shores. Here, you could go through each day in a more relaxed state and not have to worry about the hassles of getting around.

Even the night's velvety darkness did little to hide the stars that shimmered up in the sky as she raised her head took it all in for a bit. "I use to love it here so much. The long walks, the early-morning runs."

"Now that you're back, you'll get plenty of those. I run our usual trail every morning with John. You can join us if you want."

"Running with you and your husband? That doesn't sound like much fun...I'm kidding. You two are the only people I've got around anymore."

"That will change once you get the diner up and running again. This is the best chance to let people know you're re-opening Frijole's. Trust me, a lot of the locals loved your dad's recipes and will be excited you're back."

"You think it's a good idea to bring it up to the people I speak to tonight?" The sea breeze blew against her face and ruffled her hair a little, and the hem of her floral print short dress. The denim jacket Holly paired with it did little to protect her skin from the chilly wind. She was starting to regret choosing a pair of sandals over boots.

"When would you rather let people know you're back in business? Now's the best time."

Scarlet has barely finished her statement when the town's priest Reuben Docherty spotted them both, waved and walked over to say hello.

"Beautiful evening to you too, Miss Barber," he said with a smile after Holly greeted him a good evening and extended a hand for a shake. "Never thought you'd be back in Cleverly Shores. It's wonderful having you around after so long."

"Cleverly Shores is home. It feels good to be back."

"It is home indeed," he answered with a nod. "And it's a good thing that you're here tonight. I would love to talk with you about joining the founder's council. Have you considered taking your father's spot? Mrs. Genesis recently passed away and she was the last representative of the Genesis family. We are now down two members, and since you're back in town, you might want to consider picking up his role on the advisory committee...Your family is, after all, one of the founders."

Holly is speechless as he laid out the offer, and she gasped at first before blinking rapidly. "I have actually never considered joining the committee," Holly blurted. "You think it's a good idea to have someone as young as me?"

"We need young ones like you. The rest of us won't be around forever," he replied in a gentle voice. Mr. Docherty always spoke softly as she remembered.

His smile reached the wrinkling corners of his eyes now, and he gently touched her hand. "Just give it some thought dear, and let me know what you decide by the end of the week."

"Thank you for thinking of me. I will definitely think about it."

"What about your mother? Have you heard from her recently?" The priest's eyes searched hers as he asked, and he linked his fingers together in front of him, posed as he awaited her reply.

His question made Holly's smile dwindle a little. Another person she never let herself think of was her mother.

Why think of a woman who walked out on her eight-year-old kid, and husband without looking back or ever calling?

Holly's throat tightened as that sunny afternoon filtered into her memory. The images flashing in her mind dampened her mood and it took a moment for her to shake off the cloud of wistful thinking.

"She's doing great. She's travelling. Last time we spoke she was in Texas. She wants to experience life in the southern parts of the country for the summer."

"That's good. Send my regards." He shook her hand one more time before nodding at Scarlet too. "I hope to see you two around more often."

"Goodnight, Mr. Docherty," Holly and Scarlet chorused. Once the man was out of ear shot, Scarlet faced Holly and arched a brow. "Travelling? You've not spoke to your mother since you were eight."

"Yeah, but they don't know that, remember? My dad never told anyone why she left. It's best we keep it that way."

They continued their stroll as Holly's mind drifted away again to the last time she shared breakfast with her family. The thick silence that morning had been deafening. At eight, Holly had experienced a lot of silence...long enough to understand when her parents either wanted to have a fight or didn't want to talk at all.

That morning, neither of them wanted to talk.

"Sheriff," Scarlet said beside Holly, and her cheery tone pulled Holly back to reality. "It's good to see you here tonight."

"Holly Barber," Sheriff Dennis Carlton said in a thick voice that Holly remembered very clearly. She could already picture his smile, even before she looked up at him. "Everyone in town keeps speaking of your return to Cleverly Shores."

"Cleverly Shores is still home, Sheriff Carlton. It is good to see you."

Scarlet excused herself as Holly slid into a light conversation with the sheriff. Growing up in Cleverly Shores, she had seen a lot of him as he was great friends with her parents. Somehow along the way, things became tense between them though. Holly didn't know how or why it began. All she recalled was that one afternoon her mom walked out. The next day, her dad got into a huge fight with the sheriff.

Nothing was the same since then.

"Yes, yes.... And what place is better than home, yeah?" His eyes didn't hold the same smile that used to spread out on his lips.

The years have aged him a lot, but Holly remembered his eyes just as they are. Dark and brooding. *As cold as ever.*

"Sometimes it's better off if you're far away from small towns like this one. They have a way of sucking you into every cycle and drama going on. It's never worth it."

The man's jaw hardened into a frown as he spoke to her, and it made Holly wonder if there was ever a time she had offended him.

"But my family has a business here. I'm re-opening Frijole's. It's what my father would have wanted."

"Yes, Pete was a good man. Every time I visit him at the cemetery, there's always fresh flowers. He was loved by so many in the community."

Both Holly and Sheriff Carlton nod as they fell into a short silence. "Either way, it's good to have you back. I can't wait to eat some of Frijole's enchiladas again. Double Flavors doesn't even compare to your father's recipe."

Holly laughed a little at the compliment, and her eyes skittered from the sheriff and landed on Annalisa Rice, who seemed to be charming her way with the town's founding families.

"I look forward to seeing you around when I finally open up."

"You might," he answered with a chuckle, then followed her line of sight and looked at Annalisa. "But you'll have strong competition. Annalisa's franchise has only grown stronger in your dormant years. My advice is you should leave Cleverly Shores while you've got the chance. Your mother was right to leave all those years ago. You should too."

Holly met his hard, dark gaze again, and this time she only nodded before he walked away from her.

The sheriff definitely dislikes me. Holly's still pondering on his chilly attitude towards her when she looked at the crowd of founding families and spotted Annalisa speaking to a man just a short distance away.

The argument seemed chaotic, and she's on edge. Her hands flailed around her in numerous gestures while she spoke. Holly couldn't see the man she was arguing with from where she was standing, but she didn't miss the tension spearing between them.

"Woah," Scarlet said behind her, and Holly turned to her friend again. "Isn't that Mr. Rice?"

"It is?" Holly didn't recognize him. "He used to have dark hair but now it's all white," she commented as a frown spread out on her face.

"Yeah. I heard he was back in town. Those two never miss the chance to argue whenever they are together. Such a shame, they used to be the sweetest couple in town before their divorce."

Holly doesn't comment back as she kept watching Annalisa. It indeed was a shame. She used to admire the Rice's when she was younger. They were such a loving family and one she had coveted.

"Well, at least I found out tonight that Sheriff Carlton still hates me for reasons I don't understand, and he thinks I should leave town," Holly said to her friend as she shifted her attention from Annalisa. "He kind of hinted at it."

"Sheriff Carlton's a tough man to get along with. John complains about him all the time. He's like that with everyone. You have nothing to worry about."

Holly and Scarlet continued their stroll to the barbecue stand, and soon John joined them too. The rest of the evening, Holly's mind drifted back to the argument between Annalisa and her ex-husband.

What happened between them? They used to be so happy.

There's a lot to catch up on, Holly thought, and if she was really going to stay, then joining the founder's council didn't sound like such a terrible idea. Her dad would have been proud to see her take a leadership role in town. He loved Cleverly Shores and was a very active member of the community.

Holly sighed to ease off the light tension in her chest as the night edged on. She didn't know what would happen next but there was an inkling in her gut that her return to Cleverly Shores was going to be eventful.

***

The next morning came swiftly, and Holly was enjoying a cup of homemade cappuccino inside the diner. As she was preparing to open for her first day, a loud shrill scream sliced into the quietness she was enjoying.

She instantly bolted to her feet, shocked, and baffled by the noise. Holly's heart rate kicked up a notch as tendrils of panic seized in her. *What could that be?*

Another shriek followed the first scream as Holly dashed out the door. "Did you hear that Chile?" Chile barked and lead the way over to all the commotion.

By the shores in front of Holly's diner, a woman was bent over to her knees, her hands groped around her belly while she screamed again. It was a piercing shriek that could make the grounds quake, and even the heavy crash of waves rolling towards the shore, did nothing to drown the sound.

"Oh my," Holly gasped, petrified. Her heart rate was beating so quickly when she approached closer to the woman on her knees. "What happened? What is ..."

There's a body on the ground, soaked from the ocean's water, and Holly didn't need to get too close to see how pale and bloated the body was.

"I found her here," the crying woman babbled as Holly came right up next to her and dropped to her knees. "I heard the diner's open, and I was coming in for an early morning coffee, and I just... The waves brought her here, and ..." The hysterical woman ended her chatter with another scream as Holly turned to the body on the ground.

She screamed from the sight as well, her hands framed over her mouth and her eyes settled on Annalisa's ashen white face staring back at her.

CHAPTER THREE

Minutes later, the police arrived and conducted a site investigation right in front of Holly's property. There's yellow caution tape that distinctly marked the spot where Annalisa laid. A small crowd gathered in front of the diner and took in the scene.

What was once a cool, vibrant morning for Holly has now become a dark one. Hushed murmurs filled the air, and Holly could feel the curious eyes of all the bystanders staring right at her like they expected some sort of reaction.

Her insides rattled with panic and there was an outburst clawing its way up her throat to the surface. Holly was not crying, but her eyes burned with the sting of tears, and her entire body was as stiff as stone. The slightest thought about Annalisa's son Tim and her loved ones made Holly want to bawl, but it wasn't the right time.

Holly pushed down her own hysteria again and found her voice even though was shaky. "That lady found her," Holly said to John Fischer, Scarlet's husband who also happened to be amongst the officers surrounding her property that morning. "I heard her scream and rushed out with Chile to see what was happening. I found her kneeling right in front of the body. She was just...there, soaked from the oceans water."

"And you didn't hear anything prior to that? No noise or disturbances nearby?" John's words were more like a whisper, and his solemn eyes stayed on hers as he asks the questions. "Take your time," he encouraged. "You're still pretty shaken up from what you just saw."

Holly's throat tightened with a forming ache as she swallowed again. Her stomach rolled hard with the forceful wave of nausea. "It was a quiet night. I woke up early and didn't go for a run because of the light morning drizzle. I was actually just minutes away from opening up for the day." She combed her fingers through her hair and sighed. "It's supposed to be my opening day for Frijole's."

John gave her a compassionate smile before he touched her shoulder lightly. "It's not going to be your first day anymore," he said to her before taking his hand off her shoulder and closing his notepad. "You'll have to stay closed for a few days now, until we get all the evidence we need from the scene."

"Who would do this?" Holly wondered, her heart was breaking a little as she let her gaze wander to the shores again. The water seemed still now, and the woman who found Annalisa's body, was much calmer as she talked to Sheriff Carlton behind his police van parked just a short distance away. There's a blanket draped over her shoulder, and she was holding a coffee mug in her right hand.

There's a heavy weight still pressing down on Holly's chest as she spoke, and she kept counting numbers in her mind to help her stay calm. There was no shaking the memory of Annalisa from Holly's mind.

It's like it's burned in there. She shuddered and rubbed her arm, hating that she had to take in that scene.

"Cleverly Shores sees one or two murders in a year. It's a very low crime rate and the town was pretty safe. I'm sure it won't be hard to catch whoever did this. That's if it really was a murder."

"You think Annalisa would do this to herself? What reason would Annalisa have to want to end her life? Her life was perfect." Her statement hung in the air for a little while because John didn't say anything, but he soon touched her shoulder lightly again.

"I should go. We might ask you to come down to the station for more questioning, but you have nothing to worry about. We'll find out what happened to Annalisa."

Holly can only nod as John walked away from her. She wrapped her hands around herself to absorb the quivers slinking through her body. She didn't realize she was staring hard at the spot where the medical examiner and his team had pulled the body from until Scarlet's soft tone cut into her drifting thoughts.

"Hey...I heard what happened. Are you alright?" Scarlet enveloped Holly in a warm hug, and she closed her eyes to enjoy the comfort of her friend's arms for a just moment. She sighed when she pulled back. Scarlet adjusted the shawl around her neck before she started looking around. "Is that the woman who found her?"

Holly nodded as Scarlet tilt her head in the direction of where John stood with the sheriff and the lady who found Annalisa.

"She's pretty shaken up and hasn't stopped crying. I can only imagine how terrified she was when she first saw the body."

"I would have fainted from the shock," Scarlet chirped in, shuddering visibly as her brows furrowed together. "How about you? How are you holding up? This is insane, who would do such a thing? Drown someone right here at the beach?"

"The waves brought her body ashore," Holly answered as she rubbed a hand over her forehead. "I can still picture her face, Scarlet. Her eyes were...They were blue and terrified. It was almost as she if she was scared when she died." Holly stuttered as she spoke, and her skin crawled when another cold tremor slithered through her.

"Don't think about it," Scarlet said and rubbed a hand over her back. "You should stay with us tonight...or for a couple of days, at least till they have some information on what really happened here. It might not be safe for you."

"Thank you, Scarlet," she said to her friend as they hugged again. "Do you mind if I bring Chile too?"

"Sure, Chile is always welcome," Scarlet agreed in an instant before smiling at Holly again. "You shouldn't be alone right now."

Holly heaved out a deep breath before she excused herself from Scarlet and walked over to John and the sheriff. Her strides were slow because her body felt strangely heavy. Holly tried not to glance towards the taped area near the shoreline because it would only remind her of Annalisa again.

"Sheriff Carlton?" she called, interrupting his conversation with John and some other officer.

He faced Holly; his hands stay propped on his hips as his eyes swept over her face. "How are you holding up? No one should have to see what you've seen today."

"I'm fine... I'm alright," she nodded towards the other woman she was with when the police arrived. "You think she'll be alright?"

"She's calm now, John offered to drive her home." Sheriff Carlton's face stayed expressionless as he spoke, and Holly wondered for a tiny second if his calm composure is because he has seen a lot of dead bodies over the course of his career. "I'll have police patrolling the beach area until we finish looking into this case. You think it's still safe for you to be here?"

I can't imagine what that is like, Holly thought as the sheriff spoke and she didn't even hear his question when it came.

"Holly," he called, distracting her again as she lifted her shaky eyes to his. "Did you hear me? Do you think it'll be safe for you to stay here in town? A body was just found on your property, a few feet away from your house and diner."

"I'm alright. I'll get though this. It's Mr. Rice and Timothy I'm worried about. I hope they take the news well." Holly touched both her cheeks as she spoke and the tears she has been holding back since the start of this ordeal finally rushed to the surface. "Oh, Tim will be devastated," she gasped and tried to blink back the tears but failed horribly.

"I'm sure Timothy will handle himself just fine. You should stay safe and consider returning to your life and job in the city. Your father used to be so proud that you worked in New York. He told everyone there that you were a sous chef in some hot-shot restaurant. That's got to be better than being in Cleverly Shores, a town where nothing ever changes."

Holly ignored his talk about her former job because her mind was still in shock over Annalisa's death. Questions whirled around in her head. "What do you think happened? You think this was a murder or suicide?" Holly wrapped a hand around her neck as she asked in a quivering whisper, then fought back her tears again. She sniffed as her cheeks warmed. "Why would she want to kill herself?"

"The department will investigate and find out what happened. In the meantime, you should refrain from asking too many questions. Cleverly Shores thrives on gossip. You don't want to be in the middle of all that."

Holly shoved down every other question tunneling through her mind after that, and Sheriff Carlton nodded to her in acknowledgment once before turning to walk away.

Scarlet came over to Holly again, put a hand on her shoulder and whispered in her ear as she lead her away. "You're okay... You're going to be fine."

Holly walked towards the diner with her friend, the crowd slowly started to disperse. Holly's breathing grew shallower as she started to relax a little, and she finally managed to glance towards the beach. She caught sight of the crashing waves as it swept across the shore and spread across the golden sand.

Usually, the sight would bring her comfort or help her relax. Instead, the ache returned harder as she looked at the blue waves, and she nearly forgot to breathe because of the impact.

Holly knew she would never look at the beach the same way again.

CHAPTER FOUR

H olly and Scarlet visited the police station the next afternoon for questioning. Holly was stiff in her seat, while the officer listened to her talk, and keyed everything she said into the system.

"And what time was this?" he asked. "What time did you hear the scream?"

"It was around eight am...I'm not so sure of the time." The officer kept his eyes on the screen in front of him and just kept typing away without ever looking up. The constant click on his keyboard got to Holly and made her even more tense in her chair. Her spine was ramrod straight as she sat up, and the longer the seconds ticked away, the tighter the knots in the pit of her stomach twisted around.

"And what were you doing around that time?"

His insistent and continuous questions started to bother Holly, especially because he kept a straight expression through it all.

"I told you already. I was in the diner having my morning coffee with Chile. It drizzled earlier that morning, so I didn't go for my run. It was supposed to be my first day re-opening Frijole's."

"Chile?" the man's brows drew together, and his nose crunched up a little. "You haven't mentioned anyone named Chile in your last statement."

"My dog...My German short-haired pointer...Officer is there a problem here? Why am I being questioned like I'm a suspect?"

"It's routine ma'am," he answered dismissively. "We need to get your story and also the other lady at the scene."

"Did you call her in too? She found the body; she probably has more details than I do."

The man was about to respond, but Scarlet interrupted. "It's not routine...I know what an interrogation feels like, and my friend here already gave a statement yesterday." Scarlet got on her feet and pulled Holly with her. "I think we're done here," she added and started to lead Holly away.

The officer did nothing to stop them from exiting the station thankfully, and once they got outside, Holly could breathe easily again. Her chest heaved and her shoulders slumped forward. "You think it was okay to leave like that?"

"Yes of course," she insisted, frowning a little as they stopped by the parking curb and looked around. "I think John's around here somewhere. I'll text him to let him know we're done."

Scarlet took out her phone and started texting while Holly was looking around and scanning their surroundings. There was a couple standing at a corner with some officers, and they were pretty engrossed in their conversation. Holly gasped when the ring of sirens suddenly cut into the air. She spent the entire day being jumpy, and even worse, the churning sensation in the pit of her stomach refused to ease up.

"John's coming. Let's talk to him before we leave."

Holly rubbed her arms to get rid of the goosebumps that had suddenly popped up. "Something just doesn't feel right," she whispered as she looked around. "That officer earlier, he asked questions as if he didn't believe a word I said to him."

"You think he suspects you're lying or withholding information?"

"Why would he suspect me? I just moved back to town. I haven't seen or spoken to Annalisa in years. There's no reason to suspect me."

"No one's suspecting you," John said behind them. She turned to see him standing there with a warm smile. "It was just routine questioning, Holly. You two don't need to worry about a thing."

John hugged and kissed Scarlet on her cheek, then rubbed her back a little. "You two heading home?"

"Yes," both women chorused. "We'll do a little shopping first. Holly's making us dinner tonight."

"I can't thank you two enough for letting Chile and I stay at your place for now. It really means a lot."

"Come on, Holly. You're family," John said with a smile. He patted her shoulder after that, then gave his wife another loving look. "I'll see you two tonight. Stay safe."

"Bye."

Holly was still smiling as she watched her friend wave at John while he walked away. The duo seemed so much in love, just like the first time they announced their relationship. Holly remembered Scarlet being hard on John at first because she didn't want to give in to him. She later came around when she realized John wasn't going anywhere.

I wish I had a love like theirs. They were perfectly happy together, and that was enough for them both.

Scarlet and Holly went to the local market after that, and the entire ride, Holly found her mind wandering back to the last time she saw Annalisa alive.

That was a pretty heated argument, as she recalled seeing Annalisa and George Rice at the bonfire that night. Holly's mind kept spinning with unraveling thoughts and nothing she considered helped her stay calm.

"Why would she kill herself?" Holly muttered before she even realized she was thinking aloud.

"Huh?"

"It makes no sense. Except, that maybe she was depressed from all the fighting. What reason would Annalisa have to drown herself?" All these questions just kept whirling around in her head. The more she thought about them, the more she questioned what happened and who could actually be involved.

Her question hung in the air for a long time before Scarlet took the turn leading into the market. They spent the next hour shopping. Once they got home, Holly went right into fixing dinner while Scarlet tended to her garden in the back.

Her florist shop was the biggest in Cleverly Shores now, and Holly was excited for her friend's success. Chile paraded around the kitchen while Holly chopped vegetables and set them aside for her soup. The aroma in the kitchen soon became a blend of smoky chipotle and cayenne.

She inhaled deeply to take in the rich notes of scented chile and cilantro. Holly tasted the soup and hummed as she marveled at how amazing it turned out, then turned off the heat. She felt a little lighter when she joined Scarlet in the garden a few minutes later. The sweet, citrusy scent of peonies and other flowers planted around the six-foot garden made her smile.

"This is lovely. Your garden is much bigger and more beautiful than I remember it."

"Thank you," Scarlet blushed as she got back on her feet with a bouquet she just harvested. "I plan on delivering these to Mr. Rice this evening at his house. I'm sure he's still in shock from the news."

"Everyone's got to be in shock," Holly answered as she folded her hands over her chest. "Annalisa was an integral part of the community.

This tragedy makes me wonder how safe Cleverly Shores is for anyone right now."

"You think Timothy will come for the funeral?" Scarlet is staring at her bouquet as she asked, and the question instantly made Holly's pulse jump. She didn't want to think of how devastating this news would be for him.

She remembered how close Timothy was to his mom when they were younger, and her heart felt a renewed ache that seemed to rock her to the core this time.

"It's his mother, he'll definitely be there." Holly tried not to think of what it would feel like to see Tim again after all these years. *How long has it been? Eight years?* When she left for college, she had cut off contact with him. Each time Holly returned to Cleverly Shores over the years, Tim was never around.

A part of her had appreciated his absence. At least she didn't need to re-open old wounds if they ever ran into each other. Leaving without saying goodbye back then was selfish, but it was the only way Holly knew she could leave without her heart breaking. She always regretted that decision, however. Not saying goodbye turned out to be much harder than just saying it.

"They've not been on speaking terms since the divorce. Tim and his mom I mean. They had a huge fall-out when he found out about her affair. You know what's strange? No one's ever seen the guy she was with. They were pretty discreet through it all."

"How do you know so much about everything and almost everyone?"

"It's Cleverly Shores, Holly. I'm a florist. When women buy flowers, they gossip. It's all they ever do around here."

They both chuckled a bit as they walked back to the house. Scarlet headed upstairs to shower, leaving Holly and Chile in the kitchen. In her time alone, Holly pondered some more about her thoughts.

Running into Tim at this time would be inevitable. *How will I react when I see him again?*

An uncertain tingle settled deep inside her, and she tried not to dwell on it even though it overshadowed everything else she felt.

CHAPTER FIVE

It rained heavily the night before Annalisa's funeral, and it still drizzled that morning as most of Cleverly Shores residents gathered at the cemetery for the brief ceremony. A solemn silence hovered over everyone as the funeral began.

Most of the attendees are dressed in black. Holly's wearing the same black dress she wore for her father's funeral, and her hand holding a small umbrella over her head quivered a little as she concentrated on the priest's eulogy.

"She was a mother, a wife, and a friend. A vital part of our community and a blessing to many," Priest Docherty recited at the funeral ground that Friday morning while a handful of the town's residents gathered by the cemetery.

"The past three weeks have been uncertain and hard for many of us. Annalisa's death has left us worried and concerned for our loved ones. But there has always been a time to live, and a time to die. A time to love and a time to part. For Annalisa, regardless of the circumstances, that time has come. We only hope that she is at peace and happy...."

Holly and Scarlet stood with John behind the crowd, and Holly's mind was numb as she listened to the priests' words. She was trying to stop the achy feeling that was growing inside her.

When she first arrived, she spotted Timothy and his father in the front row. They stood with a woman Holly had never met before, and judging from how the three held hands tightly, Holly could tell the woman was close to the family.

I can only imagine what this loss was like, she thought as everyone chorused "Amen." Remembering how close Timothy was with his mother, and how his grief surrounding her death and all the circumstances might only make it harder for him to heal and move forward.

Realizing she was worrying about Tim made her suck in a deep breath. The funeral ended a few minutes later, and Tim lead as everyone started to drop flowers on Annalisa's headstone. When it was Holly's turn, she dropped a single red rose she carried with her from the house, and sniffed when she backed away.

Tim was standing by her side as she whispered a silent goodbye. She contemplated walking away like she did not notice he was standing right there. While Scarlet and John dropped their flowers, Holly heaved in deeply again, then moved closer to him.

"Hey," she greeted in a shaky and barely audible voice. "I'm really sorry for your loss, Tim," she continued even though he didn't respond at first. He was standing stiff beside her, both hands clasped in front of him as he watched everyone pay their respects.

"Thank you," he finally answered without looking at her. Holly noticed the hard bob in his throat as he swallowed, and she dared to let her gaze flicker over his face so she could take in his full expression.

The years had changed Tim a lot. His chin was more defined and harder than Holly remembered, and he had grown a little stubble that made him look much older. His striking cheekbones framed his face perfectly and gave him a carved look. The kind that would make every woman look at him twice.

Holly noticed his eyes were a deeper shade of blue when he glanced her way and met her gaze. Her breath hitched in her throat, and a familiar warmth spiked through her immediately. They were still as penetrating as ever.

Tim's hair was a darker shade of blonde, and even though he had his mother's blue eyes, the rest of him was so much like his father. His wavy tresses were styled in an upsweep cut and his skin was the same pale white.

Truth was, Holly knew seeing Tim again would invoke some kind of reaction in her, but she didn't expect it to be warmth. *Definitely didn't expect this tingle either.* But his eyes had always had that effect on her.

"Is there something else you want?" Tim asked her while she was lost in the moment, staring into his eyes. "Miss Barber?" His tone dripping with a hint of sarcasm.

Holly swallowed, "I ...I just want to know how you're doing. It must be difficult for you...Your mom just died and..."

His brows snapped together very quickly, and his jaw tightened. "It doesn't concern you," then angled his body so he was facing her fully. "How I'm feeling doesn't concern you, Miss Barber."

"Miss Barber? Come on Tim...Look, I know the past years have been.... I know we haven't spoken in a while with all that went down eight years ago, but that doesn't mean I don't worry about you. You just lost your mom and the entire town's grieving...You are grieving."

"I am," he said with a shrug, then shoved his hands into his pants pockets. The black woolly coat he was wearing framed his wide, muscular build and the sleeves hugged his biceps. Tim was always way taller than Holly, but his wider frame made him look like he could engulf her in one move. "I am grieving, and I have people who care enough to ask how I am coping with all this. I don't think you are one of those people Holly."

The light wind circling around the cemetery slightly blew in their direction. It picked up Holly's hair with it, ruffling it all over her face, so she used her hands to tame it. Tim stared hard at her, his lips parted a little before he pressed them together again.

She was about to speak again when he gave her one long look, then moved to walk past her. "Tim," her heart breaking a little. Holly didn't expect the first conversation they would have in eight years to go so well. She knew deep down; Tim could still resent her for hurting him that way. But she had hoped he would at least understand her sympathy.

Tim stopped after taking a few steps away from her. He was still within hearing range, he glanced over his shoulder to look at her again, and she saw the flicker of pain in his eyes.

"I heard you were back in town when I got here a week ago. Cleverly Shores is not very good at keeping secrets. Everyone's talking about you and my mom. I was hoping I wouldn't have to run into you but since I have, then it's best I make this very clear...I don't want to talk to you if we do run into each other while I'm in town. We're not friends. We stopped being friends when you walked out on me and didn't bother to say goodbye. I'm over it now though, but I'd like to keep things as it is."

Tim walked away from her without another word, and Holly watched him approach his dad and the young lady they stood with during the funeral. She was still watching with a heaviness in her heart as the three of them headed over to a small crowd of people.

Scarlet and John joined Holly a few seconds later. Scarlet adjusted her shoulder bag as she asked, "Did you see Tim? Did you speak to him?"

It took a moment for Holly to find her voice. She sighed and nodded, "I did, and he wants nothing to do with me. He says we're not friends."

Holly turned to her friend and saw that Scarlet's expression sobered. "I'm so sorry, Holly. I know you're really worried about him."

"I am," she answered with another deep sigh, not knowing how else to ease the tension budding through her. "But I don't need to be. Tim will take care of himself. He's always been strong. I just hope he knows how sorry I am."

Scarlet rubbed Holly's shoulder a little, making her smile, and they headed towards John's truck parked outside the cemetery. Holly spotted Tim and the lady talking as she got to the truck and opened the door.

He paused for a second to stare at her, the smile on his lips faded off, and their eye contact lasted a while before he looked away first. He opened his truck door for the lady to get in, then walked over to the driver's seat.

Holly tried not to imagine who the lady might be to Tim. *A friend? A girlfriend? Perhaps a distant family member?*

She tried to remind herself that it was not her business, but her mind kept running wild with her questions. She knew she would be seeing more of Tim for as long as he was in town, and she also realized that pretending not to know him would not be possible.

Chapter Six

Two days after the funeral, Holly was back at Frijole's and could finally open for the first time since her return. Her unexpected three-week vacation, because of Annalisa's death, was over and it was time to figure out how to run the diner again. *And on my own this time.*

As she put out the 'We are open for business' sign on the porch and stepped back a little and swiped her palms over each other, she let her mind reminisce about some old memories of her and her dad opening the diner together.

It had always been Frijole's tradition to have daily specials listed on the menu, but they always had some regulars like sandwiches, tacos, hamburgers, flautas and much more. Today, Holly's idea for the daily specials was bacon and egg burrito for breakfast, something simple for lunch like a cheeseburger and fries, and fajitas with beans and rice for dinner.

Holly took out some chalk from her apron's pocket and started to write out today's menu on the small black board hanging outside. Once she was done, she decided to sit on the porch and wait for her first customer.

The morning's breeze slithered her way at intervals as she sat outside the first hour alone on the porch. Usually, people would stroll down the path of the beach in pairs to enjoy the day, some would come in groups for a meal before heading out to the beach bar for some games. Children would often run along to get more tacos and free sunscreen from her dad.

Holly smiled as the fond memories filled her mind while she sat out there. Soon she glanced at her watch to see time had flown by very quickly and it was nearly noon.

There's still no one here. Not even a single soul. Holly's clenching stomach started the early onset of nausea. Her ribs grew tight as she rubbed the back of her neck, and she weaved her right hand through her brown hair, releasing a frustrated sigh.

Not even one customer? Really?

Rising to her feet, she walked inside to get herself a burrito and when she returned to the porch, a red truck pulled to a halt in front of the diner. Her heart rate kicked up a notch when the door opened, but the sudden rush of excitement dropped immediately when she saw Tim get out of the driver's side.

Holly was still standing at her doorstep as he paused in his stride to look at her, then continued till he climbed the porch stairs. The plate with her burrito on it lied there forgotten as her heart started to pound.

What is he doing here?

"Hey," he said and brushed his left hand over his hair. "I heard the diner was finally open and my dad won't let me hear the end of it until I come and get him some of your most cherished enchiladas. He says he's missed them."

"Hi," Holly blurted out in a shaky voice, still surprised to see him. A tiny smile teetered on her lips but disappeared when Tim didn't return it.

Tim looked around the porch like he was sizing up what she had done with the place. When his gaze settled on her again, he cocked his head to one side.

"Right," Holly said in a high-pitched tone that barely sounded like her voice. "Enchiladas...We don't have that on the menu today, but there's egg and bacon burritos or cheeseburger with fries if you'd like some." Her pulse jumped as she made a gesture with the hand holding her plate.

She tried to hide the nervous tics flowing through her with another shaky laugh, then continued, "I just opened, and I haven't had any customers all day. There's a lot of bacon and egg burritos in there and I'll be eating them for breakfast, lunch, and dinner for the rest of the week if I don't sell them."

"Alright...I guess he'll take some burritos then," he agreed, and relief flooded through Holly.

"Come on in, let me get it together for you. How many would you like?"

"Two is fine," Tim walked in after her, but he paused at the doorway and looked around. Holly felt the need to hear what he thought of the place while he spent his time carefully looking around. Besides Scarlet and Annalisa, no one else has been in here since she returned.

Her insides were still fluttery when she made it back to Tim with a bag of his burritos a couple minutes later, and handed it over. "There's an extra for you," she said with another smile. "I remember you used to like them. I even added a couple containers of my special green chile salsa."

"Alright, thanks," his fingers gently brushed over hers as he took the paper bag out of her hand.

Holly felt a spike in her pulse, and a breathless flush started to climb out of her when he looked her way. The silence between them seemed tense, and Holly's nerves were a mess because of it. *I want to talk to him, but I don't know what to say.*

As she shivered inside, she wracked her mind for a way to talk to Tim and find out how he was doing.

"So...what do you think of the place?" Holly finally blurted out, waving her hand around. "I thought of changing the walls, maybe some new paint and some art on the wall," she babbled. "Maybe some new decorations too."

"Less is more," Tim said to her before peeking into the bag she handed him. "New paint, some fancy writing on the wall is not what made this place special. What made Frijole's was its recipes, not its ambiance."

"You think so?"

"I know for a fact. Everyone used to rave about how amazing this place was. And they weren't talking about the paint color."

Holly saw a ghost of a smile appear on his lips. It disappeared as fast as it came, and he cleared his throat right after. "Just give it some time. Frijole's has always been a favorite for so many in our community. I'm sure this place will be streaming with customers soon enough."

His words warmed Holly's heart, and she didn't mind beaming at him again even though he still maintained his blank expression. "Thanks for the vote of confidence, I really needed it."

Tim's reply was a nod, and he turned to head for the door before Holly spoke again, "What about you?"

He stopped in his tracks when she asked. "You'll only be in town for a little while?"

"Yeah, I don't plan to be here too long. Till the investigation is over and I can find a buyer for the house."

Holly's forehead furrowed with deep creased lines. "They launched an investigation already? You're selling the house?"

Tim answers both questions with a nod. "The sheriff ruled out the death as a suicide after the autopsy was concluded last Friday. She was dead before she ended up in the ocean, so that's foul play and is enough to launch an investigation."

"Oh, wow," Holly gasped. The queasy feeling she carried inside her since Annalisa's body was found suddenly returned. "But the house? Tim, you grew up there...You sure you want to let go of all the memories you made in that place? It's your family's home, and Cleverly Shores is ..."

"Cleverly Shores stopped being home for me a long time ago," he cut-in and sook his head. "And this is not your business, remember?"

"You're right, it's not," Holly walked towards him to buttress her point. "But I still care about you, and I know you're one to cherish memories. Selling the house might not be the right choice. Perhaps wait and think about it when everything is not so hurtful and confusing?"

"There's nothing to think about, and if I didn't know you any better, I'd think you're really concerned about me."

"Tim, come on..." Holly tried to touch his arm now, but he shifted out of her reach.

"Just stop it, Holly." His tone was harsh, and his eyes hardened as they latched to hers.

"I do worry about you. I know you probably hate me...I was wrong. What I did was selfish, and horrible, and I was wrong...Tim, but I'm sorry. I've regretted that decision every day. I know it doesn't change anything, but you just have to know that I really am sorry, and perhaps you can hate me less?"

His abrupt laugh was cold, and shocking. A chill ran down Holly's spine as it rumbled over her, and the corners of his eyes hardened.

"I don't hate you. And you don't know anything about me or my family. Not anymore, so just stay out of it."

Holly snapped her lips shut and said nothing else as Tim walked away. For a long time after he left, his cold brush off reply lingered in her mind and messed with her thoughts. He probably didn't hate her, but he didn't like her either.

Holly didn't know how to handle the unsettling stir of emotions rising in her. Tim's coldness stung more than she imagined it would.

When she finally sighed and turned from the doorway to walk to the kitchen, a car honked outside and got her attention. Holly rushed out of the diner, hoping that it was another customer.

Her expectations sunk a notch when she saw it was just Scarlet getting out of her car and waving.

"I saw Tim driving off on my way here. Did he want something?" Scarlet asked when she climbed up the stairs to meet Holly.

"Yeah. He saved me from a week of eating only bacon and egg burritos," Holly replied dully. When Scarlet arched a brow in question she explained more in depth. "He came for some enchiladas, but I didn't have any so I made him buy my burritos instead. Apparently, Mr. Rice is the only one who is interested in eating here. Not a single soul has come by this place today, other than you and Tim."

"Did you say Mr. Rice wanted your enchiladas?" Scarlet asked in a lower tone and her face turned very pale. Her eyes widened, and the color on her cheeks deepened. Holly didn't think her friends flush was because she was embarrassed. A dreadful feeling climbed through her, making her temples ache steadily as Scarlet whispered words Holly didn't hear.

"Did something happen? Scarlet? You're scaring me with your silence, what is it?"

Scarlet's lips parted with a deep sigh before she announced, "I don't think Tim knows this, but I saw the police pulling up to their place on my way here. They arrested Mr. Rice, Holly."

CHAPTER SEVEN

An early morning run was always the best way to start the day and clear one's head. Holly could feel the air moving all around her as she ran down to the beach of Cleverly Shores. The air lifted the hairs on her skin, leaving her with a slight tingle that she enjoyed. There was a hint of rain coming too, Holly could smell its freshness and felt it tickle her nerves.

She hastened her speed, needing to feel the adrenaline pump all the way to her blood.

The rush left her breathless but energized for the day.

She made it to her usual turn off, turned right, and continued down the beach shores. Holly intended to run in a circle, using the familiar Terrie Street route to get back home.

This was her running trail the entire time she lived here. Holly remembered it like the back of her hand.

A few blocks down the road, Holly spotted Tim running ahead of her.

He was wearing a headset; his pace was slow, but steady, and she tried to catch up with him.

Seeing him reminded her of their argument the previous day. She slowed her pace when her chest started struggling to take in more air.

Holly didn't think Tim would remember their jogging trail as well as she did.

Every morning back then, she had run this trail with Tim. They were both in better shape, but he was always more determined to get to their set finish line, while most times, Holly gave up along the way.

The memories brought a smile to her face, replacing the echoes of his sharp tone from yesterday in her mind.

Tim slowed down like he knew someone was trailing behind him. He started jogging in one spot, then glanced over his shoulder as she started to get closer to him. The moment his eyes leveled on hers, a whoosh washed over her, causing her to struggle for air again.

"I give up," she blurted once she got to him, then dropped her hands on her knees, bending forward to brace herself.

Her heart raced from its recent exertion and a tingle zapped through her because of Tim's gaze.

"You're not a quitter, Barber," he urged while maintaining his pace on that same spot. "You're a runner...Runners don't quit."

"Yeah, well, I've got to quit today," Holly panted, still not able to control her gasps for air. Tim finally stopped jogging and bent over to help straighten her up.

Holly's hair clung to her sweaty forehead and cheeks. She swiped them out of the way with her hands, then released a breathless laugh. "Thanks."

Her chest heaved as his eyes searched hers. Tim smiled at her, his lips curving outwards till the corners of his eyes wrinkled. The smile lasted a second before it vanished, and Holly's head swooned a little. She pretended to cough before speaking. "I heard about your dad," Holly said to him, not knowing if bringing it up is best, but deciding to do it anyway. "Is he still in custody? They think he did it?

Tim lifted one shoulder in a carefree shrug before posing with one hand on his hip. "I haven't been to the station yet. I don't know what they found...Before I got back from your diner yesterday, they had arrested him."

Holly's eyes widened in disbelief, and her tone spiked a notch. "You haven't gone to visit?"

A couple jogs past them after she asked, her eyes trailed after them till they were out of sight before she turned back to Tim again. "He's your dad, Tim...Don't you want to know how he's faring? Or what they have on him? I mean...They accused him of killing your mom. That doesn't bother you?"

Her brows furrowed together as she assessed him. The guy Holly remembered would worry about his dad. They were a tight knit family back then. *Inseparable.* Holly had admired that.

Tim's reply brought her back to reality. "What bothers me doesn't matter," he answered in an edgy tone. "The police have questions, and frankly, I think he's got to answer them. Someone must make sure he's accountable for his actions."

His statement was more like an accusation as he combed his fingers through his hair, looked away, then back to Holly again. "It doesn't change the fact that I'm leaving town."

"Right, and nothing is going to change your mind about that."

Tim just didn't seem at all like the guy she used to know. *There's a lot that has changed about him now. He's indifferent.*

"Try coffee after your run," Tim told her as he picked up his jogging pace again. "It helps with an extra boost, so you don't feel tired during the day."

"I knew that already," Holly shouted after him as he jogged away, leaving her to wonder why he didn't care about his father's arrest. *Or at least, why he's pretending not to care.*

Holly spent the rest of her day back at Frijole's cleaning up her father's old room with Chile by her side.

The entire time she hoped a customer would show up.

I just need one, she thought as she lifted a pile of old books from his table and dumped them into a cardboard box.

She sneezed into her elbow when she inhaled dust, then wrinkled her nose a bit. Holly was about to turn away from the table when she spotted the blue diary lying on the edge. Chile barked as she reached for it, then jumped to snatch the book from her hand.

"Hey," Holly scolded immediately, shifting her hand out of her reach. "That's bad Chile...Bad dog."

I didn't know dad journaled. Holly frowned at Chile when she barked and jumped again. This time, Chile's ears drooped low before she sat and started panting.

"Lay down Chile," Holly said to her dog as she opened the first page of the diary and found it empty. She flipped through more pages, wondering why there was nothing written in it. Holly got to the last page, flipped the diary around, then noticed the carved out key holder in the back.

Without hesitating, she took out the key and stared hard at it. "What could this key belong to?"

Her father's room was his sanctuary when he was alive. Holly rarely ever came in here. Every year on the day her mother left, her dad would retreat in here alone with just a book to keep him company.

She often wondered if her mother's absence was a relief for him. *He seemed much happier after she left.* Although the diner didn't thrive as much in her dad's last years, he was still happy.

Still staring at the key, Holly walked over to his shelf to try and open it. She spent the next thirty minutes trying to unlock every door and drawer in the house with it.

Holly gave up after a while and decided to fix herself a meal instead. Her mind kept spinning with thoughts about Tim and his dad. What could the cops have on Mr. Rice? And was whatever they had true?

CHAPTER EIGHT

Another day rolled by with an empty diner, and Holly was tired of waiting for customers who might never show. She finished cleaning the entire building, so there was nothing else left for her to do besides practice her recipes and eat them all with Scarlet's help.

"How about seafood tacos?" Scarlet suggested the next evening when she dropped by Frijole's to buy dinner for her and John. "That's always good right? Fish or Shrimp, maybe both?"

"Oh yes, I'm also thinking about dishes like fish and chips too. Then, I'd like to add more sandwiches and burgers to what we currently have on the menu." Holly sighed and brushed a hand over her hair. "I can't believe I'm saying this, but this is the best time to up my game...Now that Double Flavors is not open for business."

Realizing she said the words out loud, Holly groaned and slapped a hand gently over her forehead. "I'm such a horrible person. A woman died and I'm thinking of riding on her exit for my own benefit."

Scarlet laughed a little. "Yeah, you're a horrible person alright," she consoled, touching Holly's arm gently. "Of all the people in this town, I think Annalisa will understand."

The diner's quiet as usual, and Holly's slowly getting used to the lack of activity.

Returning to Cleverly Shores to run her family's diner sounded like a good plan when she first thought of it, but now that she is here, it didn't seem so rosy anymore.

Feels like the entire town's moved on from my dad's famous enchiladas.

"I hear they let Mr. Rice go this morning," Scarlet revealed, cutting into Holly's thoughts as she wrote down another item on their list. "John says they didn't have anything on him besides a text he sent to Annalisa the night after the bonfire. They think he was the last person to see her alive, and after that heated argument at the bonfire, it's only natural he'd be suspected, right?"

"John tells you these things? Aren't they like...confidential or something?"

"I have my ways," Scarlet answered with a shrug and her usual vibrant chuckle. "He's my Johnnie, he can never hide anything from me." Scarlet dropped her voice a notch as she added, "Mr. Rice had an alibi for that night though. I don't know who it is, but he had one. Maybe it was Tim."

Holly shook her head. "I don't think it was Tim. He seemed... unconcerned when I asked about his dad being in custody. I don't think they're on good terms." Holly frowned as she recalled the brief conversation she had with him.

"I just can't get Tim out of my head you know," Holly continued with another sigh as she slid her dad's diary close. She made her new menu list in it, and planned to put it to good use since her dad hadn't used it at all.

"Ohhhh, you're thinking of Tim now?" Scarlet's grin turned mischievous and her eyes sparkled with an amused glint as she winked at Holly.

"Not in the way you think," Holly countered, ignoring her friends teasing laugh. "I'm just worried about him. His mom passed away, his dad was locked up as a suspect for his mom's murder, and it seems like he doesn't have anyone to lean on at the moment."

"And you want to be there for him? A shoulder to lean on?" she taunted as her words were spaced out with her giggle.

"Don't think I don't hear your sarcasm." Holly was grinning and shaking her head lightly as Scarlet burst into another rumble of amusement. "It's nothing like that," she added. Trying to convince herself that her worry for Tim had very little to do with her wanting anything else other than to be just his friend again.

*We were good friends. R*emembering the sound of his laugh, and how easy it was to invoke one from him. Holly feared the years had changed him. It didn't seem like he was the kind who smiled easily anymore.

Holly found herself fiddling with the key in her apron pocket as her thoughts swam in an abyss. She was distracted when Scarlet propped her chin on one hand and asked, "You think perhaps he's lonely? Tim was pretty close to his mom."

"They were a very close family. It's just so sad...All of it's sad. And he's not talking to me. He practically cuts off every sentence I start. I don't think he's ever going to stop hating me for leaving."

"Tim could never hate you. He was practically obsessed with you at some point. When you left town, he kept asking about you. That guy practically planned his entire life around you during high-school and you messed that up...he deserves to be angry."

"I can handle him being angry. At least that way, I know there's a chance he'll forgive me at some point. It's the silence I can't handle."

"Maybe you should try talking to him? Do something he likes, I'm sure you remember what he likes, you two were like inseparable."

Holly pursed her lips and weighed her options. Tim liked to hang out at the beach. She was almost certain if she tracked him down one evening, she'd find him sitting by the shores, enjoying the view of the waves, and listening to music from his phone.

She realized she missed those moments with him. Holly had hoped they could stay friends after this long. *It's not going to be that easy.* She knew there would be a lot of unresolved issues between them, but still, his cold attitude affected her more than she could have imagined.

"Find a way to get through to him. Sometimes people just need a little push," Scarlet encouraged her as she got up from the chair. "You have any more chips and salsa around here? I can't seem to get enough of them."

Holly took the key out of her apron pocket and stared at it for a minute, trying to figure out what it could open. *A secret locker somewhere? Or a door?* She just couldn't place it.

Scarlet returned with a plate of chips and some salsa verde. "Mmmm, this salsa is seriously so amazing," she complimented as she sat down at the table again. "I could hire you to make me this every single day. I never get tired of it."

Holly sat down and ate some chips and salsa with Scarlet, then licked her fingers when she dripped salsa all over them. "We should go grocery shopping to pass the time. I think I can attract a few customers with my new and improved menu. What do you think?"

"Let's give it a try," Scarlet supported with ease. Holly took off her apron once she was on her feet, and she made a quick trip upstairs to check on Chile and ruffle her hair a little before she joined Scarlet for a drive to the closest grocery store on Main Street.

***

Holly was taking a tour of the canned foods section for a few minutes while Scarlet wandered off to find more corn tortillas for their stock. She's reading the ingredients listed on a can of tomatoes when a deep velvety tone slithered behind her.

"I find it strangely comforting too," he said, causing Holly to turn around from shock. The gentleman behind her grinned wide as he motioned to the can in her hand. "Reading the back of every item I get. I like to know what's in it. It's comforting."

Holly took in his look as his musky masculine scent surrounded the area around them and infiltrated her senses. He smelled strangely familiar. Holly was certain she had sniffed in the blend of musk and oak in his cologne somewhere else recently.

His brown locks fell to the sides of his face in waves and his dark eyes had an unending depth. Holly felt like she'd seen him somewhere before too.

"Oh," Holly laughed, then glanced from the can in her right hand to him. "Yeah, it is strangely comforting."

"I'm Kenneth Green," he introduced himself and extended a hand to her. "Most people just call me Ken though."

Holly noticed his cart contained mostly pet food and grooming items. She shook his hand, returning his smile. "Holly. I see you're a dog lover," she blurted out before she could stop herself.

"Yeah, you?" Ken didn't let go of her hand as his smile widened and his eyes lingered on hers. Holly noticed the tiny dimple cramped into his left cheek and the cute way it deepened as he smiled.

"I've got a German short-haired pointer wandering around my home at the moment. She's quite expressive."

"Mine's a Husky...Rambunctious little demon. I find her great company though, especially since I'm new in town," he said as he finally released her hand. "I could use a friend, and you're ..." he stopped and leveled her with that admiring look again. "You look friendly, so

I was thinking…How about lunch sometime? I hear there is this place with well-loved enchiladas in town. I think it's called Fri…"

"Frijole's," she completed with a breezy chuckle before he ended his statement. They both laughed. "Yeah…Frijole's. I own the place."

"Oh really? I'll be coming to Frijole's for breakfast, lunch, and dinner then. That's if you'll have me of course."

"Of course, you are always welcome," Holly answered in the same light tone he used, and their laughter mingled into one. She just so happened to look around on her left side and saw Tim standing at the far end of the row. His eyes pinned to her, and a deep scowl etched into his handsome features.

Tim averted his gaze from her after a few moments, he picked an item up from the shelf, and walked away before Holly could finally drag her gaze back to Ken.

"So, I'll see you tomorrow then. At Frijole's."

She nodded. "I guess you will."

She was still grinning when Scarlet returned with five bags of corn tortillas. "Don't ask," she said when Holly's lips parted for a question. "I want you to make as many tortilla chips as you can."

Scarlet dropped the bags in their cart then asked, "Why are you all smiley?"

"I think I just made a friend and a customer. He's a pretty cute one too."

"That's good news," Scarlet celebrated as Holly followed her down the row and walked past Tim again.

Something about the way he looked at her earlier spiked tension all through her. If Holly didn't know better, she would assume Tim had been jealous seeing her speak to the handsome stranger.

CHAPTER NINE

"**Y**our dad's pie were always the best around here," Reuben Docherty said to Holly the next evening at Frijole's. Holly burst into a wide grin at his compliment. "I mean it," he continued, returning her smile before he grabbed the take-out bag she handed over to him.

"Thanks for stopping by Mr. Docherty."

"Please, it's Reuben. It's good that you're bringing this place back to life. Many of us have missed your dad's amazing recipes. This place truly holds a sentimental value to so many of us here in town."

"I would probably argue that fact." She suppressed another laugh. "I've not had one customer come in here in days now. You're actually the first customer today."

"It gets easier with time," he encouraged. "Speaking of...Did you put any thought into joining the council? We have a meeting tomorrow at the community hall to discuss the upcoming founder's ball. It would be great to have you there."

"I don't think it would be so terrible to give it a try." She hadn't given it much thought honestly, but what could it hurt to try out something beneficial for the town? "I won't say I'm joining for sure, but I'll attend the meeting tomorrow, just to get a feel for what it's like."

"I can't ask for more than that." Holly was still smiling when Reuben walked out of the diner. She clapped her hands together a moment later, inhaled the hints of vanilla and buttery pie crust residue in the atmosphere. After sucking in another deep breath, she turned to walk into the kitchen, but the door opened and Kenneth Green walked in.

Seeing him instantly made her smile. "Hi," she greeted him. He looked around, scanning the entire dining area before he grinned at her. She didn't think he would show up here today as he mentioned, but Holly was glad he did anyway. Having someone other than Scarlet walk in here was a rarity and today seemed to be her lucky day.

"Hey," Kenneth greeted back, his dark eyes assessing her. "I'm here," he announced, sticking his hands into his pants pockets before he met her eyes again.

"I see that," Holly rubbed the back of her neck, suddenly nervous as she let out a light chuckle. "Please, sit," she blurted after a second of silence. "I didn't think you'd show up."

Holly sat down in the seat opposite his, and Kenneth sighed. "Yeah well, I thought, why not surprise you?"

When he looked around again, she tried to figure out what he thought about the place. Holly hadn't made many changes to the walls and décor yet, but the thought of changing the wallpaper had crossed her mind a few times.

"Sorry, it's not as bubbly as you might have expected. I'm just re-opening for the first time in a while." Holly's light ramble ended with a short laugh. "Would you like something? I've got fresh lemonade and some pecan pie."

"Pie sounds great. Well, actually, I was thinking we could take a stroll down the beach, you know, get to know each other. We can have the pie later?"

"That sounds fun," she answered with enthusiasm as another light chuckle burst free from her. "I've not had many customer today anyway."

"Slow day?"

"More like slow week. Just a minute," she added, rising from her seat to take off her apron. She swung the apron over her neck, and the move tossed her father's secret key to the ground.

Kenneth bent into a squat at the same time Holly did to pick up the key, and she inhaled his musky scent again, triggering a familiar memory she just can't seem to place.

How do I know this scent?

"You've got a music box?" he asked as he handed the key over to her.

"A music box? No...I don't think so."

"Hmmm...Okay. It's just your key reminds me of this Italian Classic music box my sister had as a little girl." Holly's eyes widened as a distant memory of her ninth birthday came to mind.

She recalled her dad's words the day he gifted her the music box and the tears in his eyes as he kissed her forehead. *"One day Holly, you'll know what it means to love, and when you do, I want you to never forget."*

Holly looked at the key again, then it suddenly hit her like a ton of bricks. *It's the music box. A*nd a fluttery feeling settled in the pit of her stomach.

Her pulse suddenly spiked in a frantic rush, leaving her breathless. Holly licked her lower lip, then lifted her eyes to Kenneth's again. "I'm so sorry, Kenneth...We'll have to take a walk some other time...I have this thing I completely forgot about. I'm so sorry"

"Oh, alright," Kenneth nodded once, his grin dwindled, and he sighed. "Sure...Some other day then. I completely understand."

Holly gave him a shaky smile, and he waved at her before walking out of the diner. She dashed upstairs and into her bedroom once she was alone, pulled her closet door open and started searching for the Italian music box her dad gifted her on her ninth birthday.

"Finally." A few minutes later, she found it sitting in one of her old boxes tucked away in the back of her closet. She wiped off the dust covering its gold plated surface, then blew air over it.

Tears stung her eyes as she found the music box and shoved the key into the keyhole to unlock it. *How could I forget this music box?* She slowly took in a deep breath, filling her lungs with more air as they began to tighten.

She had loved this music box as a kid. She remembered the slow tune it played each time she lifted it open.

Her vision blurred with her tears as she lifted the lid of the music box, and she whimpered as the music started playing.

It ended after a minute, and a smile spread out on her lips as she let her mind dance down memory lane. Holly wiped her eyes with her right hand, then sniffed. She was about to close the lid when she noticed a piece of paper folded neatly inside the box.

She took it out, walked over to her bed to sit down, then unfolded the paper gently. "Dad?" Holly whispered as she realized it was a hand-written letter from her father. Holly fought back the tears as she read his words aloud. The burn on her cheeks intensified as she struggled to keep them at bay, and her lungs constricted slowly, making her gasp in larger breaths of air to help ease her anxiousness.

Dear Holly,

If you are reading this, it means the time when I don't get to see you smile, or watch you grow, has come.

I'm grateful for the years I had...the years we had together kiddo. I loved every moment with you, and I am proud to be your dad.

But if there's one thing I've learned in life, it's that we owe it to the people we love to tell them the truth. Even though I hope you never find this letter, I can only pray that if you do, then you'll be alright after reading this.

I should carry this secret to my grave, but that wouldn't be fair to you or to anyone else involved because you deserve to know the truth.

Whatever happens next, Holly, you should always remember one thing. I love you. I always have and I always will.

Love, Dad.

Sniffing, she flipped the paper over to the other side to see what was written there.

A paternity test? A frown settling in on her features as she stared at the medical center's letter head printed behind her dad's letter.

Her frown deepened as she scanned through the test results, realizing the two main test subjects were Pete and Holly Barber. *Me and dad?*

A pain grew in her already tight chest as she began to look over the document. "Pete Barber is excluded as the biological father of the subject," Holly read aloud. A chill settled through her as the words she just read actually started to sink in. "My dad's not my real dad? How can that be?"

Holly's question kept echoing around her over and over. A lump formed in the base of her throat and an anguished sob burst out of her lips as she covered her mouth with her right hand to muffle her whimper. *How is this possible?*

CHAPTER TEN

B y evening the next day, the burden of Holly's discovery was still weighing down on her. She strolled the beach with Scarlet but was distracted the entire time.

"You're awfully quiet today," Scarlet commented when they arrived at the famous X-Beach Bar.

The Drew's have owned this place for as long as Holly can remember, and Harry Drew still looked as vibrant as he did when Holly was younger. She slowed her pace with Scarlet and took off her kimono to lay it down on the sand, then sat right by the shores to face the beach.

"Is something wrong? You've been quiet since you got back from the council meeting. Did something happen there?"

Holly sighed and shook her head. "No...it doesn't have anything to do with the meeting." Her throat clogged up again as she thought of her discovery. The paternity test results were folded up in the pocket of her jean shorts, but the results were imprinted in her mind. "It's just you think you know someone, and then you find out that everything you once knew was a lie."

Sitting by the shore should be a great distraction, but it's not this time. Nothing can keep her mind from racing and wondering about what she should do next.

Do I believe the results? Should I dig deeper? Who's my biological father? These questions form a whirlwind in her mind till her temples started to ache.

"What is it?" Scarlet touched her shoulder lightly. "Holly...you are starting to really worry me."

"I found something yesterday tucked away in my old music box," Holly confided, then reached into her pocket to take out the results. Scarlet's brows squished together as she opened the paper and read over it in silence. Holly was watching her and trying to gauge her expression.

A few seconds later, Scarlet's eyes bulged wide open, and she shifted her gaze back to Holly, then to the results again. "Oh...My...Goodness. How is this...Is this real? How did you find out?"

"My dad left it for me," Holly whispered, her tone cracking as fresh tears rushed to her eyes. "I don't know what to think, Scar...I don't know what to do."

She whimpered and gave into the tears again as they flowed freely from down her cheeks. Scarlet hugged her tightly and rubbed a hand over her back.

"It's alright," she whispered in Holly's ear. "You'll be fine...You'll be just fine."

After a few minutes, Holly lifted her head and cleared her throat. She looked at her friend and forced a smile on her face even though her heart was still heavy. "My dad was my only family. He was everything to me, and now I find out he's not even my real father and ..."

"He's still your dad," Scarlet interrupted, her tone ever light. "He was there for you through it all. It doesn't matter if you don't share DNA. He's still your dad."

"I know that. It's just...If he knew all these years, then why didn't he tell me? Why did he wait to tell me when he was no longer here?"

"Perhaps he didn't want to see you so sad. I can't imagine how difficult of a decision this was for him. I bet it tore him up not being able to tell you the truth. So he did it the only way he knew how."

Holly looked to the waves again and heaved out a deep breath. The cooling breeze helped her breathing get slow and steady again. The glow of the sun on the horizon was lower now, and its golden embers no longer burned.

In the cool evening, a lot of beach visitors can ditch their sunscreen, take off their shirts and play around in just a swimsuit or their flimsy tank tops.

Holly enjoyed the feel of the wind on her skin too, so she put her hair into a bun, and decided she was going to just enjoy the night out with her friend.

When she looked to Scarlet, her friend was watching her closely, those brown eyes wide and worried.

But Holly just couldn't let it go.

"You know what I think? I think he should never have let me find out the truth. What good is it? I don't care about finding whoever my biological father is anyway."

Holly felt the slow rise of anger burn through her heavy nerves. "My mom walked away from us...she never looked back or called. This doesn't change anything for me."

My mom's the only one who can tell me who he is anyway, so what does it matter? Holly stopped dreaming of finding the woman as a teenager, and she hadn't cared since then.

"You shouldn't worry about these things, Holly," Scarlet said and patted her shoulder. "Pete was a great dad and you loved him. As far as I'm concerned, he's your dad. Nothing else matters."

"Exactly," she agreed, nodding. *I don't care about the results.* She released another huge breath before pushing her earlier tinge of sadness aside. "Shirley Temple?"

"I'll take a Shirley Temple anytime," Scarlet said with sass and chuckled as Holly jumped to her feet and walked away from the shore.

She was dusting the back of her pants off by the time she reached X-Beach Bar, and she found a smile when she saw Harry Drew standing there grinning at her.

"And if it isn't the famous Frijole's owner. Holly Barber. Heard you were back in town. I was starting to think you'd forgotten all about me."

"How could I ever forget you? How are you doing, Harry?"

"Never been better. What can I get you?"

"You know what I like," Holly answered. He grabbed a bottle of lemon-lime soda and started to fix her a drink in his famous apocalypse style. "Make that two please."

"A mix of lemon-lime soda, grenadine syrup, whipped cream and three cherries," someone said beside her. Holly turned to see Tim sitting right next to her. "You never change Barber."

"What can I say?" she answered, leaning over the bar with a smile, "Harry loves me as I am."

Tim didn't smile as his eyes lingered over hers, and Holly wondered if that would ever change.

"You okay?" he asked after a second passed and she didn't avert her eyes from his. For a moment Holly forgot all about the recent discovery that shook her to the core the entire day.

I didn't even get the chance to enjoy my first council meeting.

"You've been crying. Your eyes are puffy, and your cheeks have this crimson shade. It's always been a dead give away with you.'"

Holly placed her hands on her cheeks and stroked them a little while Tim watched her.

"I hear you're now a new member of the council. That must be terrible for you."

"Why does it have to be terrible? Your family is part of the council as well."

He swept his hands through his hair and set his drink on the table. "There's an old saying here in town, Holly. The founders never sleep. You get to carry everyone's baggage and try to hide the truth from the community. That's what being a founder really means."

Tim took out cash from his wallet and put it under his drink before he faced her again, "See you around, Barber."

He was walking away from her, and she considered letting him leave like that for a moment. Holly thought about her return to town, and her struggle with getting Frijole's back on its feet. Every burdened feeling hosted inside her sprung to the surface and spurred her next actions.

"You can hate me, Tim," she yelled after him before she could stop herself.

"Excuse me?" he turned back around to face her, one brow raised, and lips drawn into a thin line.

"Hate me. I'd rather you hate me than act like you and I were never friends because we were. I messed up bad when I left town...When I left you. It was selfish and I'm sorry. I really am Tim. So, I need you to hate me as hard as you can so that we can finally get to the part where you forgive me."

Tim held her gaze for a long time, his jaw hardening as every second ticked away. "I could never hate you, Barber," he finally said in a thick voice before he turned and walked away.

Chapter Eleven

A week later, Frijole's had its first busy day. "Have a nice day," she said to the last customer as she left with her enchilada take-out. Holly turned to Scarlet once they were alone, and smiled. "That was such a high," she commented, grinning wide as her insides hummed with excitement.

Scarlet high-fived Holly before laughing. "Congratulations. You just had your first full and vibrant day."

"I'm exhausted," Holly said as she walked over to a chair and lowered herself down on it. "Exhausted but happy," she continued, rubbing the back of her neck.

"Prepare for many more days like this." Scarlet walked over and sat down at the table where Holly was sitting. After an entire day of fixing meals for others, one would think Holly would be ready for bed. Instead, she felt pumped and was ready to do this again tomorrow.

While Scarlet talked about how the next day would go, Holly's mind wandered as she was thinking about the paternity test again. She tried not to think about it the past week, but each time she was alone, her curiosity spiked and she thought of all the different possibilities.

Who is he? My real father. Knowing her mother must have had an affair many years ago left Holly with a twisting knot in the pit of her stomach. *I don't think I can ever forgive her.* For leaving and for lying to dad and I. She can't help but wonder if that is the reason why her mom left all those years ago and never came back.

Holly didn't realize she was silently nursing her thoughts till Scarlet touched her arm. "You're thinking about it again, aren't you?"

Scarlet had always been able to read Holly since they were kids. When Holly first realized she had a crush on Tim in high school, Scarlet was the first to notice. Holly liked that she had a friend she could confide in, and trust with her deepest thoughts.

"I still want to know," Holly said after a few seconds of silence. "I'm curious and I have lots of questions. How did dad find out? Did he order the DNA test? Why did he suspect that I wasn't his biological daughter?"

"There's one person that can answer all the questions you have though," Scarlet chimed in, but Holly didn't want to think about that or even consider going down that path.

"No." She shook her head and got up from her chair. "No...I'm never reaching out to her. Not after this much time has passed."

"She's the only one who can tell you what really happened, Holly...Think about it."

Holly combed her fingers through her hair. "She abandoned me. I was only eight years old and she walked away without a second thought. She left me with my dad, and she left him too. I'll never be able to forgive her for the selfish decision she made."

Scarlet stood up too. "I know, I know. I just thought this might be the person you need to talk to in order to get the answers you are wanting right now and help ease the pain you are feeling."

The gnawing feeling in Holly's stomach wouldn't subside, so she turned away from Scarlet and closed her eyes. "There's another way," she whispered before looking back at her again. "I can start with the clinic where the test was done. I find the technician who did the test, and I can ask who ordered it."

Scarlet nodded and took Holly's hand in hers. "Whatever you want to do, I'm right beside you...I just want you to know that."

Holly's tensed muscles slowly started to relax as Scarlet whispered her encouraging words. "I got you, Holly. You don't have to do this alone."

They hugged it out before Holly headed to her bedroom to grab the test results and her denim jacket.

"Stay Chile," she said to the dog when Chile prowled around the place and barked. "Sit."

Chile obeyed and sat in a corner next to her bowl of water. "We'll go for a walk tonight. I bet you'll like that huh?"

Chile growled and Holly laughed at her expressive response. "Alright, I'll see you later."

She headed out the door and Scarlet followed right behind her. It's a twenty minute drive to the clinic address on the test results that Holly was carrying with her.

There was a red-haired receptionist at the front desk when they walked in.

Holly greeted her first before asking, "I'm here for Dr. Derek Parker. Does he work here?"

"Yes ma'am, he owns the clinic," the receptionist answered with a smile. "Do you have an appointment?"

"No, I ..."

"We're from the sheriff's office," Scarlet lied before Holly could come up with something. Holly glanced at her with an alarmed look, but Scarlet kept her smile as she stared at the receptionist. "Can you please tell him we have a message from the sheriff?"

"Hold on a moment."

Scarlet winked at Holly, giving her a triumphant smile as they wait-ed for the receptionist. She picked her phone up and spoke to someone on the other end.

"Dr. Parker is available and is waiting for your arrival down at his office. Please come with me."

"You're crazy, you know that," Holly whispered to Scarlet as they walked down the hallway till they get to Dr. Parker's office. His name was boldly written on the black wooden door, and once it swayed open, Holly saw the older man sitting behind a sturdy desk. His at-tention was buried in a medical magazine.

"Ladies," Dr. Parker greeted when the receptionist left the office. "I hear you've got a message from my dear friend Sherriff Carlton." Dr. Parker's lips widened into a smile as he tucked his magazine away and looked at them. "Please, sit."

Scarlet and Holly waited till they were comfortably seated facing him before Holly answered. "Yeah, that was a lie," she said, loving how his brows quickly shot to his hairline, and his already dark eyes darkened.

"What?"

"We're here because of this." Holly set the results on his desk and slid it over to him. "Sorry I couldn't make an appointment, but I wanted some questions answered about the test results that I found. This is your signature on the results, isn't it?"

"Pete Barber...I remember him very well," Dr. Parker said as his gaze flickered from the test results in his hand back to Holly. "He ordered this test years ago. I remember because he asked me to do it as a favor..."

Dr. Parker's lips suddenly parted without him saying anything else. "You're the daughter, aren't you?"

Holly didn't know what to think as she stared at Dr. Parker. *It was dad? He suspected something was wrong, so he ordered the test.*

She didn't know how to feel as Scarlet's hand covered hers. Holly let Dr. Parker's news settle in her for a moment before she drew in a deep breath. "Thank you," she told him, numbing every feeling and banishing every other thought that came to mind.

She had figured out her father had ordered the paternity test. *But why?*

Reflecting on her childhood, Holly suddenly understood why her parents never had a moment of peace, till her mother left. As a child she didn't get it, but now it made more sense. It was all beginning to make sense.

Mom had an affair and dad found out.

The drive back home was longer than the twenty minutes that it took them to arrive to the clinic. Holly was quiet the entire time, but she was aware of Scarlet stealing glances at her.

Holly stayed in the spiral her mind created till they arrived at Frijole's. Scarlet slowed her drive and pulled to a halt directly in front of the diner when they noticed the police cars surrounding her property. Their sirens saturated the air, making it difficult for Holly to hear anything else.

The evening wind blowing against her skin suddenly filled her with a chill as Sheriff Carlton announced into his receiver. "Stand down...Stand down."

"What's going on?" Holly murmured to Scarlet, turning to her as Sheriff Carlton strode towards Scarlet's car.

"Holly Barber," Sheriff Carlton called taking out his cuffs, and a warrant that he flashed at her. "You're under arrest for the murder of Annalisa Rice, and you have the right to remain silent as anything you say can and will be used against you in a court of law."

"What? Murder? I didn't ..."

"What are you doing?" Scarlet protested before Holly could defend herself. Two other officers stopped her from making any move. "You can't arrest her...She didn't do anything! Sheriff!"

Scarlet's words fell on deaf ears as he proceeded to cuff her. Holly was frozen to one spot the entire time. The cold metal bit into her skin, her head flinched back slightly from her shock, and her mouth parted even though no words came out. Her heart thumped wildly in her chest and her first instinct was to run.

No, that only makes you look guilty, she thought as sweat broke out on her forehead.

Sheriff Carlton's hard gaze didn't soften as he lead her away without another word. Holly's mind blanked from her confusion, and her body heat spiked. *What do they have on me?* She thought as an officer got behind the wheel and started the engine. *How did I get entangled in this mess?*

CHAPTER TWELVE

Holly's still dazed by the next morning when Scarlet arrived at the station with a lawyer. She always thought she looked good in orange, but today she didn't feel too elated about the color. Especially because it was an oversized jumpsuit she never imagined she would ever wear.

"He's the best," Scarlet told her when the officer brought Holly out to an interrogation room so she could speak with Felix Sterling. "He can get you out of this."

Holly rubbed her eyes and sighed. "I never imagined I would one day sleep in a holding cell my entire life," she told Scarlet. "This still feels like a horrible dream."

"One that'll be over soon," Sterling chirped in, making Holly shift her eyes over to his. The man seemed confident as he adjusted his tie and added, "I have already spoken to the sheriff. They searched your place while you were away and found evidence...Implicating evidence."

"What?" Holly blurted, nearly choking on her words. "I didn't do anything...what evidence?"

"They found Annalisa's bloody clothing in your house, her cell phone, wallet, and some other personal items all tucked away in a cardboard box hidden in your closet. The phone was turned on re-cently, so they were able to track it there."

Holly blinked from her shock, loomed to Scarlet, then burst into a rolling laugh that made her hug her sides with her cuffed wrists and lower her head to the table. "Did you say bloody clothes?" she asked as she laughed harder. "Annalisa's bloody clothes? That's just insane right?"

Holly looked to Scarlet, then back to the lawyer who was simply watching her with an amused smile.

"I just got back to town, and I spent the entire night with Scarlet after the bonfire. How and when did I get the chance to murder Annalisa Rice, drown her in the ocean and then get back home to hide her items in my closet?"

Tears stung her eyes as she laughed till her sides hurt, then she burst into a loud sob. Scarlet left her seat to comfort Holly even though the officer in the room stared at her with a scowl on his face.

"Mind your own business," Scarlet said to him and Holly leaned into her embrace, loving the warmth of her hug.

A few seconds later, Holly finally stopped crying, she wiped her cheeks with both hands, then looked to the lawyer again. "How do you get me out of this?"

"We establish that you have an alibi," he answered her almost im-mediately. "All they've got on you are the items they found at your place, and they could have easily been planted there. They'll run the bloody shirt for prints and if they come back clean, you'll be free to go."

"What if it doesn't?" Holly asked and glanced at Scarlet, then back at the lawyer again. "I mean, I was with Scarlet most of the night, and I went to bed right after she left. It was almost midnight at the time she left."

"Your alibi's not solid proof because the victim's time of death has been estimated to midnight, but the DNA prints can get you out of this."

Holly shuddered at the thought of spending one more night in that holding cell. She didn't get much sleep last night, her back hurt, and her head would not stop pounding.

"I might be here a while, right?" The dreadful feeling settling in the pit of her stomach was enough to make her feel nauseous, but she fought that feeling too, and drew in a deep breath instead. "Can you look after Chile while I'm here? Poor girl, she's probably so hungry and lonely."

"I took Chile home last night. You have nothing to worry about. You will be out of here very soon."

The conversation with the lawyer lasted a few more minutes before the officer in the room announced, "Time is up."

Time passed slowly, while Holly lied awake in the holding cell, waiting for a miracle to happen after Scarlet's visit. The next time she heard the rattling of the cell's gates opening, she looked up to see Tim standing out there, and the sheriff by his side.

"Make it quick," Sheriff Carlton said and walked away without saying a word to her.

Holly sat upright on the ground but didn't move to get on her feet. Tim was the last person she expected to see, and she didn't think he wanted to be here either because he was scowling at her, his eyes unflinching.

"I didn't kill your mom, Tim," Holly gasped as she managed to meet his hard gaze. She swallowed hard to push the tightness in her chest down. *Does he really think I'm capable of murder?*

"I didn't think you did," Tim answered, releasing a deep breath before he shoved his hands into his pockets. "I heard what happened. Everyone in town's talking and it's only been one night."

"Yeah well, news travels faster than light in Cleverly Shores, so I'm not surprised."

She rubbed a hand over her face and got on her feet. "Why did you come?" she asked him as she walked over to the gate and held the bar. Standing close enough so she could inhale his breezy mountain scent, Holly closed her eyes and subtly let it fill her nostrils.

"You look like crap," Tim said to her as she slowly opened her eyes and looked at him.

Tim drew in a deep breath when their prolonged eye contact ended with Holly looking away first, and he stepped back from her a little.

"Come to gloat? And say I deserve to be locked up here?" She didn't even try to hide her sarcasm.

"Scarlet tells me she got you a lawyer." His tone was cool and calm like always. It's hard to read him because he masked everything he felt with a frown or a blank expression. Holly remembered Tim used to be so expressive.

When he smiled, his eyes would light up, and the corners drew upwards till his lids were half-closed. Holly realized she missed his smile.

I don't think he'll ever smile at me again.

"Yeah...They don't think I stand a chance though. My alibi isn't reliable, and the police have evidence that incriminates me. I might be stuck in an orange jumpsuit a while I guess."

"You won't be here long. You're innocent, so they won't have a reason to keep you."

"You trust that I am?" Holly asked in a shaky voice. She gasped, and her heart picked up its pace when Tim lifted a hand and stroked her chin gently. His touch is feathery light, and her lip's parted slightly as she leaned against the bars holding her apart from him.

"I know you, Barber...You could never hurt anyone." He dropped his hand, swallowed, then took out a tiny drawing pad from his pocket. "I got you something to cheer you up." He handed her the drawing pad.

Holly opened the first page, saw the sketch of a puppy on it, then smiled. "You still draw?" Grinning wide, her chest started to feel lighter just from looking at the drawing.

She flipped to the next page and saw a sketch of her. It was a younger version of her though. Holly's hair was longer, and her cheeks rosier as she smiled wide. Her stomach sunk as she recalled Tim painting her each time they hung out at his family's beach house together.

You're a muse, he told her once while she posed for his painting. She was so happy with him back then, but also torn between staying back and leaving for college.

"That should cheer you up till you get out of here," Tim whispered, distracting her from the path her thoughts took.

"Thanks." Her lips parted with a full smile that showed teeth. Tim returned the smile, and for once, it was genuine. Holly's breath hitched in her throat as his eyes crinkled at the corners and a lone dimple flashed in his left cheek.

"See you around, Barber," he said as he backed away from her.

Holly's feeling much lighter after speaking to him. She waved him goodbye while holding onto the sketch pad. For the first time since her return to Cleverly Shores, it didn't feel like her chances of being Tim's friend again was completely ruined.

There's hope. And Holly let that encourage her to stay strong.

CHAPTER THIRTEEN

"You're free to go," Sheriff Carlton said when he walked up to Holly's cell the next morning and opened the gate for her. "There's an officer waiting in the front with your personal items, and John will drive you home."

Holly stood in the same spot on the floor even after he opened the cell's gate and held it open for her.

"You didn't find anything, did you?" she asked, eyeing him closely as he planted his hands on his waist.

"We got a warrant because we had proof Annalisa's missing phone was on your property, and we found the items we were searching for," he explained. "But we ran the prints on her bloody clothes and other items, and they don't match yours. That means we have no reason to hold you here and forty-eight hours have elapsed so...You're free to go."

Holly got on her feet now, and scoffed. "You don't seem to like me very much, do you?" This time she walked over to him so she was close enough to stare deep into his eyes.

"What are you talking about?"

"You didn't seem pleased that I'm back in town trying to restore my family's business...You jumped at the chance to arrest me without giving me the benefit of the doubt, and now you're speaking to me like I'm still a suspect even though you've got nothing to prove that I'm involved in this case."

The sheriff's frown deepened as she spoke, proving Holly's suspicions. "It's not about you," he said after a second of silence.

"Then what is it about? My parents? Whatever issues you had with them I don't want any part of it. I'm back in Cleverly Shores to stay and I don't need you judging me for that choice."

"You're over-thinking this, Miss Barber." He stepped aside so she could leave the cell. "I warned you not to stay in town because I know Cleverly Shores has a way of sucking everyone into its drama, but you wouldn't listen. It was just some friendly advice...it has nothing to do with how I feel about you."

"But..."

"No buts, Miss Barber. You're free to go now. Are you going to leave, or do you want to stand there and accuse me of being impartial towards you because of some past baggage you think I've got towards your family?"

Holly pressed her lips together, dismissing everything else she was going to say to him. Chin hiked high; she walked away from the sheriff and found the officer with her items. She walked out of the station, grateful to breathe in crisp, fresh air once again.

"You're a free woman," Scarlet said behind Holly, making her turn with speed. Holly ran towards her for a hug. They stayed in a tight embrace for a while, ignoring John till he cleared his throat.

"I didn't think I'd ever get to do that again," Holly commented with a short laugh when she pulled away from Scarlet. "I thought I would wear an orange jumpsuit forever."

Scarlet's light chuckle burst free from her. "You know I would never let that happen."

"Thanks for helping, you truly are the most amazing friend a girl could ever ask for." Holly hugged her again, then did the same to John before she walked to his patrol car with them.

When she arrived at Scarlet's house a few minutes later, Holly was grateful for the warmth of their home again.

"Why don't you take a shower, and I'll fix you something to eat. Can I make you some soup?"

"Yeah, I'd love that." Chile barked when Holly entered the kitchen. She instantly went down on her knees to cradle Chile close. "I missed you too, girl...I truly did."

Holly played with Chile's hair and kept hugging her close for a long time before she lowered herself all the way down and sat on the floor.

Solemn thoughts raced through her mind as she recalled the sketch pad Tim brought her at the station. She took it out of her pocket, stared at the sketch on it for a while, then smiled. Holly was still grinning at the sketch pad when Scarlet asked, "Is that from Tim?"

"Yes, he brought it to me while I was at the station yesterday. He still draws."

"I didn't know he came to see you." Scarlet was walking around the kitchen trying to fix them a meal while Holly remained on the kitchen floor, her knees too weak to move.

"He shocked me too, and he was nice to me for the first time since he's been back." Holly stroked her image on the drawing pad. "I think he's finally coming around."

"And that excites you right?" Scarlet has her usual teasing smile on as she asked, and her suggestive tone made Holly roll her eyes. "Admit it, Holly. You still like him."

"I don't," Holly denied but Scarlet arched a brow in disbelief and slanted her a suspicious look till she gave in. "Okay, fine...Maybe I still like him a little. There is just something about him."

"I knew it!"

"It doesn't matter anyway...He's never going to like me that way again. Not after how I hurt him."

Holly's heart sunk a little. She had ruined whatever chance she could have had with Tim already. All she could ask for now was a friendship at least.

That must be enough.

"Go on in the bathroom and take a shower," Scarlet said to Holly as she got on her feet again.

Holly massaged the back of her neck as she wandered out of the kitchen and headed in to take a nice, warm shower. The past forty-eight hours were the longest of her life and she was grateful it was finally over. But there was one question jabbing at her, even though all she wanted to do was drop on the bed and sleep her exhaustion away.

The police didn't find anything to implicate her, but it didn't mean it was over yet. *Someone tried to frame me. Why else would Annalisa's personal items suddenly get into my bedroom closet?*

Whoever it was, Holly knew she must be more alert of her surroundings now. *A killer's lurking in the shadows.* She turned on the shower and let the warm water slither down her skin and ease the kinks out in her muscles. *I have a feeling he's coming for me.*

CHAPTER FOURTEEN

A few days later, Holly was back at Frijole's, and it was a bit busier than usual. She grinned at a customer as she handed over a take-out bag of tacos. "Have a great day."

"You too," the woman responded before leading her son out the door.

For a second after that, Holly placed her hands on her cheeks in disbelief. "I just can't believe this." She turned away from the door and headed to her kitchen again. Frijole's luck had changed since she returned from her two nights stay at the station. Holly made more pancakes than she ever had this week, and she spent the entire morning shuffling between kitchen and dining area cooking and serving so many customers.

At this rate, she might need her first waitress by the end of the month. *Hopefully.* Another fluttery wave of excitement settled inside her. She stepped out of the kitchen when she heard the front bell ring again, indicating that someone had walked in.

"Welcome to Frijole's," Holly announced as she walked into the dining area. Her follow-up line was cut short when she saw Tim stroll in and stop in front of the counter. "Tim," she gasped, her pulse skittering up a little as she met his gaze.

Holly hadn't seen him since he visited her at the station, and now he's smiling at her with a softened look in his eyes. "You look better in regular colors," Tim said to her as he placed a hand on the counter. "Orange just doesn't do you justice."

"Really?" she answered instinctively as a chuckle bubbled free from her. "I've been told I look good in orange. It brings out my eyes, you know."

"You've been lied to," he responded before their laughter blended into one.

"Here for some enchiladas?" She tilted her head to one side while assessing him. Holly's voice sounded lighter than she intended it to. It's almost as if she let it get breezy on purpose. *Like I'm flirting.*

Tim shook his head. "Actually, I came to check on you...See how you're holding up after your wonderful two nights stay at the station."

"Funny," she replied with a laugh. "You ever going to stop teasing me about that?"

"Not really."

It's easy to flow into a conversation with him like this when he's smiling, and Holly soon let herself forget all the reasons why she hadn't seen him smile since she got back to town.

"Well, since you're here anyway, and there's no customers, mind sitting on the patio with me? I've got chips and salsa."

Tim looked like he was considering her offer as he pursed his lips, and Holly gently nudged his arm. "Come on, I've got your favorite, green chile salsa. You know you can't resist that."

Holly held her breath in anticipation of his reply. She worried for a second, he'd ruin the light-hearted moment by declining her offer.

Tim shocked her with his affirming nod a few seconds later. "Only if you pair that with your legendary raspberry lemonade. I've missed those."

Holly doesn't hold back the side-tickling laugh that erupted through her. She's still grinning when she wandered into her kitchen and returned with some chips and salsa for them to share.

Tim sat on the patio, and she returned again a couple minutes later with two glasses of freshly made raspberry lemonade.

She took off her apron and pulls her hair into a low ponytail before joining him at the table. Some strands of hair were stuck on her neck, and she peeled them away gently before meeting Tim's gaze again.

"That's an interesting pendant." His gaze dropped to the key she was wearing around her neck.

Holly slipped the key into the braided cord necklace she found amongst her old stashed away items the other day.

"Oh, thanks," Holly twirled the pendant around her fingers as she relaxed in her chair. "Weird right? It's a key I found the other day. Scarlet and I ordered the cords from Esty back in high school. So I decided to make a necklace with them both.

"Why are you wearing it around your neck?" Holly sucked in a deep breath when he stared at it again. A knot twisted in the pit of her stomach as she recalled the trip to the clinic, and Dr. Parker's revelation about her father's request.

"It's just something important I want to keep close to me," she responded to Tim while her thoughts wandered around a little. "It's just ..." Holly trailed off, suddenly realizing that in the past she would have told him something this important. Tim used to be her go-to person. They would spend long hours strolling the beach, indulging in far too many chips with spicy salsa, and dancing on the shoreline.

"Holly?"

She swallowed hard to push down the lump at the base of her throat. "Sorry," Holly answered with a breezy chuckle. "Was lost for a moment there. It's just a very important key," she added, then licked her lips. "I never want to lose it again."

Tim assessed her for a moment before he reached into his pocket and showed her the key he had tucked away too. "I also have a key I never want to lose either," he said as he twirled the key around his fingers. "Found it in my room with a note from my mom the night she passed."

"You were back in town then?"

"No," he answers in a raspy tone. "But I was supposed to meet her that night." Couldn't make it, so it had to be the next day. It was too late by then."

Holly noticed a tic in his jaw muscles as he spoke, then he blew air out of his lips and swallowed hard. His next smile was wistful, Holly noticed the shimmer of tears in his eyes.

"I'm so sorry, Tim. About your mom. I'm so sorry." Holly placed a hand on his and she only realized what she'd done when Tim released a shuddering breath then looked into her eyes again.

"Sorry," she apologized again and removed her hand from his.

"Don't be. You were right. I couldn't leave town with everything as crazy as it is right now. I have to stay till they find the person responsible for the death of my mother."

A tiny smile worked its way to Holly's lips as she stared at him, but Tim's forehead contorted in a frown when he noticed. "What?"

"Nothing. Just...I knew you wouldn't be able to leave till they found out who did this. She's your mom, Tim. No matter what happened before now and the feelings you had towards her. She's your mom."

"I guess maybe you do know me better than I give you credit for."

He picked his lemonade glass up and sipped from it. "So, what does the key open?" He directed the conversation to her, and once again, she considered spilling all about her recent discoveries to him.

I'm not sure he's that open to being my friend again. This is the first time we're even holding a conversation that's not tense, and she wanted to savor the moment for as long as it lasted. *Before he goes back to hating me again.*

"A music box," she revealed, but ended it there. "Yours?"

"A safety deposit box. I don't think I'll ever open it though."

"You should," she blurted out, and he arched a brow before she slowed her breath and repeated it in a much calmer tone. "If your mom left you the key, then you should open it. She probably has something she wants you to have."

"Like a parting gift?"

Holly nodded, "Yes, exactly like a parting gift. Somehow those seem to make the thought of losing someone you love easier to handle."

"I wish you left me a parting gift," Tim whispered and his words made her chest cave in with the weight of remorse again. "Would have made missing you easier."

"Tim I'm..."

"Don't apologize," he cut in, his voice squeaky. It sent a ripple of unease up Holly's spine, and she was scared their brief moment of renewed friendship had come to an end. "You did what you had to do. I don't resent you for that even if I do hate the fact you did it."

He offered her a shaky smile, and Holly exhaled a pent-up breath. "Thank you," she whispered in a throaty voice. "Does this mean we're friends now."

"Don't push it," Tim replied sternly with a hardened glare, but that lasted only a second before a loud chortle emerged from him. "I'm kidding. Sure...We're friends again."

"Great!"

Holly was out on the porch alone later that evening after Tim left, and a black sedan pulled up in front of Frijole's. An unexpected customer walked towards the diner.

CHAPTER FIFTEEN

Holly tried to figure out who the gentleman looking around her diner was. *I know I have seen him somewhere before.* She couldn't place his face the entire time he looked around, and when his eyes settled on her face again, he smiled.

"Nate Fallon," he introduced.

"Oh," Holly gasped, then placed a hand in his extended one. "Nice to meet you, Mr. Fallon. Can I get you something? We have our famous enchiladas, or some tacos if you'd like."

He nodded and smiled again, his eyes skimming over her. "You're young," he said. "Do you stay here alone? I mean.... Since your father passed and you moved back to town."

The hairs on the back of Holly's neck stood erect at his question. Her brows furrowed into a tight line. "I didn't know you knew my father. Or me for that matter."

There's something chilling about his smile, but his eyes stayed focused on hers before he laughed. "Of course I knew your father, Holly. This is Cleverly Shores...Everyone knows everyone around here."

"Right. So, what can I get you?"

"Ceviche. I haven't had in in awhile, it's my favorite. Hopefully you can make that for me."

Holly was about to refuse his order when he continued, "Double Flavors serves the best ceviche. I keep hearing about how good this place is, and since they're out of business for now, I thought I'd drop by here and taste test it for myself. Surely, you're as good as your competition, right? I was really hoping it was not just talk?"

"I can assure you it's not just talk. It'll take a few minutes Mr. Fallon, but I can get your order out very soon."

"I have all the time in the world Miss Barber, no rush."

They exchanged smiles again, and Holly left him to sit in the dining area while she went back into the kitchen. The first few seconds, she spent it staring at nothing in particular, in her kitchen. She was very curious what he was doing here, but she didn't have time to think about that right now. She got straight to work after a deep sigh.

About twenty minutes later, she arrived with the plate of ceviche freshly made and marinated in lemon juice. She had also added an extra dash of spiciness to it.

Holly waited till he took his first bite of the dish. She could tell from his smile and nod her recipe met his approval.

"I guess they were right...Double Flavors really does have some tough competition."

Holly's not sure his words are a compliment, but they make her smile anyway.

The rest of the evening after Nate Fallon left, Holly worked on more of her recipes to make sure she could keep the community talk going about her food. For a moment that night, she wondered if Frijole's would have any recognition if Double Flavors had not shut down.

It's a horrible thought, but it's there in the back of her mind as she knew deep down that Annalisa's murderer took out her competition.

CHAPTER SIXTEEN

Music from Holly's earbuds had her forgetting everything going on during her run the next morning. She realized her heart was hammering in her chest, she must have been running at an extremely faster pace than normal. Holly thought so at least because she was almost out of breath and she just barely finished the first two miles.

She slowed her pace a bit to catch her breath. The whiff of the morning's crisp air invaded her lungs, bringing a smile to her lips.

Holly hoped she would run into Tim while she was running down her usual path around the beach.

She continued to slow her pace when she felt her lungs struggle to keep up with the racing of her heart. She stopped and dropped her hands to her knees for a moment, leaning slightly forward.

Holly glanced at her smart watch for a bit to monitor her heart rate and lost track of her surroundings. She didn't hear anyone approach till a hand tapped her shoulder gently.

"Hey," Kenneth greeted when she turned to him, then she took out her earbuds. His dazzling smile reached his eyes, and he jogged in a spot for a moment longer before he finally stopped right next to her.

"Hi Kenneth..."

"Didn't know you ran," Kenneth said with another charming grin. "You do it occasionally? Or you a junkie like me?"

"I wouldn't say I'm a junkie," she answered with a short laugh. Holly noticed his chiseled biceps showed off by his tank top. They glistened with the sheen of sweat on his skin, and veins were bulging out of them, proving he's hardcore into strength training. "I just do it once in a while because I love the sea breeze."

She framed her hands on her waist and smiled at him again. "So, you have a trail? Or you just run?"

"I have a trail. Maybe you can join me on it one morning? We never got around to hanging out the other day."

"That's right," Holly laughed again as she recalled finding the music box because of his comment. Kenneth let his gaze trail over her face and his smile broadened again.

He mimicked her pose and nudged his head in one direction. "So, what do you say? You'll run with me? Or are we having dinner instead? Not at Frijole's though...I don't want you cooking dinner for our date."

His mention of date made her smile fade a notch. "You're asking me out on a date?"

"Yes, I guess I am," Kenneth answered with a light chuckle. "If that's okay, I guess. I mean, you're not seeing anyone are you?"

"No," she answered almost immediately. "I mean...Not really. No one right now."

"Well then, I guess I'm in luck." Kenneth had an easy laugh, and the wind carried it her way as she stared into his eyes.

The light breeze picked up some strands of Holly's hair now, ruffling it over her face. She lifted a hand, but Kenneth moved faster, and helped tuck some strands behind her ears. His hand lingered over her cheeks in a light fluttering touch, and the flirtatious smile that kissed his lips didn't go unnoticed.

"Thanks." She was about to say something else when a familiar voice called out her name.

"Tim?" She spun around to see him closing the distance between them. Tim stopped right by her side and huffed out a breath before he looked from her to Kenneth.

"Kenneth, this is Tim. He's a friend."

She expected Tim to extend a hand to Kenneth, but both men exchanged hardened glares instead, and the smile on Kenneth's face completely disappeared as his eyes narrowed at the corners.

"We've met before," Kenneth grumbled, his lips twisting into a smirk that made his eyes darken further till they were thick, bottomless depths.

"Yeah," Tim replied as Holly shuffled her gaze between both men. "Kenneth's new in town," Tim continued, his jaw hardening. "I'm sure he's told you all about how he moved here a year ago and has decided to build a home here."

Holly's right brow rose to her hairline. "A year?" she questioned, looking at Kenneth briefly.

"I should probably do. See you around, Holly."

"She won't be seeing you," Tim replied instead of Holly, and Kenneth didn't respond.

He picked up his pace quickly and jogged away from them. Holly looked over to Tim and shoved down the first tingle that sprouted in her chest. "What was that all about?"

Tim moved lightly, taking up the spot where Kenneth stood a moment earlier. "That was you meeting my mother's boyfriend."

"What?" she croaked, before bursting into a low laugh and shaking her head. "Boyfriend? Kenneth's like..."

"Ex, actually. They broke up after three months. He probably mentioned being new in town and needing a friend, right? The guy's a young, ladies' man my mom just happened to have the hots for before she divorced my dad."

Holly blinked from the shock of his revelation. Her mind spun as it registered what Tim had just said. "Are you saying Kenneth's the reason for the divorce?"

"No, he's not the reason. Their marriage was pretty much over years ago. I didn't know it at the time. They agreed to stay together so they could raise me as a family, then part ways once I graduated high school. Neither of them were faithful the entire time. They didn't think I could handle it so they never told me."

Holly's jaw dropped, but she snapped it back up immediately, hoping Tim didn't notice her sudden shock of emotions.

She had pictured them as the perfect family for years. *All of that was a sham? From the outside looking in, they looked so perfect.*

"Anyway, Kenneth and I didn't exactly have a great relationship."

"No one can blame you for that. It's a tough situation, I'm not sure how I would've handled it either. If it's any consolation, I recently found out that my dad kept a huge secret from me too. He didn't think I could handle it while he was alive, so..."

"Guess we didn't know them as good as we thought we did."

"Yeah, I guess so. We sure didn't."

"How many miles have you covered?" she asked, directing her thoughts back to their reality.

"Six. You?"

"Two and some. Want to finish our run out together?"

"Only if you buy breakfast after."

She suppressed a chuckle and let her flush sweep through the rest of her. "I'll do you one better...I'll make you another one of your favorites, avocado toast once we get back to the diner."

They grinned at each other and then headed off down the shore to finish their morning run, running in a rhythmic pace like they did every morning many years ago.

CHAPTER SEVENTEEN

D ays later, Holly's still thinking of the DNA results she discovered, and her father's last words. Her time with Tim spurred more curious thoughts. Finding out his mother left him a key to a safety deposit box, that probably contained her will, made Holly think of her father's last letter.

You'll always be my little girl. Those words brought a smile to her lips each time she thought of it. But a part of her still craved for more. *Answers, the truth.* There's only one person who can provide them.

My mother, and she ignored the fresh ache that trembled through her heart at the thought of speaking to her again after eighteen years.

''You sure you want this? You really want to do this?" Scarlet asked as they serve dinner in Scarlet's kitchen. Holly decided to spend Saturday evening with her friend, relaxing, after a long afternoon at Frijole's. They prepared chicken casserole together while talking about Holly's decision to contact her mom.

Holly dropped a batch of freshly made brownies on the table before she shrugged and turned to her friend.

"I don't know," she answered honestly. The thought of reaching out to her mother after all these years made a knot twist deep in her gut. "She never reached out to me. Not even a birthday card or

Christmas card in eighteen years. She's been radio silent. What would I even say to her after all these years?"

"You could start with, hey mom...Good to know you're still alive considering you've been a whorl for over decade. Anyway, I just found out my dad isn't my real dad, and I'm guessing you know who my real dad is, so ...I really need some answers. Send a card if you can't call. Bye."

Scarlet's high-pitched tone as she suggested what to say made Holly laugh so hard. "You're kidding right?" Holly said as her body shook with the force of her raspy laugh. "you are crazy. I'm not going to say that to her."

"Of course you won't, I'm just kidding. Seriously though, just speak from your heart, Holly. Tell her how you feel and ask her what you need to know. You deserve to know the truth."

The familiar ache in Holly's heart made it difficult to decide, so she shook her head and dispelled thoughts of reaching out to her mom from her mind. "You know what? It's not worth it. She didn't want me, and it's been this long already. I don't need to ask her anything. I'm fine not knowing."

Scarlet turned to Holly and arched her brows softly. "You sure about that?"

"I am." She ignored the prick in her chest, determined not to let it affect her decision. *This is how it is.* She walked over to a chair at the table. John walked in a moment later and greeted Holly with a smile.

"How's it going?" he asked before kissing his wife on the cheek and taking the seat next to hers.

Each time Holly saw her friend beam at her husband, she was reminded of what true love was all about.

I hope to find that one day. As she dug into her casserole a moment later, the spicy taste of ginger blended with cayenne reminded her of her mom. By the time Holly was six years old, she had spent so much time with her mom in the kitchen at Frijole's. There were times she even helped with the cooking too.

Both her parents ran the diner, each taking turns to whip up dishes for their loyal customers. Those times, Holly remembered there were very few fights, and lots of love and laughter. She would stroll the beach shores with her mom in the evenings once Frijole's closed, and dance salsa at X-Beach Bar while perched on her dad's neck.

They were so happy. Until they weren't. The fighting began in the summer right before she turned seven, and shortly after that it became nastier. Holly would hide in her bedroom while their voices thundered all the way up from the diner downstairs.

Back then, she had wished she could drown out the sounds with her pillow, but her young mind always listened anyway.

Holly was lost in her thoughts; she barely heard her friend when she asked, "You okay?"

"Holly?" John called a second later, his gentle but insistent voice lured her back to reality, and she cleared her throat before forcing on a smile.

"Yes, sorry," Holly lied. "I'm good, I just..."

"You need a minute?" Scarlet asked, her brows drawn up with worry lines.

"Yes, I think I do," Holly moved her chair backwards to free herself. "I just need some fresh air for a minute. I'll be right back." She walked out of the kitchen, leaving her casserole half touched.

Too many memories. They flooded her mind regardless of what she wanted, reminding her of the good times she shared with her parents. Holly's still standing on Scarlet's front porch, enjoying the heavy gust of wind ruffling her hair and tickling her nostrils.

Chile's sprawled on the front porch too, but she got up to stand by Holly's side. It's like she knows something is wrong. Holly smiled at Chile when she sat by her feet.

Holly decided she was going to take her for a long stroll later that evening. It will help her clear her mind and she knew Chile would enjoy getting out of the house as well. She is locked up in the house most days, so taking her out for a stroll this evening is a natural reward for being a good dog.

Holly hugged herself tight as she rocked back on her heels and tried to handle the flood of emotions tunneling through her. Her chest tightened, her throat felt raw, and the only thought on her mind was the struggle between letting go of what she found or continue searching for more answers.

Do I really want to know? Realizing that her parent's marriage probably ended because of her mom's choices, was already a tough pill to swallow. *Do I really want to know who the other man is?*

"You know," Scarlet began softly without touching Holly. "John's with the sheriff's department. He could pull some strings and ask around if you wanted him to. I'm sure he could find her and get some information on her. Maybe that would help you decide."

She angled her head to look at her friend, and the solemn look on Scarlet's face made Holly's heart ache even more. Sighing, she stepped back, put her left hand around Scarlet's waist, then gave her a side hug. She leaned her head on Scarlet's shoulder for a second before she whispered, "You're my family…You're my sister…You're my friend. You and Chile are all I need right now."

A long moment of silence passed before she added, "I think I'll be content not knowing. My dad's forever going to be my dad, so I just need to learn to be okay without knowing."

Scarlet said nothing as they stood in that loving embrace for a few minutes longer. The cool breeze eased most of the tension budding through Holly, and finally she started relaxing while leaning against her friend.

"Alright then. Come back inside and finish your casserole."

Holly offered her a shaky smile before pulling away and turning to the door.

"John's available if you change your mind. All you need to do...All you ever need to do, is ask." Scarlet's words made Holly freeze in her tracks. Her hand hovered over the doorknob before she shoved off every tiny tingle of curiosity still sprouting in the back of her mind.

"Thanks, but I won't change my mind," she said with certainty. "I have no reason to."

CHAPTER EIGHTEEN

It's time for a change! Holly stared at the new wallpaper on Frijole's walls with her hands framed on her hips. She spent her entire morning on this project keeping her mind off all the other thoughts that had been constantly going through her head. Now that the wallpaper was completely different, she realized the walls still needed a little something more.

Something more...Maybe art, maybe colors. She can't decide what it needs exactly, but she's sure she'll find out once she gets to the art store on Cleverly Shores Main Route.

The drive down there was a measly ten minutes. Holly pulled her hair back with both hands, then placed her sunglasses over the top of her head to keep her stray aways in place. She huffed in a deep breath before strolling into the store for a quick peek at the paintings they had displayed on the wall.

She was lost staring at a geometric abstract piece when someone cleared their throat behind her. Holly turned quickly, and gasped when she saw Tim behind her with a charming smile on his face.

"Abstract art?" he questioned, taking a step towards her to stand by her side so they could admire the paintings together. "You've never been one to understand art, or even like it much for that matter."

Holly laughed a little before shaking her head. "I still don't, but Frijole's is in dire need of some change, and I'm thinking art pieces are the perfect thing for the walls."

"Ah, have you tried life art pieces?"

She looked up to him with a puzzled smile, and he took her hand before she could muster up a reply.

"Here," Tim said, slowly letting her go before he pointed at an art piece on the wall. Holly stared at the painting of a woman for a few seconds, admiring the curvy lines that display her back, and the delicate representation of her black hair falling to waist level.

"That's uh..... It's very expressive," she said as a flush stung her cheeks.

"I actually painted it," Tim revealed as he stared at the painting with a smile.

"Oh really," Holly gasped, and this time, a stinging bite of jealousy ruffled her insides when she wondered who the woman in the painting was. *Girlfriend? Wife?* She doesn't know much about Tim anymore, and in their eight years apart, a lot could have happened to him too.

He probably fell in love, made plans, and executed them.

"That's not exactly what I had in mind..." Holly's words were drawn out as she looked around the collection of art pieces on the store's wall. "Unique...And vibrant."

Tim showed her another painting with a wave of his hand. "Do any of these seem to fit what you had in mind? I painted all of these too."

She didn't miss his proud smile as she looked around the collection he showed her. "Wow, that's a lot of paintings," she breathed out.

"Yeah, I know. I probably have you to thank for all these paintings. After you left eight years ago, I needed an outlet, so I locked myself in my studio for days unending and didn't step out unless I needed water or food to keep me going. My parents understood. They were pretty upset when you left without a word too. "

When Holly looked away from him, he chuckled.

"It's water under the bridge though," he continued with a short laugh. "We're friends again, aren't we?"

"Friends. Yes, yes.." They smiled at each other for a second longer before Tim bent over and lifted one painting from the ground.

"Take this one. It has warm colors and research said they are suitable for invoking hunger."

Holly stared at the vibrant painting. "Thanks, I actually really like this one. I think it will go perfect on the walls," she said before her eyes flickered to the painting of the woman again.

Tim noticed her flickering gaze as he removed his hand from the painting they both held. "You want that too?"

"No," she blurted with a nervous laugh. "I don't...I just..."

"College, second year...She was a model, and we had a thing for about one semester," he explained. "She transferred schools after that, and I never heard from her again."

"What? You don't need to explain yourself to me Tim, I was just..."

"I can tell what's on your mind from the expression on your face, Holly," he interrupted while she tried to deny the fact that his explanation didn't relieve her.

Holly bit her inner cheek to tune down another flush, and Tim's wandering eyes finally met hers.

"You're all flushed because you're nervously wondering who the woman I painted was. You're nervous because you want to ask but you're not sure it's the right thing to do. I can read you, Holly. Not much has changed about you."

"A lot has changed about me," she denied in an attempt to lighten the mood.

"You know I'm right about you. Your hair's the same color even though it's shorter…You use the same hair products because your hair smells just like I remember it. And you can never meet my gaze when you're nervous."

"Tim…"

"Your laugh is still the same," he continued, stopping her from voicing her shaky words.

"You didn't need to tell me…About the woman in the painting."

"I know that. But I wanted to."

He shrugged, slipped his hands into his pockets, and assessed her for a few seconds before adding, "Do you want some help? With hanging up whatever paintings you decide to get."

"That's really nice of you to offer, but I'll manage. I can always call Scarlet, she loves to come help." Holly stared at the painting in her hand. "I'll settle with this painting for now. But I definitely want to get a few other things like beach decorations and some fake potted plants. Just to give the place life."

"Great choice."

"Thanks." It's awkward after that, and Holly wished she could think of something else to say to him to cut the tension.

"Great talk, Barber," he said before she found anymore words. "I'll see you around."

Tim's eyes met hers one last time before he turned away.

Oh boy. She shook her head as she moved to the counter with her art painting. It'll be easy to fall for Tim again, but that's not an option.

Focusing on Frijole's is more important right now. And the killer on the lose!

She's heading out of the art store a few minutes later when she spotted Tim's truck parked in the corner of the art store's parking lot.

He was leaning against his tailgate, his arms crossed in front of him while he spoke to Nate Fallon.

Holly was about to start walking over to him when she saw Nate Fallon point a warning finger at Tim, spoke harshly, then stormed away.

What is going on? Tim stormed off from his truck and was about to walk away when he turned in her direction and suddenly met her gaze.

Holly held her breath, watched him and waited to see if he was going to say anything. Instead, he simply hardened his jaw and walked away like they didn't just smile at each other just minutes ago.

CHAPTER NINETEEN

At the next founder's meeting, Holly tried to focus on the topic of discussion the entire time she sat with the other founding members. Tim was on the far end of the table, his fingers constantly caressing his chin and Holly found herself wondering what thoughts were running through his mind.

Mr. Docherty mentioned the upcoming founder's ball again and that got her attention. "We have the planning committee putting together the entire details of the night, but I urge any of you that have the time and resources, to also help out putting it all together. We can never have too many hands-on deck."

There are quite a few people already nodding their heads signaling they'll help and assist the planning committee. Holly took note of Mrs. Branson, and Penny Colon murmuring to each other about the founder's ball, then noticed Tim watching her intently again.

He does that whenever he's lost in thought. She sucked in a deep breath and regarded him closely. He seemed lost in thought, and whatever ran through Tim's mind, Holly doubted it had anything to do with Sheriff Carlton's talk about the recent uprising rate of petty thieves in town.

"I'd like to ask the progress on the recent murder case of our dear council member, Mrs. Rice?" Mr. Nate Fallon, another council member, asked as he rose from his chair and adjusted his black suit. He adjusted his tie and his keen blue eyes scanned every face in the room. "The entire town wants to know what's being done about it."

Holly noticed how Tim's head spiked up and he fixated his gaze on Mr. Fallon.

When Mr. Fallon showed up at her diner the other day, he was very nosy and full of so many questions.

His brows drew together, and his chin hardened. Tim's definitely attentive now, and Mr. Fallon's expectant gaze moved from Sheriff Carlton's to the other founding members seated at the table.

"There's an ongoing investigation, is there not?" Mr. Fallon continued. "There's been a few suspects, yet, nothing tangible. Are we in anyway close to finding the killer? Or are we just going to let the killer roam free for a while and leave the other residents living in fear? Perhaps we should start by questioning anyone who might be directly involved in the case? Like Annalisa's known enemies and competitors for example?"

Grumbles arose around the table, and Holly noticed some people glance in her direction while she was careful not to react in anyway. She held onto a woman's stern glare for a long moment before looking away. Tim was staring at her again when she looked in his direction, and there was no hiding the intensity on his face right now.

"We are still investigating this case. At the moment, we have no suspects," Sheriff Carlton answered to ease the restless grumbles sprouting around the table. "I assure every one of you that we have it all under control. We don't throw out accusations until we have concrete evidence."

"Are there any leads at least?" another woman asked. "We need to know what to tell our folks at home. Everyone's worried...One of us died, and..."

"The department's doing everything they can at the moment, I assure you that," Sheriff Carlton interrupted again. Clearly, his explanation was not enough for anyone in the room. Their dissatisfied glares were evident, and tension was rising in the thick air around Holly.

The meeting ended a few minutes later, and Tim left the room without a word to anyone. Holly said hello to the town's priest first before rushing out after him. She adjusted her bag on one shoulder as she tried to catch up.

"Tim, wait up," she called, and picked up her pace again when he slowed down to talk to her. "Hey, are you okay?"

"Yeah," he answered before raking his fingers through his hair. "I just really need to get out of here. I don't think I can stand one more word out of Fallon's mouth. The man's been a thorn in my flesh since I got back to town. Can't even get through a day without seeing his smug face. He's literally everywhere."

Frowning a little, Holly tipped her head to one side. "I don't understand...Mr. Fallon's a thorn in your side, how?"

Tim sighed, shook his head, then rubbed his chin. "It's nothing serious. Just...Fallon had this business deal with my mother before she passed, and he's been bent on moving forward with it even though the restaurant's been closed since the incident."

"Oh wow, that's interesting. So, are you going to move forward? With this deal? He showed up at Frijole's the other day for some ceviche. He hinted he was a frequent customer at your mom's restaurant."

"Yeah, he was. He never missed her ceviche. He was there every week, even during their back and forth with the entire property deal."

Tim released an exasperated sigh. "I don't know what to do yet. All I know is my mom wanted to expand," he blurted out and swallowed hard. "I just need more time to think it through I guess."

"Maybe do what you think she would have done. I mean, you do know what your mom would have done, right? You knew her better than anyone, you would know if she wanted to go through with this deal."

"I know she had her doubts with Fallon," he murmured, this time, placing his right hand on his hip. "But...She had her doubts about many things and lots of people. My mother wasn't a very trusting person."

Tim's obvious worry spanned out on his expression. His neck looked stiff, his posture stooped, and the wrinkles on his forehead didn't diminish.

"I'll get it figured out. Its fine." A shaky smile played out on his lips before his gaze breezed over hers. "I'll see you at the founder's ball Friday night?"

Holly nodded her reply. "Yes, I'll be there."

"Cool," he acknowledged her with a nod before walking to his truck. Holly watched him drive away first, then moved to get into her car. She noticed the sheriff watching her when she turned around briefly.

Priest Docherty was speaking to him, but every angle of his body was turned away from the priest, his arms folded across his chest while his disapproving stare lingered.

An unsettling feeling increased in the pit of Holly's stomach as she got in her car. She could never shake off the shivering dread that overcame her senses each time the sheriff was near.

***

"The founder's ball," Scarlet commented as Holly strolled around the beach shores where the dinner was hosted for the night. Usually, the ball took place at the mayor's large office, but this time, the council had voted for something different and Penny Colon's team made it happen.

"Ever thought you would attend one of these as a founder?" Scarlet asked as a light laugh eased out of her and she rubbed her hand across Holly's back. Holly loved how Scarlet looked in her red sequined colored dress that evening. The full sleeves and bodice framed her petite figure perfectly, and the color highlighted her creamy skin tone just right.

"If my dad were here, he would have been very proud. I would have saved him my first dance tonight."

"So, who will you be saving it for instead?" Scarlet asked in her teasing tone, and winked at Holly before nudging her head towards the crowd in front of them. "Is it the blonde one? Or the handsome, dark-eyed one?"

Holly instantly knew she was referring to Tim and Kenneth. She glanced towards the dessert bar a few feet away and spotted both men speaking with hard expressions on their faces.

Her heart doubled its speed once she saw Tim, and the slow burn of heat rushing to her cheeks made her grin wide.

"It's definitely Tim," she said to herself.

Tim whipped his head up in her direction a second later, and Kenneth followed his gaze. Both men stared at her for a long time and Holly wondered what the deal between them was before she looked away first.

"You gonna walk up to him or what?" Scarlet teased again before John joined them and kissed her cheek. "Holly's into Tim, but Kenneth has a thing for her and now she has to choose."

"Scarlet..." Holly cautions as Scarlet burst into a loud laugh. "That's not true...That's so not true."

John held his wife's waist as he laughed with her, and Holly rolled her eyes at both of them, grinning too as their bubbly laugh teased her insides.

"But you do have a thing for the chef, don't you?" John asked her, his eyes drifting over her face.

"Chef? Kenneth?" She looked to where Kenneth was standing again. Tim was now alone, and Holly scanned the crowd to look for Kenneth, but he was nowhere in sight.

"Yeah, I thought you knew that. He worked with Annalisa at Double Flavors for like six months while they dated, then shortly after, he decided to start up his own restaurant. The place is in shambles, and he hasn't done much with it yet. Rumor has it, he needs funding, so he drew up a proposal to get Annalisa to invest but Mr. Rice wouldn't let her. Things were pretty tense between Kenneth and Annalisa after that. He always tried to get her on board, but she kept refusing to do business with him."

Holly suddenly recalled Tim mentioning that about his mother's deal with Mr. Fallon. "Do you know anything about a deal between Annalisa and Mr. Fallon?"

John nodded again. "Yeah...Annalisa was going to buy his property off Shelling Street. The two talked about it for a long time actually, but it turns out, she wasn't very forthcoming." John grinned before adding, "I work with the sheriff, I hear about a lot of things."

Tim was speaking with Mr. Fallon again when Holly looked his way, and she sees them shake hands. "I'll be right back," she mumbled before heading towards Tim.

CHAPTER TWENTY

"**H**ey, you," Holly greeted when she got to Tim a few seconds later. On the walk over, she paused to greet the town's priest and a few other familiar faces. There's no ignoring the curious gaze she got from some of the town's residents too. *And the murmurs. Lots of talk all around her.*

Holly was used to gossip. Cleverly Shores survived on it. Tim grinned at her when he turned around. His black tux suit framed him perfectly, giving him a dashing look Holly was certain she would never forget.

"The last time I saw you in a tux, you were homecoming king," she said to him as their grins matched. "Boy, you've grown up since then."

Tim was all muscle now, and his taller frame towered over Holly. His blue eyes held onto hers for a second that felt longer than usual, then he dropped his gaze to her lips and stared for a second longer.

"Yeah, I'm all grown up now," he answered in a confident tone. "But so have you, and you look..." he slowed his words, then moved his head from side to side before releasing a shuddering breath. "Ravishing in that dress."

Holly blushed before she looked down at her black dress. It was flowing all the way to her ankles, and covered her legs, but the thigh has a long slit that exposed her leg on one side.

"It's just a dress," she whispered, and her toes curled up in her heels. "Picked it out from my mom's old stuff. Didn't even think it would look very nice, actually."

"Well, you look nice," he stated, and she looked at him again. "Beautiful actually."

A slow song started playing in the background now, and Tim cocked his head to one side before asking. "Care to dance?"

The request shocked Holly, but she agreed with a nod anyway, and placed her hand in his. Tim moved her to the dance floor in fluid motion, and others around them paired up for the dance as well.

Their bodies aligned like they were always meant to be together and they swayed as one. His eyes never left hers while they danced. He spun her around towards the bridge of the song, and drew her back into his arms again.

"So, you settled the deal with Mr. Fallon? I saw you two shake hands."

"I wouldn't call it settled yet. We're still talking about it. I can't take such a huge decision lightly."

"But did you know your mom didn't want to take the deal with Mr. Fallon? I hear she kept putting him off for a long time. Maybe there's a reason why she wasn't considering it?"

Tim twirled her around again. "Have you been speaking to people about my mom?" He sounded slightly edgy, and his brows furrowed together to show his annoyance.

"People? No...Just John and ..."

"Don't," he cut her short, then released her abruptly, ending their rhythmic dance. "Don't speak to anyone about my mom or about me, got it?"

"No Tim. It's just that, a few days ago you thought the man was condescending and everywhere. Now, you're about to do business with him? You should consider the reasons why your mother held back in the first place."

He stormed away, and Holly followed, rushing to meet up with him before he made it too far across the room. "Tim, wait..."

Tim spun around quick, grabbed her by the shoulders, and plastered his lips to hers for a brief, shocking kiss that sent tidal waves of electricity jolting through her very being. The brush of his lips was quick and rough, but it screamed passion. Holly's lids stayed closed for another second after he released her.

"Holly," Tim growled now, then raked a shaky hand through his hair. "Don't butt into my life." His ears and cheeks reddening as he slanted her a furious glare. "Don't say we're friends either because I was wrong...We're not friends. Don't know why I kid myself into thinking I could be friends with you."

"Tim...Wait, just..."

"I'm leaving. As soon as they find my mom's killer, I'm leaving Cleverly Shores. You shouldn't stay here either, Holly." He stormed away after that, leaving her speechless and shaking with the rush of paralyzing heat that rooted her to that spot.

"Hey, did something happen with Tim?" Scarlet asked behind her a few minutes later. Holly's still reeling and struggling to find words when her friend placed a hand on her shoulder. Scarlet's cold touch cut through the heat rushing inside Holly and brought her back to reality.

"Is Tim alright? Why did he storm off like that...Did something happen?"

Holly only nodded. "I should get home. I uh...I have this thing I need to do, so I should get home."

"John can drive you; we're heading home anyway."

"No," Holly blurted out almost immediately. "I mean...Sure." She's still dazed from the kiss, every nerve ending in her body is heightened, and the strong urge to go after Tim has yet to pass.

She went with Scarlet and John quietly, taking each step one at a time so she didn't trip. Holly's head swooned the entire walk to the reserved parking spot on the beach where most of the guests had their cars. Once she got in the back seat of John's truck, she exhaled deeply.

Scarlet met her gaze through the rearview mirror. "You sure you're alright?"

Holly rubbed the back of her neck. "I'm fine," she lied, wishing she had some chocolate or a piece of her father's pie to help calm her nerves.

The short drive to her place lasted three minutes, then Holly waved her friends goodnight, kicked her heels off, and carried them into the diner.

She sighed when the familiar scent of lavender she used in the diner greeted her nostrils. Holly set her purse on a table, drew in a deep breath, then spent the next few seconds massaging the back of her neck to ease the kinks there.

She walked in through Frijole's front door, then took the stairs leading up to her apartment.

"Chile?" Holly called, expecting her dog to greet her with a riotous bark and lots of tail wagging. "Chile?"

She flipped on the light switch, hoping to see Chile run out of her bedroom somewhere. Holly gasped from shock when her gaze landed on the chaos her house was in. Her sofa was ripped in different spots, every item on the living room mantel was crashed onto the ground.

A scream bubbled to the surface inside her as she hurried into her room and found Chile tied to her bed, a muzzle was over her mouth so she couldn't growl or bark. The room was in chaos, her bed was turned upside down, and every item in her closet lied on the ground scattered everywhere.

Holly cried out and rushed towards Chile, ignoring the giant mess her house was in. "Oh, thank goodness, you're alright," she sobbed before reaching for the muzzle and releasing it from her snout. Chile barked now, her grunts and growls were repeated, and she didn't stop till Holly wrapped her arms around her body and pulled her into a tight embrace.

"Good dog," she whispered, stroking her head till her agitated bark slowed into more of a grunt.

After getting Chile to calm down, Holly got on her feet again, and motioned for the dog to run with her down the stairs. Holly made it to her purse in the kitchen and dialed 911 as soon as she got to her phone.

"911 what's your emergency?"

She drew in a shaky breath and held it still before announcing what had happened. "Someone has broken into my house!"

CHAPTER TWENTY-ONE

"Nothing's missing," Holly explained to her friend the next day while they were on the front porch. She spent the entire day cleaning up the mess the intruder left upstairs and was now relaxing outside to ease the tension in her muscles. "I can't think of anything I have that someone would want. The police were here last night to take my statement, and they had a patrol car stay right outside of the diner until early this morning. They'll be back tonight too."

"This is insane," Scarlet commented. "I mean, whoever it was tied Chile up, and messed up the entire place without remorse. Who would do that? Cleverly Shores is usually more peaceful...Safe...It gives me chills to think of someone breaking into your house."

Chile barked once when Holly looked to her and sighed. While talking about the intruder is very important, Holly's mind was still consumed by other thoughts. *The kiss...His eyes.* What did it mean?

While thinking about it, she brushed her hand over her lips and sucked in a deep breath.

"Are you thinking about that kiss again?" Scarlet asked.

Holly turned to her friend. "You saw that?" she asked in a shaky voice as color mapped her cheeks again. "I didn't think..."

"Everyone at the founder's ball saw that kiss, Holly. You're one lucky girl. Having Tim still hung up on you after all these years."

"He's not hung up on me," Holly denied even though she wished that were true.

"But you're hung up on him.'"

Holly slapped her friend's arm before Scarlet burst into a loud giggle. "You so are," Scarlet continued as Holly blushed. "That look on your face says it all."

Holly sucked in a deep breath as she allowed thoughts of Tim to flood her mind again. "I just don't know where that came from. He kissed me and then stormed away like it meant nothing. I don't know what to think. Does this mean he still likes me? That there's a chance?"

"You need to talk to him. Iron things out."

"Yeah, I know," she answered, then bolted to her feet. "Yes, that's what I need to do. I need to go over to his beach house and talk to him."

"Need me to drive you?"

"No," Holly laughed. "You stay here, I can handle this. I appreciate your support, but I really do need to handle this on my own." Chile moved to follow as she jogged down the few porch steps. "Stay Chile...Stay," she ordered, moving her hand to motion for her to sit.

Chile obeyed like a good dog, her ears drooped low, and she barked again, moaning this time before she looked to Scarlet.

"Good dog, I'll be right back very soon. Then I'll take you for a walk along the beach when I get back."

"I hope I won't be waiting long," Scarlet called out with a loud bubble of loose cheeriness as Holly hurried away still smiling. The walk is just a few minutes to Tim's beach house.

When she arrived, Holly sucked in a deep breath before heading to his front door. "Tim?" she called when no one responded after her first three knocks. Holly walked around the house to check the back door once she still didn't get a response.

She had spent lots of hours hanging out around this house with Tim in the past, so she remembered the place very well. They used to spend long hours talking in the rocking chairs on the back porch. Seeing that the chairs still were in the exact same place, brought a smile to Holly's face.

Tim had a cat once, and he buried it down at the very end of the backyard. From where she stood on the back porch, she could spot the little grave he made for the cat. Holly was smiling to herself when she heard a crashing sound from inside the house.

"Tim?" She was about to twist the doorknob open when she saw Kenneth storm into the kitchen through the half transparent glass on the back door. Her heart began to pound in her chest, and she quickly lowered herself to a squat so he didn't see her.

What the heck is Kenneth doing in Tim's house?

Holly crawled away from the porch and hid in a corner seconds before the back door opened. She heard Kenneth curse loudly before he hurried away from the house. Holly stayed in hiding until she could no longer hear the heavy thuds of his footsteps.

When she finally got up, her heart was still pounding, and her lungs struggled for air. *If Kenneth broke into Tim's house, then there was a good chance he did the same to me right?*

Her mind raced with different thoughts as she stood there. *But what could he possibly want?*

She strolled towards the front of the house when the roar of a truck's engine was nearby. Holly hugged herself tight as she saw Tim get out of his truck, then lifted some bags from the bed of his truck. He slowed his stride once he made eye contact with her, and Holly tried to ignore her doubling pulse.

"Hey," she whispered when he finally stopped in front of her, then set the bags down at his feet.

"What are you doing here, Holly?"

Tim's intense eyes stayed on hers, and she struggled to find the right words to explain why she came to see him.

"I ..."

"Look Holly, if you're here to talk about the kiss last night or tell me what you think about doing business with Fallon, then you really need to start minding your own business. I don't want to talk about Fallon with you...I don't need your advice on what I'm going to do, so just back off."

Holly swallowed hard from his outburst, and her speech concerning the kiss she can't stop thinking about, vanished from her mind.

"Right," she whispered, ignoring the panging ache that settled deep inside her. "I was here to talk about the kiss actually, and ...Well, it doesn't matter now," she stuttered. "I should just go."

She moved to walk past him, but he held onto her wrist, spun her around to face him again.

"Holly..."

"You should know that Kenneth broke into your house just a few minutes ago. When I got here, he was already in there. I highly doubt you gave him a key to just let himself in so..."

"Kenneth was here?" Tim's eyes widened before he released her and bolted away with speed. "In my house?"

Holly followed, shocked at his outburst. When she rushed up the stairs to Tim's bedroom, she found him on his knees in front of his bedside drawer.

"Thank goodness," he sighed while holding up a box. His hands were shaking, and Holly slowly moved closer to him so she could see what he was holding.

"Tim are you okay?" Holly noticed the tears in his eyes when he faced her, he got to his feet gently before he blew air out of his lips.

"Tim?" she placed a hand over his and enjoyed the feel of his warmth seeping into her again.

"I'm fine, it's just...My mom left me the key to a safety deposit box, and in that box contains everything she'd ever worked for."

Holly nodded when he met her eyes again. "Everything?"

"Everything! All of her money, the restaurant...It's all in her will, and she left me strict instructions to make sure Kenneth doesn't get what he wants." When Holly raised a brow, Tim added, "The money. Kenneth wants the money and she wanted to make sure he never got his hands on any of it, so she asked me to buy out Fallon's property with it instead. She was going to take the deal, Holly. That night when I was supposed to meet her, she was going to tell me all about it."

His voice was hoarse as he spoke about his mother and Holly's heart ached for him. "So, what do we do? We don't have proof that Kenneth was in here, but we can tell the police."

"I don't want you to do anything. This is all my problem. I'll make sure Kenneth doesn't get a dime, but I need you to just stay out of it please."

"But I wanna help Tim, let me help..."

"No," he insisted.

"Tim..."

"Look, we kissed once, but that doesn't mean I'll let you in on everything that happens in my life. You're not my girlfriend, you're not my family...You're just...Just stay out of this, Holly, okay?" he snapped. "Just stay out of it."

Holly stepped away from him when he turned his back to her. The lump in the base of her throat pushed down hard, making her chest ache. She blinked back the tears burning in the back of her lids.

"Right," she whispered. "I'm not your girlfriend...I'm not your friend...I'm nothing," she said to him, sniffing hard to push back the burn in the back of her throat. "Then why did you kiss me at the founder's ball?"

"Holly that..."

"Was a mistake?" she interrupted. "Yeah, you're right. It was a mistake for me to think it meant something when it clearly didn't. She stormed out before he could stop her. Thinking there was a chance that Tim would honestly let go of their past was foolish.

CHAPTER TWENTY-TWO

Hours later, Holly still can't get Kenneth off her mind. *Or Tim.* Perhaps thinking about Kenneth was a way to distract her thoughts from Tim. *Why do I keep thinking about him?*

Tim made himself very clear at the ball. She was nothing to him. Those words shouldn't hurt so much. *What did you expect?* But still, her heart ached, and her throat burned.

While trying to fall asleep, she rolled over to her side and found Chile staring up at her. She had those big round eyes that gave a 'why are you so sad' kind of stare. Holly sighed, shoved her sheets off her body, then motioned for Chile to join her in the bed.

"You're sad too, right?" Holly murmured to her as she snuggled under the covers and curled up next to Holly's body. Chile groaned and Holly sighed again. "Yeah, me too. I thought we were making progress you know...I thought we could be friends. I guess I was wrong."

She laid awake for a long time that night, her mind spinning with different thoughts.

What could Kenneth be looking for in Tim's house? Annalisa's money? Her will? Holly tried to piece it all together since she couldn't sleep even a wink that night. After she'd been lying in bed for a while tossing and turning, so many thoughts were racing through her mind, she jolted up in her bed.

"Tim's got her money...All of it," she thought out-loud. "What if Kenneth wants that? The money."

Her pulse spiked a little as John's words came to mind again. Kenneth and Annalisa broke up and he tried to start his own restaurant, but she wouldn't invest in it even though she could afford to. She opted to purchase a property that would expand her business and make her a stronger competitor.

There's a tingle at the base of Holly's neck and she frowned a little before throwing off the covers to her bed and paced very slowly around her bedroom. She repeatedly rubbed her face, her gaze flit around her room, not settling on one object for too long.

Chile paced with Holly, her tail constantly wagging as she marched around the room making every step Holly made.

"That's it, right? I mean, Kenneth wanted her help, and her husband refused. Mr. Rice also has a say because they were partners before the divorce. Annalisa tried to invest her money with Mr. Fallon instead, and Kenneth probably didn't want that to happen so he...."

Holly drew in a loud gasp as all of this instantly started making sense. *No, it can't be. Kenneth Green couldn't be the killer.* Or is he capable of murder?

She shuddered as an image of those dark eyes came to mind. He smiled so easily, but she had to admit there was something strange about the way he looked at a person. *Like he was trying to pick apart your thoughts...His eyes are that intense.*

The burn of bile in the base of her throat was enough to send her reeling. Holly got in her bed again, and Chile jumped right back up there to protect Holly from her thoughts.

"Oh, Chile...I think this is bad...This is really bad." The nausea twisted up her guts as the implication of what she was thinking slithered through her mind. If Kenneth's up to something, then she had to find out.

Or perhaps inform the sheriff? Holly shook her head after playing out a scene involving Sheriff Carlton. The chances of him listening to her thoughts were slim. The sheriff already disliked her. Telling him these suspicions would probably get her no where. *He'll probably tell me to sit tight and stay out of his investigation.*

The hard thudding in her chest wouldn't stop. *I've got to do something.* Holly spent the rest of the night tossing around in her bed with very little sleep.

The next morning, she opened Frijole's early, hoping customers would flock in and distract her from her thoughts. Holly's frustration grew when the early hour of dawn passed, and no one showed up. All she was left with was her obsessive, suspicious thoughts about Kenneth.

"We've got to do something, Chile. Rather, I've got to do something. If Kenneth's involved in this then he needs to be stopped. He's messed with me too!"

Chile yipped with enthusiasm as Holly changed into black slacks and a black hoodie. She twisted her hair up in a bun, covered it with the hoodie, then grabbed a pair of mittens from her drawer.

"We can figure out what Kenneth is up to. Of course, not you and me...But I'm gonna need a partner and I can't involve Scarlet in this because her husband's an officer and I don't want to get him in trouble."

She walked to her dresser mirror and Chile padded softly behind her, trailing her every move while wagging her tail. Holly rubbed her covered hands together and huffed out a deep breath. "Who do I call?"

Scarlet is usually her partner in crime, but this time, Holly preferred she stayed out of this. *I can tell her and John when I'm more certain of what's actually going on.*

Chile gave her a wide eyed look, then she barked once like she was trying to pass a message. Holly squatted to touch her head, then sighed. "There's only one person to call, and he might not listen to me either. Oh well...I'm gonna call him anyway."

She left the room after double checking all the doors were locked to make sure Chile stayed safe, then she hurried down the stairs with her purse.

Tim's line rang a few times before he finally picked up the call. "Tim, hey..."

"Holly..."

"Wait, just listen," she stopped him while hurrying out her apartment through Frijole's front door. "I figured something out...It's important and it has to do with your mom. I need your help to make sure I'm on the right track. So please just...Let's get over our personal stuff for now and do this together."

It took some time before Tim replied gruffly. "What do you need?"

"I'm gonna break into Kenneth's house. And I need you to help me with it."

CHAPTER TWENTY-THREE

"I can't believe I let you talk me into this madness," Tim complained for the third time while they were hiding in front of Kenneth's house. "He's in there. How are we gonna break into his house while he's in there?"

Holly's heart kept pounding, and her palms were sweaty even though she tried to hide her obvious nervousness. "We wait till he's out, then we go in through the back and find a way to get in. It's that simple."

"It's a crime, that's what it is," Tim countered and rolled his eyes. "You haven't changed much. You still like to meddle in everyone's affairs and get yourself in trouble."

"I'm not meddling. Kenneth messed with me first when he broke into my house."

"Oh yeah?" Tim faced her now and slanted a brow. "You've got proof of that?"

Holly's next reply hooked in her throat, then she pressed her lips into a frown instead.

"That's what I thought," Tim continued, then raked his fingers through his hair. "This is stupid. We're about to commit a crime...Breaking and entering is a felony, and we could go to jail for this. Didn't you learn from your first stint behind bars? Did you think of that before coming up with your brilliant idea?"

"Do you got a better one?" Holly retorted and gave him a heated glare now. "Besides, he broke into your house too. Aren't you curious about what he knows? Or why he did that? It's not like we can ask the question directly."

Tim huffed then looked away from her, focusing on Kenneth's house across the street again. They were parked a few blocks away, so the chances of him noticing their presence was hopefully small.

"Look, I get that you don't like me...But the past is the past and I'm just trying to help you figure out what happened to your mom so you can get out of town like you so clearly want. I wouldn't have to ..."

"Shush up," Tim ordered, silencing Holly for only a second before she gasped.

"Don't you dare tell me to..."

"Really, shush Holly, and look." Her squinting gaze followed Tim's pointed finger, and she spotted Kenneth leaving his house on a power bike. "He's leaving, now is our chance. Do you want to do this, or do you want to continue sitting here, yelling at me?"

Holly is out of the car once Kenneth drove away, and she jogged towards his house while Tim followed directly behind her. They made it to the back of his house, and she peered into Kenneth's kitchen through the window.

"How do we do this?" she asked Tim in a hushed voice as he tried the back door. "Oh right, because he's gonna leave his doors unlocked when he steps out?"

Tim's jaw hardened as he took out a pin from his pocket and stuck it in the keyhole. "I was a boy scout, and we had a young instructor back then who didn't like to follow rules."

The door opened with a click, and Holly laughed. "And he taught you to pick locks?"

"No, but some other notorious kids did," he replied with an easy smile, pushed the door forward, then let Holly enter the house first.

Tim closed the door as soon as he was in the kitchen too, and once it clicked shut, a beeping sound erupted loudly all around them.

"He's got a security system. I should have thought of that."

He tried to open the door again, but it was locked. He attempted to use his pin again, but there was no way out.

"We're in so much trouble," Holly cried out as she took off her hoodie and slapped a hand over her forehead with another sarcastic mutter. "This is not good. This is not good at all."

"Well, we're in here, aren't we? We might as well find out what he's really up to," Tim suggested, making her look at him again.

A mischievous smile quirked his lips up, and Holly laughed before shaking her head. "You're just as horrible as I am," she told him as he lead the way past the kitchen.

They spent the next few minutes going through everything they could find in Kenneth's bedroom and living room. Once the police sirens filled the air, Tim and Holly moved to the kitchen to wait till the sheriff and his officers swooped in to arrest them.

Sheriff Carlton was standing outside with Kenneth when the police lead them out of the house, their hands were cuffed behind them.

"Sheriff Carlton," Tim spoke first when they got to him.

"This was all my idea," Holly rambled immediately before Tim could say a thing. "I convinced him to do this with me, so if you're charging anyone, it should be me."

Sheriff Carlton's gaze hardened as he stared at Holly, and she swallowed hard to shove down the lump that formed in her throat.

"You know you could face felony charges for this, don't you?" he scolded, his eyes not leaving hers even as she licked her lips nervously.

"Yes, but...I had my reasons and..."

"Your reasons?" Sheriff Carlton roared. His nostrils flared with his noisy breathing, and the wrinkles around his eyes tightened. "You should have brought them to me...I'm the sheriff here, you're a civilian and you have no business breaking into someone's home regardless of your reasons."

Kenneth's smug smile withered before he leaned into the sheriff and whispered something to him.

Sheriff Carlton cleared his throat after that, and eyed Holly for a long time before turning to Tim. "Mr. Green here's quite fond of you Tim, and he considers this a mistake, so he won't be pressing charges on either of you two."

"What?" Holly gasped, and Kenneth winked at her, causing a deeper frown to kiss her features.

"You're free to go," Sheriff Carlton said before an officer unclasped the cuffs around Tim and Holly's wrists.

Tim placed a hand on her shoulder and they walked away from Kenneth's house together.

"Did you see that? Kenneth's smile? Did you see that? He's definitely got something to hide...Why wouldn't he press charges?" She glanced behind her as Tim lead the way, and Kenneth was still speaking to the attentive sheriff.

"There's something fishy," Holly whispered as they got to Tim's truck.

"Let's just be grateful we're not spending the rest of the day locked up in some grungy cell. I know that you have some expertise in this area now, but I'd like to stay out of an orange jumpsuit."

"Ha, ha," Holly answered, then jumped in Tim's truck. He keyed his engine to a start and they drove off down the road. Holly can't stop staring at Kenneth and the sheriff through the side mirrors as Tim drove away.

Her instincts were never wrong. *I'm sure he's up to something.* There's no shaking off the dreadful sensation settling deep inside her. Holly realized Tim had taken a different route a few minutes later, and she glanced over at him.

"Where are we headed?"

"I don't know about you, but I'm famished," he answered without taking his eyes off the road. "We're going to that place you like on 3rd Street. What was it again? Chops and Hops?"

Holly laughed and pressed a hand over her lips. "The way you say Chops and Hops makes it sound like it's some Chinese name...Chops and Hops."

A smile teased Tim's lips too, and he finally looked her way, their gaze lingered for a second.

"I thought we weren't friends. Why are we having lunch together?"

Tim looked away briefly, and by the time he glanced at her again, his eyes lit up. "Who am I kidding? I can't stay away from you, Barber. Isn't that obvious?"

"Right," she said softly as her grin widened. Holly fixed her eyes on the road again as the flutters of hope filled her heart. *So, there really is a chance we might be friends.* Suddenly her day felt brighter, and she forgot all about Kenneth for a while.

CHAPTER TWENTY-FOUR

"A greasy burger? That's your idea of a healthy meal?" Tim teased as Holly sat with him on the patio at Chops and Hops. "That's a load of carbs."

"Who cares?" she asked with a laugh, then took a huge bite. "I can have a load of carbs if I want and eat healthy if I want. Loosen up, Tim...Life's supposed to be enjoyed. You really shouldn't spend every second of your day counting your calories...It's not healthy."

He laughed and she joined him, they both got a good chuckle from their conversation. Holly's heart thundered, and the excitement coursing through her lasted just a few seconds before she recalled their earlier predicament.

"I still can't get my mind off Kenneth. He's hiding something, I can feel it in my gut."

"Anyone ever told you that you're obsessive?" He shook his head and took a few more bites of his salad again.

"It's just..."

"Let it go, Holly. We got in enough trouble as it is already. No need to keep digging up more problems. If Kenneth's involved in my mom's murder somehow, the sheriff will figure it out."

Holly reluctantly dropped the topic and focused on her burger for a bit. There's a thick silence hovering around them for a few minutes before Tim shocked her with his next words.

"I said a lot of things I didn't mean at the founder's ball, Holly," Tim said in a sotto tone now as he met her gaze again. "I was...I needed space to think...Needed to breathe, and you make it very difficult for me to do either of those things."

Holly assessed him for a while to note how serious he was, and when she saw how his eyes reflected his solemn words, she sighed.

"I'll take that as a compliment," she said with another laugh. Holly can't stop feeling the urge to burst into a bubble of excitement whenever he was near, and the energy rushing through her resonated with her light-headedness.

"I didn't think you'd ever return to Cleverly Shores though." His bowl of salad was close to empty, and Holly was done with her cheeseburger and fries.

"I didn't think I'd ever come back either, but then...My dad died, and I got fired at my job as a sous chef, so I figured it was time for a change. Life in the big city isn't nearly as peaceful and serene as it is here, you know."

"I wouldn't know," he answered her before gulping from his bottle of water. "Never lived in a big city."

"Right, you told me...You moved to Westerville, which is pretty close by, and opened up your art studio there."

Tim nodded. "I find that I prefer the slow pace of a small town. I do things however it suits me, never need to worry about the crazy traffic or long lines waiting for a Starbucks or fast-food restaurant. Life's just easier over here."

"That's so true," Holly agreed with a laugh, then they continue their discussion for a while, neither of them realizing how much time passed while they were on the patio enjoying each others company.

The sun was setting by the time Tim drove Holly back home, and she thanked him again, waving a hand before he got back in his truck and drove off.

Chile was waiting eagerly when Holly made it to her bedroom upstairs. She took off her hoodie, let her hair loose from the hair tie holding it in place.

Holly held onto a dreamy sigh as she fell back on her bed, then spread her arms out wide. "I think we're in a good place now."

Holly petted Chile's head when she came close, then sighed and held onto her smile. Holly never imagined getting back together with Tim when she first saw him after eight years, but in that moment, it was all she could think about.

***

"We're in a good place," she muttered three days later when Tim hadn't reached out to her even once. It was torture waiting for his call or text, but it was all Holly could anticipate since they nearly were charged for a felony and spent the rest of the afternoon together.

"He's supposed to call. Right?" Holly resumed her pacing. Her hands buried in her apron pockets as she walked to the end of the dining area, then reversed and walked back in the opposite direction.

Scarlet slanted her a questioning gaze and paused what she was writing to look up at Holly. "Can you stop pacing? You're freaking me out."

Holly nodded, then sat down, and rubbed a hand over her chin. "What does it mean when a guy says he can't stay away from you, then he doesn't call for three days? He's so busy he can't even send a text message?"

Scarlet dropped her pen again with a sigh. "Is this about Tim, Holly? Did you two get back together?"

"What? No..." Holly blushed beet red and cleared her throat. "Wait, why would you think we're together?"

"Because a girl only worries about a guy not calling, then disappears, when they are in a relationship. It generally just means he's not interested."

"Or it could mean something came up and he couldn't reach out even though he so desperately wanted to?"

Scarlet's next laugh was full. She tipped her head back and gave out a very loud chuckle. Her eyes twinkled too. "Sure, you can play it out that way if it makes you feel better." She shook her head as another chuckle left her lips, and Holly frowned deeper. "Just call him already, instead of getting yourself all worked up like this."

"I did...Three times now. He didn't answer or call me back. I don't want to seem desperate, but I think I'll drop by his place...What if something is wrong?"

"What could possibly be wrong?" Scarlet rolled her eyes. "I'm sure he's fine. Probably just caught up with other things and he'll call or show up soon."

"You really think so?" Holly asked in an unsure voice. Her fingers drummed over the table, and she tapped one foot on the floor repeatedly. Scarlet placed a hand over Holly's to stop her tremors.

"I'm sure he's fine. You've got nothing to worry about. He'll call, or show up soon, okay?"

Scarlet's encouraging words kept Holly calm for the rest of the day, but her patience finally elapsed by the next morning. Holly got to Tim's beach house in the early hours of dawn and found his dad sitting on the front porch. A magazine in one hand, coffee in the other, he looked very content sitting in the rocking chair.

"Holly Barber," he greeted the moment she walked up to him and offered him a shaky smile. "It's been a long time," Mr. Rice continued as he smiled at her. Holly noticed how the years have aged him. His once vibrant blonde strands now have a mixture of platinum blonde locks in them, and there were many wrinkles on his oval-face. They make his eyes look smaller, like he's constantly squinting.

Mr. Rice sat upright in his rocking chair and patted the arm of the other rocking chair right next to him for Holly to come sit. "How was life in the big city? Did I hear correctly that you are back in town now? Or will you be leaving soon."

"New York was good, but after being back, I realized just how much I missed being in a small town. Actually, I think I'm here to stay, or at least for a good while," she told him with a smile. "Frijole's is my main priority right now."

"Alright...That's very good to hear. I'm sure your dad would be so proud to see what you are doing with the place. Cleverly Shores needs more great chefs like yourself."

When he smiled at her again, Holly rubbed the back of her neck. "Thank you for those encouraging words. It was so great to see you again Mr. Rice, but I was actually looking for Tim. Do you know if he's in?"

His nose wrinkles up as he asked. "You kids dating again?"

"No," Holly denied with a vivid blush. "No, we're not, it's just... We're not dating."

She bit her inner cheek when his eyes flickered over hers one more time. Mr. Rice picked his magazine up again and opened it up to the place he left off. "Alright then. Tim's not here. Haven't seen him in a couple of days so I figured he left town again. He does that often. I rarely ever know what he's up to these days."

The stinging feeling bottling down inside Holly was too great to ignore. "I think something's wrong," she insisted as she got on her feet again. "Tim would not have just vanished after our last conversation, and I can't reach him on his cell...I really think something's wrong Mr. Rice. I just have this gut feeling that I haven't been able to shake."

Mr. Rice lowered his magazine to the chair, and the instant frown that saddled his features made Holly's heart dive faster against her ribcage. An ache erupted at the back of her throat, making it hard to swallow, and her limbs quivered slightly. "I have to call the sheriff!"

CHAPTER TWENTY-FIVE

Sheriff Carlton barely heard a word Holly said to him as he ordered his men around.

"Sheriff," Holly called again, her frown deepening. "Are you even listening to me?"

Holly tried to keep calm the entire time. Her panic was slowly crawling into an alarming zone, and she was barely keeping it together over the thought of Tim in some kind of trouble.

Don't think of the worse.

"Tim's missing. No one has seen or heard from him in two days. I think this has to do with Kenneth. We tried to break into his house, and he refused to press charges even though he had every reason to. We have to do something sheriff."

Sheriff Carlton walked into his office and she followed behind him. The door bounced closed, and she stood right in front of his desk. "Sheriff..."

"Enough Barber," he interrupted in a stern voice. "The deputies and I have it under control. We have a lead and we're working on it as I speak. Tim will be found, and he will be alright."

His eyes were serious but it's the first time his voice was soft towards her. Holly sucked in a deep breath and nodded.

"Okay, so what do I do?" She questioned, waiting for the sheriff to assign her a task. When he slanted her an incredulous look, she added quickly. "No, please, I need to do something. I need to..."

"You will sit right there with John and stay put until I get back. Got it?"

"But..."

"You stay here Barber, or I'll have you cuffed to the desk if I have to."

He stormed out of his office after that and a second later, rushed out of the station with some other officers.

Holly quieted her insides and walked over to John's desk. He lifted his head to her when she tapped her fingers over the top.

"The sheriff's only looking out for you," he said slowly. "This is a murder case. There's nothing you can do to help at this point."

His words didn't help Holly feel any better. "I know Kenneth's up to something," she muttered while pacing around John's seat. "I just have a feeling."

John released a raspy chuckle. "A feeling?"

"Like a gut feeling."

"You think a guy is guilty based on a gut feeling?" He laughed some more while shaking his head.

"I can't just sit here and do absolutely nothing."

She looked around when a few officers hurried out of the office while speaking into their radios.

"What's going on?" She asked after John also listened to someone speaking on his radio. He got on his feet immediately and was about to rush out of his office when she called him in a stern voice.

"John."

He spared her a glance. "It's a report about shots fired on 7th Avenue."

Holly's brows furrowed together as the meaning of his words settled in. "7th Avenue? Kenneth lives there, John."

Her heart pounded faster in her chest now. Her breaths turned quick and shallow. Her limbs fluttered with a tremor and her pulse was racing.

John left his office in a hurry and Holly remained standing rooted in one spot for the next few minutes, unable to think or breathe.

*That's Kenneth's house. S*he felt a wave of nausea when a knot formed in her gut. *What if Kenneth has Tim?*

Without weighing her options fully, she moved around to the back of John's desk and started going through the documents he had laid out on top.

"Statement, autopsy, DNA reports," she muttered while skimming through anything and everything as quickly as possible.

She froze when she stumbled on a file labeled 'Kenneth Green'. Holly flipped it open immediately, and gently lowered herself into John's chair.

A chill spread through her as she began to read every line in the report.

Kenneth Green had an alibi on the night Annalisa was murdered, according to his statement.

Holly felt her blood pressure elevate while she took in every sentence in his report.

We met that night, but she had to meet with her husband shortly after, so she left early. Annalisa and I had an understanding. I didn't resent her even when she refused to help me out.

Kenneth's alibi for the night of the murder was solid according to the report. He spent the early hours of the night at a pub on Main

Street, and his neighbors testified they saw him drive back up to his house later that evening.

His car also stayed parked in his driveway the rest of the night.

Holly closed her eyes for a second and analyzed all she had learned. If Kenneth had an alibi for that night, then who was the killer?

She picked the next file up labeled 'Joseph Rice' and flipped through every page as her keen eyes read the report.

"Joseph Rice was the last known person to see Annalisa alive," she muttered while reading his statement.

We met at the beach that night to talk about the project. She insisted on buying Fallon's property and I tried to talk her out of it.

The property in question is a sham...the repairs would have cost her millions, and in the end, she'd be bankrupt before she even brought the restaurant back to life.

Her money was better invested in Green's restaurant project. She stormed off that night and I headed home.

The last document Holly picks up was an envelope with a forensics report.

Her jaw dropped as she read the crossmatch result proving the blood stains found on Annalisa's shirt didn't match Joseph Rice or Kenneth Green.

The only reasonable suspect left is Fallon, she said to herself, and her rolling stomach dropped with a nauseated feeling.

"I can't believe it," she commented, her eyes widening at her discovery.

John walked in while Holly was holding the forensic results. His frown deepened once he spotted her and realized what she has just done.

"What do you think you're doing?" John snatched the results from her hand. "You weren't supposed to open that. It's a sealed document for the sheriff, Holly. There are policies that have to be followed here."

"Where did you say the sheriff was headed?" She asked in a shaky voice and combed her fingers through her hair.

Holly's trembling breath quaked through her, leaving fierce heat in her chest.

"John," she yelled this time. "Where was the sheriff and his men headed?"

"7th Avenue. Why?"

Holly shook her head and blurted out the words that left her with a shrill ache. "It's Fallon."

"What?"

"The last forensic results I just opened...It was Fallon's blood on her shirt that night."

"Holly...."

She is already hurrying around his desk as he tried to stop her. "I need your keys, John. I need to get to Fallon. He probably has Tim. Tim has his mother's will and all her money, and Fallon wants it. He's always wanted the money."

"You're spiraling Holly, there's no proof and..."

"Will you help me, John, or will you blame yourself when Fallon hurts Tim in the end?" Holly's outburst shocked even herself too. Her heart has never trembled in fear this much.

Tears stung the back of her eyes that very second, as it hit her.

John reluctantly took out his keys. "You better be right about this," he warned as Holly exhaled loudly. "I'm driving."

Holly didn't think she could handle a steering wheel right now anyway. Her limbs were shaky and there was no iota of calm nerves in her.

John lead the way, and they flew out of the station parking lot while he contacted the sheriff to fill him in.

"We're headed down Main Street towards Boulevard Road, Fallon's house is located there. We believe he kidnapped Timothy Rice, and we need all units en route to 6th Boulevard Road right now... I repeat, all units en route to 6th Boulevard Road now."

CHAPTER TWENTY-SIX

It was the longest ten minute drive of her life. Holly nibbled on her lower lip the entire time and tried to keep her nerves at bay. The cool breeze filtered into the car through the lowered windows, and John threw worried glances at her every second.

"Tim will be fine," he said a moment later as he drove onto Boulevard Road. Police sirens filled the air behind them. Holly looked through the side mirror and saw patrol cars trailing behind them.

She sniffed and shunned the panic rising inside her. "You don't know that," she whispered, fighting tears. "You don't know he'll be okay."

"Holly..."

"Just...Let's just get there in time," she interrupted, then pressed her lips into a thin line again. Holly held her breath as they got closer to Fallon's house. John pulled to a halt outside of the house.

Holly jerked the door open and was out of the car before he could say anything to her. She ran towards the house, tossing every caution to the wind. "Tim," she yelled at the top of her lungs as she made it to the front porch.

"Holly," John yelled behind her. "Holly, stop..."

Holly tried the doorknob with force, and it gave away for her to stagger into the house. "Tim," she yelled again, her tears sliding down her cheeks now. The living room was empty, and the house smelled like roses. Holly sniffed in deeply and looked around.

"Holly," John called as he finally caught up to her as quickly as possible. "You can't be here...This is..."

The vibrating echo of a shot fired went off in the air before John could finish his sentence. Holly screamed as John shoved her to the ground. Her ears rang as the echo slowly faded. There was a residue of smoke in the air, and Holly's heart quivered as she thought of what just happened.

"Oh no, Tim," she cried out, ignoring John's words as she got back on her feet. "I think Tim's dead...Tim's dead..." she sobbed, shaking violently. She thought about the bleak years her life would be without Tim's smile or voice, flashed before her eyes.

Police surrounded the house, and John handed her over to another officer before setting out to search the house for the shooter. Holly was standing outside, a blanket wrapped around her body when the sheriff arrived a few minutes later.

"What happened?" he asked, walking towards where Holly was standing with an officer. "What is she doing here?"

The ache in Holly's heart was all she cared about as the officer filled Sheriff Carlton in on what happened.

"There was a shooting," he explained. "Deputy Fischer is searching the house with a unit for the shooter. We suspect Timothy Rice is in there with Nate Fallon."

"You suspect?" the sheriff thundered. "Is there any concrete evidence why we're searching this gentleman's house at the moment? Or have you all gone..."

"Tim's in there," Holly cuts in before he scolded the officer. "I read the forensic report on Annalisa Rice. The blood stain found on her shirt matched Nate Fallon's DNA. He has reason to want her dead too. I thought it was Kenneth at first, but Mr. Fallon he ...He wanted Annalisa's money, and he probably eliminated her out of his way so he could deal with Tim instead."

Sheriff Carlton faced her with his blazing gaze now. "You're speculating, Barber...You have no concrete evidence that proves Mr. Fallon has anything to do with—"

Another shot fired silenced the sheriff, and he sprung into action immediately.

"Make sure she doesn't leave your sight," he ordered the officer standing with Holly, before sprinting away.

"Don't move," the officer ordered Holly when she tried going after the sheriff. "You take a step and I'll be forced to tackle you, Miss Barber."

Holly stood still and waited the next few torturous minutes without moving. She hated the helplessness of standing there alone with no clue as to what's going on.

Her thoughts trailed off when Tim's familiar baritone voice called for her. "Holly..."

Holly's head snapped up, and she saw Tim standing with the help of Sheriff Carlton and John. "Tim," she called out, relief flooding through her to see him standing there, breathing.

"Tim...'"

Holly ran towards him without thinking. She flung her arms around his neck once she arrived, hugged him tight, and sobbed into his chest.

Two other officers lead Nate Fallon out of his house, and Holly's insides relaxed when she saw the cuffs holding his wrists together.

"I thought ...When I heard that gunshot, I thought..."

She gasped, and held him steady, realizing then that blood was soaking his shirt. "Woah..." he groaned, then his legs gave out.

"Tim," she panicked as she slid to the ground with him.

"An ambulance is on its way," John said when Holly looked up at him. She lowered her gaze to Tim again, noticing his labored breathing.

"Easy," Holly whispered as tears stung her eyes. "An ambulance is on its way. You didn't feel the pain at first because of the adrenaline rush, but you'll be fine." A smile broke out on her lips, and she sniffed to push back her tears. "You'll be fine."

His lids fluttered closed just then and he released one last sigh.

"Tim?" she cried out, tears flowing down her cheeks now. "Tim.. .Tim..."

Her hysteria ran wild. She struggled with the officer trying to pull her away from Tim so they could lift him into the ambulance.

Holly's heart gave way to a deep, aching darkness that she knew she would never recover from. She could not stand the thought of losing someone else she cared about.

CHAPTER TWENTY-SEVEN

Hours later, two surgeons walked into the hospital's waiting room where Holly and Scarlet spent the last four hours.

"Holly Barber?" the doctor called, and she jerked herself out of her chair, waking Scarlet from her light sleep.

"I'm right here," Holly answered, and wiped her cheeks with both hands. She held her breath for a moment, anxiously waiting to hear what the doctor had to say about Tim. "How is he? Is he..." her voice cracked before she swallows hard. "Is he alright?"

"We managed to stop the bleeding, and we took out the bullet," the doctor replied with a soft smile. "He's not conscious yet, and we're keeping him in the ICU to monitor his vitals for the night."

"Is there anyone that can stay with him tonight? I understand you're not his family and..."

Sheriff Carlton walked into the room with Joseph Rice in that very moment. Holly watched them start making their way over, before offering the doctor a shaky smile.

"Yeah...I'm not his family. That's his dad right there."

Mr. Rice arrived where Holly stood with the doctor, and she listened quietly as the doctor reported his status before excusing himself.

Sheriff Carlton patted Mr. Rice on the shoulder before turning to Holly.

"A word?" His usually snappy tone had returned, but Holly didn't care.

In that moment, all that mattered was Tim, and hearing he would recover, filled her with unexplainable joy.

"Sheriff Carlton," she began when she walked with him over to the corner.

"What you did today was reckless and ignorant, Barber," he said, cutting short whatever she was going to say to him. "You never run into a crime scene like that. You're not a detective or an officer, you're not trained...."

"Sheriff," she tried again, sighing because her head hurt too much for his scolding.

"Let me finish," he stopped her, his jaw hardening some more. "You shouldn't have been there today. What you did was dumb, but it was also brave."

Holly's eyes widened at the compliment, and he nodded softly before adding, "You saved Tim's life today. We were barking up the wrong tree, and it might have been too late by the time I saw that forensic report for myself."

"Thank you," Holly whispered in a shaky voice, stunned that he complimented her efforts today.

"You crossed some lines today though, and I won't commend you for that. The next time you snoop through the sheriff's office, or try breaking into someone's house, I'll make sure you don't get off so easily. Got it?"

Holly suppressed a smile. "Got it," she answered just before he walked away from her.

She sighed deeply when Scarlet rushed over to her, and put an arm around her neck. "Was Sheriff Carlton scolding you?"

"Yeah," she answered, and smiled without realizing it. "But he also said I did good. I saved Tim's life today."

"You did," Scarlet agreed, and hugged her tight.

They are still in that embrace when Mr. Rice walked over to them.

"Holly Barber," he called and she faced him slowly. "Sheriff Carlton says your instincts saved my son's life today. I want to personally thank you for that. I can't even begin to tell you how grateful I am and I don't think I'll ever be able to repay you for this."

"It was nothing, Mr. Rice," she said with a soft smile, hugging herself tight.

"Tim was right about you," Mr. Rice continued now with a slow nod. "Eight years ago, when you left, you broke his heart. He was right to wait for you…"

"Wait for me?" Holly's pulse rapidly increased and her brows furrowed into a tiny frown. "I…I don't understand," she stuttered.

"His mother and I pressured him over the years to date again or bring a girl home for Thanksgiving…We wanted to see him happy. He insisted…He knew that one day you'd come back, and he wanted to be available if there was ever a chance."

Holly's heart swelled as she listened to Mr. Rice's words. "That's…"

"Unbelievable," he continued, filling in the words for her. "It's unbelievable, is what it is. No one waits for a person they aren't sure will ever come back."

Mr. Rice released a small laugh before sighing, "After the divorce, I kept thinking Annalisa would change her mind and come back to me. She moved on pretty quick, and I kept holding out hope, wishing that she would change her mind. I guess my marriage was long over even before it was officially done."

"Mr. Rice…" Holly sympathized, but he shook his head and blinked multiple times.

"You should be the one here when Tim wakes up," he whispered in a hoarse voice. "He'll be happier if it's you. I'll come back in the morning. The sheriff and I have some things to iron out about the case right now anyways."

Holly only nodded because her throat was too tight to make out any words.

"Thank you," she finally murmured before he walked away. It's just her and Scarlet left, when she wiped her tears away and drew in a deep breath.

"John's in trouble because of you," Scarlet says now. "If he gets suspended, you're so cooking us dinner for the rest of the summer."

"Cooking just happens to be my strong suit," Holly answered as they both laughed and walked towards the chairs again.

Scarlet left with John several hours later, and Holly went into the ICU to see Tim. "He's breathing on his own," the nurse monitoring him whispered. "That's a good thing."

It's the early hours of morning when Tim finally groaned. His soft sound woke Holly out of her light sleep, and she lifted her head to see his lids flutter open.

"Tim," she called, taking his right hand in hers almost immediately as a low laugh erupted from her. She exhaled with a whimpering sob, and she sniffed before greeting, "Hi...Hi there."

"Holly," he whispered as she tightened her grip around his hand. "I'm alive."

"You're alive," Holly laughed. "You're here at the hospital right now."

"I'm tough, Barber," he murmured, his voice still weak as he broke into a wide smile before swallowing hard.

"Yes you are," Holly agreed, then took his hand in hers. "But you don't need to be tough right now because I'm here if you need anything. You lost your mom, and then nearly died...You get a free pass on anything right now."

He laughed and his eyes light up as he stared at her. "I just want one thing..."

"Name it..."

"No breaking into any more houses, got it?"

She tipped her head back and laughed. "Cross my heart."

Chapter Twenty-Eight

S heriff Carlton visited the hospital the next afternoon while Holly sat with Tim in his hospital room.

"Nate Fallon will face trial and pay for all his crimes. We have him in custody while we tie up all the loose ends."

"Loose ends?" Tim asked in a faint voice as Holly massaged his arm. "He knocked me out...Dragged me into his car and kept me locked in his basement for I don't know...A few days? All because he wanted my mom's money?"

"Turns out Fallon is in a lot of debt. He's gambled away all he had, and he planned to sell your mother's property for an outrageous amount. All of this happened because he needed the cash urgently. He didn't have the luxury of waiting till she made her decision...He thought he would try and convince her, but ended up losing his cool that night at the beach."

"He confessed to her murder?" Holly asked the sheriff.

"He confessed to what happened that night on the beach. He's facing murder charges, as well as kidnapping and assault...He's looking at spending the rest of his life behind bars."

"So, the clothes found in my house...How did they get in there?"

"That was all Fallon too. You were the perfect suspect, considering you had just returned to town and Frijole's was a known competitor of Double Flavors."

"Wow, I just can't believe he did all of that. I'm glad it's finally over," Holly said before exhaling deeply. When she faced Tim again, he smiled at her.

"Actually, it's not over yet," Sheriff Carlton said as he stood near the door. His hands were rigid at his sides. "If Fallon decides to plead guilty to the charges against him, then we might wrap this up before the end of the summer. If not, there will be a trial and it will be all over the local news channels. You two will have to testify in court, and so will your dad and Kenneth. It might be a lot to handle, so you two need to get prepared."

His eyes skimmed over to Holly's briefly before he looked to Tim again. "My deputy will be here to take your statement as soon as you start feeling stronger. In the meantime, focus on your recovery."

"Thank you, Sheriff Carlton," Tim said, and he nodded before turning to walk out of the room.

Holly followed after him as the door closed. "Sheriff," she called before he was out of sight.

He stopped in his tracks, and she hurried across the room to meet up with him.

"Sheriff...About John Fischer...He didn't do anything wrong, so I was hoping you could be lenient on him with whatever punishment you dish out."

"You mean punishment for letting a civilian run into a possible crime scene without stopping her?"

His harsh reply made her suck in a deep breath, and she exhaled before adding, "Yes...It wasn't his fault. There's no way he could have stopped me from going after Tim. I had to do something."

Sheriff Carlton looked at Holly for a long time. His eyes never left hers before he sighed, "You're just like your mother."

"What's that supposed to mean?" A frown creased over Holly's face as she looked at him.

"It means exactly what I said. Your mom...She...She never gave up when she wanted something. She has always been resilient, and I admire that about her."

"Admired," Holly interrupted, her breath snagging painfully in her chest as she blinked. "You mean admired...Because ever since she skipped town when I was just a little girl, she hasn't been in touch with anyone...Not me...Not my dad..."

Sheriff Carlton's expression softened as he stared at Holly, and it dawned on her right then that she was wrong this entire time.

"She's been in touch with you, hasn't she?" Holly whispered. The ache in her heart left her breathless till she gasped for air. "All this time, you've...You've known where she was all this time?" Her words ended on a hiccup, and she closed her eyes for a brief second before swiping a hand over her face to get rid of the tears that were forming. "It doesn't matter...I don't care anyway."

"You should care. Whatever happened, she's your mom. I know she made choices that you'll probably never understand. But I know she made those choices out of love, for you."

"Yeah right," Holly snapped. "She abandoned me when I was eight and she never bothered to call or send a card the entire time, but she kept in touch with you? I'm supposed to care why?"

"She wanted to. She always wanted to...But it was better this way."

"How was it better for me not to know her? For me not to have a mother in my life?"

Holly's eyes searched for his. "Why are you defending her?"

Right then, Holly noticed the flicker of pain in his eyes.

A distant memory of an argument her parent's had flashed in her mind, and air left her lungs as she recalled her mom returning home on a rainy night in the sheriff's car.

Cold swept through Holly and left her shaking in that moment. "It was you..." she murmured, too stunned and too cold to speak. "It was you, wasn't it? The reason why they fought all those nights.... You're the reason why she left."

"Holly..."

"Oh...My...Gosh," Holly gasped and framed her hands over her mouth. "It's you...All this time you've been...Are you my biological father?"

The second the question left her lips, Sheriff Carlton's hard façade crumbled, and his eyes turned watery. "You know about that?"

His question bounced over Holly, leaving her trembling with a slow, rising bout of anger.

"I know alright," she threw at him, then bit back a bitter scoff. "You ruined my parent's marriage."

Sheriff Carlton's silence gave Holly all the answers she needed. The lump in her throat hardened and a gut-wrenching ache split her heart in two.

"Wow," she laughed, tossing her head back as hot tears burned the back of her eyes. "You folks really do know how to keep a secret around here, don't you?"

"I didn't know you found out."

"Thanks to my dad, I did," she retorted before sniffing and wiping her eyes furiously. "You can tell my mom I turned out great. Tell her..." Holly paused and forced the words past her tightening throat. "Tell her I did just fine without her. Tell her I'm happy and I run Frijole's now. And please tell her, I wish her the best far away from Cleverly Shores because I hope she never returns."

She left the sheriff standing there and returned to find Tim sitting up in his bed. "Hey," he called as she rushed to his side and buried her face in his sheets to muffle the sob tearing through her. "What's the matter?"

It takes some time to find the words. When she looked up at Tim, he stroked her cheek and leaned closer to her.

Holly tried to control her tears. "I'll tell you all about it later," she whispered to Tim, wanting to share all she had just learned with him. "You just need to get better first."

She smiled at him while hoping the ache tearing through her would one day fade. *With time.*

A part of her wished she didn't return to Cleverly Shores. That way, she never would have found out that her mother really didn't care about what happened to her.

But as she stared deep into Tim's eyes, and matched his smile, another part of her was grateful she had returned. She would have never had the chance to reconnect with him.

***

Kenneth Green visited a few hours later while Tim was still asleep. Holly spoke with him outside of the room.

"I'm very sorry," she apologized, lowering her chin a little to avoid his gaze.

"For accusing me of breaking into your house? Or for accusing me of killing the woman I was in love with?"

Holly looked at him now, and Kenneth smiled briefly before his expression turned solemn again. "I didn't break into your house," he clarified. "But I did break into Tim's house."

She frowned and he shoved his hands into his pockets before clearing his throat.

"I needed something to remind me of her...Annalisa I mean. We had some very few good moments before she passed away, because of the constant arguing, and I just...She didn't believe in my dreams enough. That's why we broke up."

"Why didn't you mention it? When we first met."

"You don't go around speaking to everyone of your failed relationships now, do you?" His question made her swallow hard. "Yeah, I didn't think so. Tim hates my guts, so it's expected for him to suspect me. I really did want to be friends with you, not because of Tim or his mom...Just thought you should know that."

Holly felt another twinge of guilt bite through her. Kenneth offered her one last smile before walking away, and she watched his retreating figure for a few seconds before going back into Tim's room.

It's late when Scarlet showed up with lunch and Holly walked with her around the hospital to clear her head while Tim was asleep.

"John got a week suspension," Scarlet announced as they made it past the elevator, and headed towards the pediatrics unit of the hospital. We decided to take the time off and travel to Palm Springs. I've always wanted to go there."

"That is so cool. I bet you both are looking forward to that nice little vacation. You should thank me for that. I got you two the chance to spend some time together for a whole week."

Scarlet laughed. "Don't joke around. You still got my husband suspended."

They both laughed, but Holly's heart still ached, so her laugh ended on a light sob.

"What's wrong?" Scarlet asked as she turned Holly towards her. "Holly?"

"It's the sheriff. " Holly went into Scarlet's widened arms willingly for a tight hug. "My biological father is the sheriff."

Scarlet's low murmur was muffled against Holly's hair as they hugged, and for a second right there, Holly let herself enjoy the comfort of her friend's arms before she finally pulled back. She wiped her hands over her cheeks and cleared her throat.

"He told you that?"

"I figured it out. This entire time, he's been in touch with my mom. She didn't bother reaching out to me, but she kept in touch with him all these years. He couldn't deny it when I looked him in the eyes and asked him face to face."

"You want to reach out to her?"

"No," Holly answered almost immediately. "She didn't want me. What good is reaching out to her? I'd rather not hear from her either. I'm perfectly okay with how things are."

Holly said the words to convince herself even though she knew deep down, she would always wonder. *Why didn't she want me?*

Holly sniffed, then blinked away the rest of her tears.

"You sure you'll be okay?" Scarlet asked while rubbing her arm.

"Yeah, I'm going to be just fine." Holly forced on a smile now, willing to shrug away all the heaviness. "Tim will be fine. That alone is enough comfort."

"Are you finally willing to admit you still have the hots for him?" Scarlet asked as a teasing laugh erupted from her and made Holly chuckle too.

"We're taking it slow. I'm taking it slow. There's a lot of water under the bridge between us." She heaved in a deep breath. "Only time will tell."

Scarlet hooked her arm around Holly's and leaned her head down on Holly's shoulder.

"It's finally over," Scarlet said in a relieved tone. "That's what matters."

EPILOGUE

Weeks later, Scarlet hosted Holly's birthday at Frijole's, and there was a bunch of locals around to share some of Holly's famous chicken taquitos and fresh squeezed lemonade.

"Happy birthday," Scarlet, John and Tim announced as they popped a bottle of champagne, and Holly's laugh filled the air around them. Her sides tickled as she stared at the most important people in the world to her.

There's a lot to be grateful for, she thought as Tim came in for a hug. "Happy birthday, Barber," he said while holding her gaze.

"Aww," Scarlet teased from beside them. Holly's smile widened. They stared at the crowd of well-wishers, and a wild applause erupted in the air around them.

After the past few weeks with Tim losing his mom and nearly dying at Fallon's hands, life was finally returning to normal and boring again in Cleverly Shores. *Just as I like it.*

Holly laughed as she took the glass Scarlet handed her, then she lifted it in the air for the toast.

"My entire life, I've had one sister, one friend, and one wingman," Scarlet began. Everyone else gathered around to celebrate with Holly. "I know the last few weeks have been crazy, and I'm sure it's left you second guessing the choice you made to come back. I know I am so glad you are back, and I can't imagine doing life without you by my side. You are the best friend anyone can ever ask for, and today...Today's your special day."

"So, everyone, raise your glass, and toast to Holly Barber."

"To Holly Barber," everyone chorused, and warmth filled Holly's heart again as she sipped from her glass, then joined in the light-hearted laugh that was coming from the crowd.

Tim turned her towards him a few moments later, then stared deep into her eyes, his smile reaching the corners of his eyes.

"What?" Holly asked him, loving his smile and how her heart skipped a beat because of it. *This is good,* Holly thought while waiting for his words.

"I have a gift for you, Barber," he said as he reached into his pocket and pulled out an envelope. Holly's brows furrowed lightly together as she thought of what it might be.

"What is it?" She took the sealed envelope when he handed it to her. Holly stared at it for a while, then she set her glass down on the table next to her.

As she peeled the envelope open, she was aware of Tim gauging her expression. "It's everything my mom left me before she died...I want you to have it. Double Flavors was her life's work, but she had no continuation plan, and now that she's gone...You're the only person I can think of who will take proper care of her restaurant."

"Tim, what are you saying?" Holly whispered in an unsure voice, her eyes searching his.

"I'm saying I want you to have it all. I'm sure you'll be much better at running it than I would."

Holly's not sure of what to say next. Her pulse raced as she held his gaze and his warm smile. "I want you to have it because I think you're the best person to keep her legacy going."

"I don't know what to say," she finally gasped.

"Then don't say anything." He grinned wide now, and she stared at the envelope. "You saved my life, Holly, and you're the best cook I know. You deserve this."

"Holy cannoli," she said as she thought of everything that had happened since her return. For the first time, it truly felt like a new beginning. Holly decided to toast this time, and everyone paid attention as she lifted her glass in the air. "I am truly lost for words right now. I have the best friends a girl could truly hope for. Thank you everyone for being here and supporting me through this new chapter and all the trial and tribulations it has brought on. It's been a whirlwind for sure, but I'm looking forward to what's in store in the very near future. To new beginnings."

Holly's looking forward to the end of the summer, and what is still to come. She has a feeling fall will bring many more adventures here in Cleverly Shores.

THE END

If you enjoyed Clues & Cruel Catastrophes, you will love Delights & Deadly Disasters.

(Click here to get Delights & Deadly Disasters)

Pastry Chef Maggie Wilkerson inherits a cafe back in her hometown. But once she moves back, she finds a dead man in her freezer. She quickly realizes she's being framed for murder. Maggie and her high school rival are trying to find out who the real killer is, before it's too late....Read the Prologue on the very next page!

SNEAK PEEK

Delights & Deadly Disasters – Sneak Peek

Walking into her newly inherited freezer and finding a dead man, isn't how she envisioned her new start.

Pastry Chef Maggie Wilkerson hates everything about New York. The opportunity to start over comes with a surprise letter from a lawyer. She is given the Cuppa Cafe.

Back in her hometown, she's excited to get the cafe up and running again...

...only to find she's being framed for murder. And Sheriff Wakefield wasted no time making her the prime suspect.

Maggie and Mindy, her high school rival, are desperate to prove her innocence before she gets run out of town by the very people she thought she knew. Who killed the former mayor? And why was he put in her freezer?

Maybe then she can settle down to the real work of creating the coffee & pastry shop of her dreams. And connect with the handsome sheriff in a way which doesn't involve a warrant for her arrest.

Maggie is racing against time to figure out all the secrets that are unraveling in her small town before the killer strikes again.

(Click here to get Delights & Deadly Disasters)

Prologue

How are you supposed to take anything seriously when it's spoken by a man with a whipped cream facial and cherries jubilee dotting his tie? Short answer? You don't.

The problem was Maggie Wilkerson's fiancée had started talking nonsense over dessert and it was the quickest way to end what was starting to become a most unpleasant conversation. She might have been mistaken though. She'd stopped listening when he started uttering phrases like, "I'd like the engagement ring back" and "Mitzie Wolship is the love of my life."

"Mitzie Wolship."

The worst part? She knew that name. She'd even met the woman at last year's holiday party. Justin had even introduced her as his co-worker. What had he called her? A 'real team player.'

Well, the player part seemed right.

She stared at her former fiancée as he blustered, still trying to get whipped cream out of his eyes. "I never planned this. Really, the whole thing is kind of funny. An accident really..."

Right. She could see how he might have gotten confused, seeing as how they had the same initials and all. Maggie Wilkerson. Mitzie Wolship. The poor man. He'd never stood a chance.

So, just like that, three years of her life came crashing to an earth-shattering halt. Lucky for him, she hadn't set the cherries on fire yet. For the longest moment her hand hovered over the little butane torch, thinking it wasn't too late to light the whole thing up.

Not that she was usually the violent sort. Justin really had just blindsided her. Maybe she could be forgiven for thinking a little emotionally. In the meantime, Justin was still babbling as if filling the air between them with words would somehow make things better. Add to that the noise from outside, sirens, the honk of horns, the babble of an entire city, was it any wonder she finally lost it? The world was just filled with too much noise and right now Maggie couldn't hear herself think.

And this, was definitely a moment which was going to take some thinking.

Chocolate would be good too. Dark and bitter, laced with nuts. Like her life.

She took a shaky breath. "Justin. Out. Now."

She'd stopped him mid-sentence, pointing at the door as if he couldn't figure out how to get out of the apartment on his own. It was a tiny space. The only other option was the window, which led to another happy thought involving trying to find out if Justin could fly or not.

Oh, yes, definitely time to move him along before something worse than cherries jubilee happened to him.

Maggie reminded herself these were only passing thoughts. Deep down she knew she usually wasn't this violent. The only thing she ever truly beat around was eggs.

Never mind what she did to the cream.

At least he was no longer making excuses. If anything, he had gone a little pale under all that pastry which he'd been trying to mop off with the tablecloth. As if napkins hadn't been invented. As if one wasn't right *next to his hand*.

One more thing she'd have to be mad at him about later.

Or now. Whichever.

"If that's the way you want it..."

"That's the way I want it."

Maggie wrenched the engagement ring off her finger where it had been sitting for nearly three years now. It caught on the knuckle, which hurt, though nowhere near as bad as his betrayal had. She plunked it onto his plate, watching with satisfaction as it disappeared into a mound of whipped cream, forcing him to look for it.

It was a small satisfaction, but right now she'd take what she could get.

Then with crossed arms, she watched as he stepped out of her life for the last time, an awkward man trailing choux and cherries. She slammed the door behind him and fell against it with a tumble of emotions, not the least of them relief.

Three years. She'd spent three years with that man.

She started laughing until tears flowed down her cheeks.

"That does it. I need a change."

She didn't even pause to clean up. She'd had an idea brewing ever since she realized just what Justin had been saying in all his lovelorn babble. Not one to waste time, she swiped at her tears and grabbed for the mail. Somewhere in the basket by the door was the letter she'd flung there earlier that day. Something from the landlord about wanting to increase rent when the lease renewed. She'd actually been upset about the extra $150 just that morning. Now it felt like those petty mundane concerns happened eons ago, to another person altogether.

Now she's ready to use it as an excuse. She was tired of the city. She hated her job where she suspected she'd never be higher than *commis pâtissier* if she stayed where she was now. She fingered an envelope and really considered how she felt for the first time in...forever.

I've been wanting so much more for so long. I want someone to call me 'chef' with that tone of reverence mixed with awe. That's never going to happen here, where there's a thousand pastry chefs vying for a handful of jobs. Maybe another city? Or I could go back to school and see if I could earn my CMPC...?

Maybe it was an odd time for a career change. For a life change. But hadn't she kind of put things on hold while engaged for so long, always waiting for the right time in Justin's career before tying the knot? Of course, in the end, maybe that was a good thing. It would be easier to unravel the life she had here and start fresh.

Wow. Starting fresh. The blossoming of hope within her breast caught her by surprise. Who knew heartbreak could hide excitement within the pain?

She wondered how much time she had before she would have to move. How long before she needed to make a concrete decision on whatever dream she was about to embark upon next.

Only, she couldn't find the letter. Frantically she flipped through sales flyers and junk mail, looking for the plain white envelope with her name in block letters on the front. Instead, she found something different. An envelope she hadn't even opened yet with a return address from her hometown.

Maggie paused over this one, startled that she'd missed it. Of course, it was probably nothing important. A notice about a class reunion? A wedding invitation? No. More likely, a request for a donation for someone's fundraiser. Small towns were like that, not shy about asking when one of their own is in need. She pulled the envelope free from the rest, drawn to the idea of connecting with someone back home. Like looking for comfort food when distressed.

It was not a reunion or an invitation. It wasn't even a request for cash.

It was from a law firm. Morris, Tate and associates.

She frowned over the pages enclosed, reading them through once, then again sitting down with silent sobs, for she hadn't realized a beloved mentor had died and it was too late to attend the funeral.

Then swiping at the tears drying on her cheeks, she read the letter again just in case her vision had been too blurred to read the enclosed documents correctly the first couple of times through.

"I own...a café...?"

Still in shock she let the papers fall to her lap.

No. Not just any café. The café where she'd learned to bake her first pie back when she was in high school. The café where she first realized dreams could include milk, sugar, eggs, and a whole lot of butter. The café which had belonged to her friend and mentor Katherine Emerson, who'd recently died of a sudden illness.

Her hands were shaking.

I really don't have to stay here.

She could start her whole life over after all.

The only catch? She would have to go home to do it.

(Click here to get Delights & Deadly Disasters)

Printed in Great Britain
by Amazon

35608404R00096

NAMES
from the
DAWN
of
BRITISH LEGEND

In Loving Memory of my Father

Ira Purdy Griffen

Names from the Dawn of British Legend

Taliesin, Aneirin, Myrddin/Merlin, Arthur

Toby D. Griffen

Other titles published by Llanerch include:

Symbolism of the Celtic Cross
Derek Bryce.

Taliesin Poems
Meirion Pennar

The Black Book of Carmarthen
Meirion Pennar.

Sir Gawain and the Lady of Lys
Jessie L. Weston.

Guingamor, Lanval, Tyolet & the Were-wolf.
Jessie L. Weston.

For a complete list, write to Llanerch Publishers,
Felinfach, Lampeter, Dyfed, Wales, SA48 8PJ.

TABLE OF CONTENTS

5

ACKNOWLEDGMENTS

Permissions for the extended quotations cited in this book have been given by Llanerch Enterprises, by The Governing Board of the School of Celtic Studies of the Dublin Institute for Advanced Studies, by the University of Wales Press, by Gomer Press, and by Phillimore and Company Limited. The responsibility for the conclusions reached in this book lies entirely with the author.

Published by
Llanerch Enterprises

CHAPTER 1

CANU ANEIRIN:
THE DAWN OF BRITISH LEGEND

Few of us indeed can claim never to have heard of the legendary Arthur. From Medieval sources such as Geoffrey of Monmouth to the more recent retellings and embellishments such as Alfred Lord Tenneyson's monumental *Idylls of the King*, we learn that Arthur was a great king presiding over a Round Table with the most virtuous knights in all Britain (or England!). He became king by drawing a sword from a stone, and he rid the island of all enemies. We may even have read of his invasion of Europe, his part in the quest for the Holy Grail, and other tales. And we certainly know about his wife Guinevere, his knight Lancelot, and his death-but-not-death in the struggle against Modred.

All of these stories have stirred us from childhood on, but they are only facets of legend. And at the basis of this legend lies a not-so-romantic period of chaos and tumult, of invasion and defeat, of valor and death known as the Dark Ages. We call this period the Dark Ages for the simple reason that we know so little of the details of what actually went on: Who *was* Arthur? What did he do? Where did he live?

Although modern scholarship has shed much light on the Dark Ages, it has brought the period only out of the darkness of night and into the twilight of dawn, when shadows appear real and reality blends into shadow. This is the twilit dawn in which Arthur and shadows of Arthur blend into the legends we have come to know.

In this short book, let us try to discern what we can

in this shadowy dawn of just who the people were who would eventually evolve into the great names of legend. More precisely, let us examine the names themselves to see what we can find out.

While there are a great many names connected with the Arthurian romances, let us restrict ourselves to four names that go back to the earliest work written in the British tongue: *Canu Aneirin* ('The Song of Aneirin') with its long series of elegies to fallen heroes — the *Gododdin* (the name of a North British nation and its people). These names are Taliesin, the foremost of all warrior poets; Aneirin, who survived the disastrous Battle of Catraeth to write the eulogy for his fallen comrades; Myrddin, better known in English as the sorcerer Merlin; and, of course, Arthur himself.

Unfortunately, little is said of these people in the *Gododdin* (with the exception, of course, of Aneirin), and we shall therefore have to bring in other works ranging from the complaints of Gildas (a contemporary of Arthur), through the histories of Nennius and the *Welsh Annals*, to the poetry of the *Black Book of Carmarthen*. In terms of history, we shall follow the simple premise that what comes earlier is more reliable than what comes later (arguments for lost books aside, for simple lack of evidence). Moreover, sources that attribute the acts of others to Arthur or Myrddin are suspect from the outset.

Above all, we shall approach the identities of these figures from the methodical (but far from unexciting) analysis of the linguist. In this respect, we need to examine the very words that have been written down the earliest to determine the fascinating answers to such questions as: What can we find in the name itself? What can the language tell us about the name and the person?

For the most part, this linguistic analysis can be done without many technical and poetic complexities. While we shall get into linguistic structure and poetic devices in these first two chapters, let us look at these in as nontechnical a manner as possible, leaving the linguistic intricacies to esoteric journal articles. Indeed, when intricacy is called for, it can often be skipped over with the trust and indulgence of the reader.

Of course, we must look rather closely at the language, and for this reason texts will be presented as necessary in Middle Welsh, in Modern Welsh rendition, and in Latin — but always with an English translation. It is important to examine the originals (or texts as close to the originals as we can get) not only for the precise form of the names and words, but also to gain an appreciation for what the words looked like and sounded like to those who knew the events and to those who formed the legends.

We shall follow a rather traditional division of language periods for Welsh. Brythonic was spoken through the eighth century (with Late Brythonic — blending into Early Welsh — during the period we are most interested in), Old Welsh was spoken from the ninth century through the eleventh, and Middle Welsh was spoken from then to around the fifteenth century. Of course, the periods are rough approximations demarcated by particular characteristics of language and poetry.

The Brythonic Source: Canu Aneirin

In examining the origins of Taliesin, Aneirin, Myrddin, and Arthur, we must be sure that these names do appear in the records of their times. This is to say that we must find them in a work dating from the earliest period of the language — Brythonic (or British).

Certainly, the names are all found in *Canu Aneirin* ('The Song of Aneirin'), which consists of the collection of poems *Y Gododdin* ('The Gododdin') and four verse tales, or *Gwarchanau*. While it may have been composed as early as the depicted events of about A.D. 600 (in the aftermath of the disastrous Battle of Catraeth), the manuscript we have dates only from about A.D. 1265 and was copied from at least two sources: one traditionally known as the A text, being more modern in its grammar and orthography (spelling rules); and the other traditionally known as the B text, showing orthography of considerable antiquity.

While the names in question do appear in *Canu Aneirin*, we must ask whether the manuscript dating only from about A.D. 1265 is indeed a faithful enough copy of the original Brythonic work that we may conclude that these names were in fact known around A.D. 600. The manuscript could, after all, simply be a much later work and the author could be referring not to actual historical figures but to those of legend — to people who never really walked the earth as individuals (an important point that will occupy our attention in chapter 6).

The test for the Brythonic authenticity of *Canu Aneirin* would seem simple enough: If the language shows elements of the old Brythonic tongue, then it must have been composed during the period right after these major figures of British legend lived. But, as we see below, archaic elements could simply have been added to a later composition to give it the appearance of having derived from a Brythonic original. What we need, then, is not random samples of Brythonic expressions and spellings, but something considerably more systematic, more extensive and patterned.

Before we can examine *Canu Aneirin* for these systematic traces of Brythonic, we must first determine what it is that will convince us that a sample of writing may be Brythonic, and not Old Welsh or Middle Welsh. While there are many different characteristics that would mark something as Brythonic, there is a problem with all of them: The scribe would have known many of these characteristics and could have simply added them to give the work the air of the Brythonic period, just as a modern English writer might add *thee* and *thou* to an historical novel to give it an Elizabethan air.

What we need is some linguistic or poetic device that the scribe would not have known about — one that, if it appeared in the Old or Middle Welsh manuscript, would signal a systematic use of Brythonic that could not have been reproduced in Old or Middle Welsh. Once again, of course, such linguistic and poetic period designations as Brythonic, Old Welsh, and Middle Welsh are not well defined, certainly not with reference to precise dates. These periods have rather lengthy transitions during which some dialects might be classified in one period and others in the adjacent period.

Nonetheless, we can broadly define these periods in terms of their linguistic and poetic devices. For example, the process of mesotomy (explained in the next section) requires a linguistic system with "pitch accent" (pronouncing the accented syllable higher than the others) and no significant stress accent (pronouncing the accented syllable stronger or louder than the others) and requires a poetic system that counts the number of syllables in a line in a process called "scansion." As such, this device could only have existed in Old Welsh, for before Old Welsh the language apparently maintained stress accent possibly without a poetic system of syllable scansion, and after Old Welsh it returned to a significant stress accent again. We can thus consider a poem with this device as Old Welsh, regardless of the particular date of its composition.

At this point, the reader who does not wish in this reading to go into the linguistic and poetic details that lead us to the conclusion that *Canu Aneirin* is in fact of Brythonic origin can skip the next two sections and proceed to the section entitled "*Dating* Canu Aneirin." These details are presented in as nontechnical a manner as possible, though; so the reader who simply wishes to read through the book quickly is urged to return to them when convenient.

Mesotomy in Old Welsh

The "mesotomic" syllable, a syllable 'cut through the middle' is one of the most recent discoveries about literary Old Welsh. The phenomenon is most transparent in the lengthy poem *Armes Prydein* ('The Prophecy of Britain'), found in the *Book of Taliesin* in the Peniarth 2 manuscript of the National Library of Wales. In the following examination, let us use the 1972 edition of Ifor Williams with the translations by Rachel Bromwich, as they appear in that edition. To keep track of the lines, we shall prefix each with AP and the line number. So that we might better see the syllable count, we shall also add a colon between the half lines.

Armes Prydein was composed in a meter called Cyhydedd Naw Ban ('nine peak line' — henceforth, CNB). In this meter, each line of the original Old Welsh composition would have consisted of two half-lines, the first of which would have had five syllables, and the second four syllables. For example, AP 1 *Dygogan awen : dygobryssyn* "The *Awen* foretells, they will hasten" maintains the proper CNB meter. But while the original poem was composed around A.D. 930, the copy of *Armes Prydein* that we find in the *Book of Taliesin* is not written in the Old Welsh of the author but is a Middle Welsh copy made around A.D. 1275 at the earliest, and after a transmission through an unknown number of copies in an unknown number of dialects.

The discovery of the mesotomic syllable in *Armes Prydein* has derived from a rather technical linguistic approach known as "dynamic phonological analysis," the particulars of which are found in other publications and need not bog us down here. Assuming that the original poet was competent (a rather extreme understatement), we can expect that although the meter is not always consistent in the manuscript, the author's original composition was indeed consistent.

If we analyze each line of *Armes Prydein*, we find that when two identical vowels precede the accented "ultima" (the final syllable), they may be considered to occupy one single "extended" syllable. For example, AP 2 *maraned a meued : a hed genhyn* 'we shall have wealth and property and peace' appears to violate the CNB meter with six syllables (rather than the required five) in the first half-line. The word *maraned* [maraneδ] 'wealth, treasure', however, contains the sequence in which the "pretonic" vowels (those before the final accented syllable) are identical in pitch and have the same vowel. These two apparent syllables are thus counted as one mesotomic syllable (cut by the consonant *r*), and the meter is justified as CNB.

This rule was possible because the sole accent in Old Welsh was on the final syllable — the ultima. Since all other syllables were equal in pitch, two repetitions of the same vowel could be considered so identical as to be a continuous unit — one long vowel cut by a consonant.

The rule of the mesotomic syllable applies with striking regularity in *Armes Prydein*. Of the 199 lines in the poem, only a minority of 92 (or 46%) adheres to the CNB meter without taking mesotomy into consideration. When we do take this device into account, 24 more lines are fully justified as CNB (an increase in 26% of acceptable lines), to bring the total to a majority of 116 lines (or 58%). Three more half-lines are justified by the device and two are brought closer to the meter. Thus, the mesotomic syllable assists in the proper scansion in 29 lines, bringing the total so far justified or assisted to a clear majority of 121 (or 61%). Moreover, every instance in which a mesotomic syllable would appear to introduce a violation of the meter is clearly due to spelling variants, foreign phonological systems, or Middle Welsh orthographic conventions. While such an increase in the regularity of the meter may not impress us from the standpoint of modern texts, given the age of the work and the number of transmissions it must have gone through, this regularity is indeed rather impressive.

As noted above, this phenomenon was exclusively Old Welsh. In Late Brythonic, the accent was not on the ultima, but on the penult; and if the accent consisted of stress in addition to pitch (or instead of it), as many scholars rather effectively argue, then there may well have been various levels of stress throughout the word, making adjacent vowels inherently different (see below). Thus, we cannot expect to find mesotomy occurring before the Old Welsh period.

Moreover, mesotomy disappeared in Middle Welsh with the development of the stress accent on the next-to-last syllable — the penult. This new pattern, whether indeed it constituted the primary accent or not, eliminated the very opportunity for mesotomic syllables. With different levels of stress occurring on adjacent syllables, no two consecutive syllables could be considered identical enough to have a single, long vowel. Thus, mesotomy could not occur in Middle Welsh. It is for this reason that the Medieval bardic grammarians, who could easily describe epenthesis and other phenomena shared by Old Welsh and Middle Welsh, knew nothing of the mesotomic syllable, which involved a set of pronunciation rules totally alien to them.

This exclusively Old Welsh nature of mesotomy provides us with a valuable tool for dating the composition of poems. Any poetic work containing mesotomic syllables must have been composed entirely or partially in the Old Welsh period. As shown above, *Armes Prydein* realizes mesotomy with extreme regularity. This regularity shows us unequivocally three things: (1) that the *Armes* was composed in Old Welsh; (2) that it was changed so little in its transmission to Middle Welsh that no case of mesotomy was affected; and (3) that whatever Late Brythonic source may have been used, the source was either oral and the work was first composed in writing in Old Welsh, or the Late Brythonic written source was extensively (if not entirely) reworked.

Mesotomic Syllables in Canu Aneirin?

As noted at the outset of this chapter, while the *Gododdin* of *Canu Aneirin* depicts events of about A.D. 600 (after the Battle of Catraeth), the manuscript we have dates from about A.D. 1265 and was copied from sources of varying conservatism (where the most conservative, least changed forms are considered to be representative of the oldest manuscript). In our examination of this collection of poems, let us use the 1938 edition of Ifor Williams, with translations into English and modernized Welsh from the 1990 harmonized text of A.O.H. Jarman (combining the various versions into one). Williams' stanzas are designated by Roman numerals, Jarman's by Arabic; and lines are prefixed CA.

It has long been argued that some aspects of the language and the poetic devices in *Canu Aneirin* belong to the Late Brythonic period. Indeed, the work shares poetic practices with the earliest monuments of Irish literature and thus reflects (directly or indirectly) an old Celtic tradition of versification.

An examination of *Canu Aneirin* reveals quite clearly that the text is devoid of mesotomic syllables. Perhaps the most transparent evidence for the lack of mesotomy can be found in stanzas with short lines — lines of four or five syllables. On the one hand, longer lines admit to more problems introduced in transmission; and on the other hand, the number of beats may well have been an important factor in this earlier poetry (or indeed the crucial factor), not just the number of syllables *per se*. Short lines would avoid both problems, providing less opportunity for transmission error and supplying a more obvious role for the syllable count.

One such stanza is LXXXIV (Jarman's stanza 82), in which the pattern is definitely one of four syllables per line. This stanza reads as follows:

LXXXIV

	Porthloed vedin
1015	porthloed lain.
	a llu racwed
	en ragyrwed
	en dyd gwned
	yg kyvryssed.
1020	buant gwychawc

                    gwede meddawt
                    a med yuet.
                    ny bu waret
                    an gorwylam
        1025   enyd frwythlam.
                    pan adroder
                    torret ergyr
                    o veirch a gwyr
                    tyngyr tynget.

                        82

Haven of an army,	Porthloed byddin,
Spear of the haven,	Porthloedd läin,
And a distinguished host	A llu rhagwedd
In forward position	Yn rhagyrwedd
On the day of battle	Yn nydd gẃnedd
In the conflict.	Yng nghyfrysedd.
They were savage	Buant wythog
After drunkenness	Wedi medd-dod
790 And the drinking of mead.	A medd yfed.
There was no escape	Ni bu wared
From our successful assault	Ein gorwylam
On the day of the mighty charge,	Yn nydd ffrwythlam,
When it was told,	Pan adrodedd
A host was broken	Torred ergyr
Of horses and men,	O feirch a gwŷr,
Tyngyr's fate.	Tyngyr dynged.

Given the two-syllable pronunciation of *lain* 'spear' (rendered in the more modern Welsh of Jarman as *laïn*) and *gwned* 'battle' (rendered as *gẃned* by Jarman), the stanza is completely faithful in keeping four syllables per line. Since the number of beats in stress accentuated poetry would probably have been either four or two, fewer than four syllables in a line would violate the beat or make it extremely awkward.

It is therefore significant that *yg kyvryssed* 'in the conflict' must be scanned as having four syllables. The noun (especially with its "proclitic" *yg* [ən] — a syllable that is attached to the beginning of a word and incorporated into the word itself) is a prime candidate for mesotomy; but if it is pronounced mesotomically, then the meter is lost. Exactly the same situation is found in the following stanza in which CA 1033a *ku carasswn* 'a dear one I had loved' is an even more obvious candidate for mesotomy; but mesotomy cannot apply.

Of course, throughout the work, the word *gododin* 'Gododdin' and also the word *mynydawc* 'the mountain people' abound. Yet, neither is ever treated mesotomically, although both are prime candidates for the process.

The rare instances in which mesotomy appears to occur are almost all accountable by the very irregularity of the syllable count. For example, CA 326 *Keredic caradwy e glot* 'Ceredig, of lovable fame' and CA 333 *Keredic caradwy gynran* 'Ceredig, lovable chieftain' would both have the same number of syllables with their following lines if mesotomy were to apply once (but not twice, as would really be required!). A glance at their respective stanzas (XXVIII and XXIX), however, reveals that the number of syllables varies rather widely, although the eight syllables of the two lines in question (without mesotomy) are indeed in the plurality.

In extremely rare cases, we might think that we have found an instance of mesotomy producing a more consistent line. For example, CA 210 *dygymynei. e gat* 'Cut down in battle' would appear to yield a better scansion with the five syllables resulting from mesotomy. Such cases, however, are so rare that we must discount them, for many lines contain an unexpected number of syllables. Indeed, if so few cases could make an argument for mesotomy, then other lines could make an argument for practically any process imaginable.

We can thus conclude with a high degree of certainty that mesotomic syllables were not a part of the language used by Aneirin or by any of the early redactors of *Canu Aneirin*, as it is found in the text.

Dating Canu Aneirin

In his insightful analyses of the orthography of *Canu Aneirin* and other early manuscripts, John T. Koch has traced developments in the spelling conventions to show that the works of literature that include *Canu Aneirin* "rest — *at some level* — upon written material older than *c.* 750" (Koch, "When Was Welsh First Written Down?" page 59). Indeed, the B text of this particular work is recognized by Koch and others as being consistently very conservative (= old) in its orthography.

However, Koch notes a major *caveat*: "We also suffer the general disadvantage of seeing the original spelling only as errors and slips poking through texts (excepting parts of the *CA* B text) reduced to wholly different orthographic standards. The ultimate wild card in any such study is the possibility that literate poets might have made use of glossaries or quarried words from old written texts. As will be seen, there is some evidence for such practices in the works of the Gogynfeirdd" (Koch, page 54).

To this we might also add the further complication that in general, poets and scribes having available some orthographic and even grammatical examples from an earlier period are prone to imitating the conventions (whether verbatim exemplars exist or not) in the composition of works in which the venerability of age is desired. This widespread device (in all written languages) is known as the "archaism."

Thus, we should not at all be surprised to find Late Brythonic archaisms in Old Welsh compositions or Old Welsh archaisms in Middle Welsh compositions. It would be unusual to find Late Brythonic archaisms actively used in Middle Welsh compositions though, simply because there would have been too great a degree of change. To cite a parallel English example, we find many Shakespearean archaisms in Modern English literature, but no Chaucerian archaisms.

We could therefore conceive of the possibility that

Canu Aneirin (even the more conservative text B) could have been composed in the Old Welsh period by a poet or poets consciously attempting to capture at least the orthographic style of Late Brythonic, since the subject matter does after all come from the earlier period. On the other hand, *Canu Aneirin* would not have been composed in the Middle Welsh period. While Brythonic spelling conventions may have been acceptably archaic in Old Welsh, they would have been quite alien to Middle Welsh. (This may well explain why the B text has managed to survive so well intact — it was so unfamiliar that the scribes could not determine how to modernize it, even to the archaic level of Old Welsh.)

So far, our conclusions are based upon orthography — letters spelled overtly across a page. These letters are obvious and can be copied and changed on the basis of older exemplars. But the syllable structure is not so visible. Although the evidence of mesotomy was there for the Medieval grammarians to observe, it had to be deduced by dynamic phonological analysis, which was not within the ken of the bard.

Likewise, the Old Welsh poet or grammarian would not have noticed the lack of mesotomy in Late Brythonic written texts but would simply have judged them to be irregular. Thus, a work that had been composed in Old Welsh with every attention to the production of convincing Brythonic archaisms would still contain mesotomic syllables.

The fact that we have no mesotomic syllables in *Canu Aneirin* could thus be accounted for in one of two ways. The first way is to suggest that there may have been mesotomic syllables in the original composition, and these may have been "corrected" by the Middle Welsh scribes. That is, rather than the modest orthographic "reform" as in the manuscript of *Armes Prydein*, in which the mesotomic syllables are faithfully maintained while other devices are changed to be consistent with Middle Welsh, the Middle Welsh scribes may have revised the manuscript thoroughly enough to have eliminated the mesotomic syllables altogether. This would appear to be the case in *Canu Llywarch Hen* ('The Song of Llywarch the Old'), for example.

There is a crucial difference, however, between *Canu Aneirin* and *Canu Llywarch Hen*. If we examine the language of the latter, we find that not only are there no mesotomic syllables, but the orthography in general has been revised to adhere to the Middle Welsh norm. As noted above, the orthography of *Canu Aneirin* shows definite traits of Late Brythonic. The suggestion that the scribes would have carefully excised the mesotomics (which they could not perceive in the first place) and yet maintained the Brythonic orthography would be highly unreasonable.

The second way of accounting for the lack of mesotomic syllables in *Canu Aneirin* is to suggest that they were not included in the first place. This would indicate that the composition was written not in Old Welsh, but in Late Brythonic.

If the written composition had been created in the Old Welsh period, the author could conceivably have imitated the Late Brythonic archaisms, as we have already discussed above. The lack of the mesotomic syllable in Late Brythonic, though, would not have been apparent to the author unversed in modern dynamic phonological analysis. We should thus fully expect to find some patterned instances of mesotomy — and we do not.

Conclusion

From our examination of the orthography, we can thus conclude that *Canu Aneirin* was written down before the Middle Welsh period, which was too far removed from these spelling conventions. Accordingly, we can assume that it was written either in Late Brythonic or in an Old Welsh with studiously applied archaisms.

From the lack of mesotomy, we can conclude that *Canu Aneirin* was not composed in the Old Welsh period.

Since its archaic orthography could not have been more recent than Old Welsh, it must have been written down in Late Brythonic, not long after the disaster at Catraeth around A.D. 600.

Nor does the Late Brythonic date of composition refer merely to the beginning of an oral tradition. An oral transmission could not have withstood the pressure of mesotomy in Old Welsh, in which the meter would certainly have had to adjust to the spoken language (in the absence of an extensive written text) at a time in which syllable count was entirely replacing beat (and with an absence of significant stress accent). Thus, the archaic orthography of *Canu Aneirin* was doubtless not the product of scribes imitating Brythonic exemplars, but the product of scribes copying with some degree of faithfulness a text written in Late Brythonic itself.

What we find in *Canu Aneirin*, then, is not an Old Welsh written composition based upon a Late Brythonic oral transmission (as could quite conceivably be the case of *Armes Prydein*); rather, it is a copy (of a copy, of a copy, ...) of a Late Brythonic written text, as accurate as we can reasonably expect given the scribal practices of the time. The depiction of events we can thus surmise to be close to eye-witness accounts.

For us and for our examination of the names at the dawn of British legend, this proof that *Canu Aneirin*, with its long series of poems to the Gododdin who fell at the Battle of Catraeth around A.D. 600, was indeed first composed in the seventh century is crucial. It means that the names that we find in the *Gododdin* poems were in fact names that did exist at the dawn of British legend, not just in later fantasies of the Medieval romantics.

While we shall certainly draw on other sources (and indeed we must), the mention of these names by Aneirin gives us a reliable anchor that keeps us from being pulled away and swept off in the tide of often fanciful legend. Now we can get on with the interesting task of figuring out what these names may have meant to Aneirin and through them who these people may have been.

CHAPTER 2

TALIESIN

The great bard Taliesin figures into many poems and tales after the Brythonic period of Arthur. Unfortunately, the only reference we have to him before Old Welsh is a single line in the *Gododdin* of *Canu Aneirin*. This appears as follows in the 1938 edition by Ifor Williams followed by the 1990 English translation and Welsh modernization of A.O.H. Jarman:

o ved o vuelin.
o gatraeth werin.
mi na vi aneirin.
ys gwyr talyessin
550   ovec kywrenhin.
neu cheing e ododin
kynn gwawr dyd dilin

	About mead from the drinking-horn,	O fedd o fuelin,
	About the men of Catraeth,	O Gatraeth werin,
480	I, yet not I, Aneirin	Mi na fi Neirin,
	(Taliesin knows it,	Ys gŵyr Taliesin
	Skilled in expression)	Ofeg gywrennin,
	Sang *Y Gododdin*	neu cheint *Ododdin*
	Before the next day dawned.	Cyn gwawr dydd dilin.

Nonetheless, there is much we can surmise about Taliesin from the poems that have been attributed to him. These have traditionally been thought of as dating from Old Welsh. As we shall see, however, the situation is — as always — not so neat and tidy. From the "untidiness" of the poems attributed to him, we shall indeed gain perhaps the most crucial insight we can into the bard and his name.

One of the most acute problems in Old Welsh poetry is the fact that the poet pronounced his poem in Old Welsh, but the scribe we must rely upon wrote it down in Middle Welsh — after, of course, an often convoluted transmission through Old and Middle Welsh. As we saw in chapter 1 for example, while *Armes Prydein* was probably composed around A.D. 930, well within the Old Welsh period and certainly in an Old Welsh dialect, the copy we have in the *Book of Taliesin* dates from the Middle Welsh Peniarth 2 manuscript of the late thirteenth century. Thus, we can never be sure on first examination which characteristics of the manuscript reflect Old Welsh usage and which are peculiar to the language of the Middle Welsh scribes.

This problem is crucial in determining the syllable-based meter. As pointed out in chapter 1, we know that the accent pattern of Old Welsh differed significantly from that of Middle Welsh: The former had a pitch accent on the final syllable — the ultima; while the latter maintained this ultimate pitch accent and also a stress accent on the next-to-last syllable — the penult.

Mesotomic Syllables Once Again

Because of such changes as the Old Welsh accent shift, we can expect certain Old Welsh poetic rules to have disappeared and thus not to have been addressed by the Medieval bardic grammarians. As shown in detail in the previous chapter, such a rule has been discovered. When two identical vowels precede the accented ultima, they are considered to occupy the same "extended" syllable. For example, the second line of *Armes Prydein* (again using the 1972 Ifor Williams edition with its translation by Rachel Bromwich) *maraned a meued : a hed genhyn* 'we shall have wealth and property and peace' appears to violate the meter with six syllables in the first half-line. The word *maraned* [maraneð] 'wealth, treasure', however, contains the sequence in which the pretonic vowels are identical and have the same pitch accent. These two apparent syllables are thus counted as one mesotomic syllable.

This rule was possible because the sole accent in Old Welsh was on the ultima, and all other syllables were equal in pitch accent. In the accent pattern of Middle Welsh, though, the mesotomic syllable was not possible, for the development of different degrees of stress throughout the word kept two sequential vowels from being considered this identical. Thus, the rule totally escaped the Middle Welsh grammarians.

For the literary scholar, the importance of mesotomy goes far beyond its justification of metrical patterns in *Armes Prydein*. In the other poems of the *Book of Taliesin* — even among the twelve believed to be accurate transmissions from the sixth-century bard — mesotomy is also found, but it occurs with different degrees of regularity. For example, as we shall see below the rule is regular in poem IX, but it seems to be completely absent from poem IV.

If mesotomy is applied differently among the twelve "authentic" poems of Taliesin, then there would appear to be more than one poet. An examination of the mesotomic syllables in these poems reveals an extremely complicated situation.

Readers who find the examination of lines of poetry tedious may skip the next section and proceed directly to the the section entitled *"Who Was Taliesin?"* Once again, however, the treatment, while involved, is presented in as nontechnical a manner as possible, so the reader who skips it now may wish to return to these details later.

The Poems

In the following analyses of three key poems, we shall use the 1968 edition of Ifor Williams. For ease of reference, poems are designated by Roman numerals,

lines by Arabic numerals, and half-lines by the letters "a"
(first) and "b" (second). The translations for entire poems
are from the 1988 edition of Meirion Pennar, but
individual words and phrases are translated by the
author, since the Pennar translation — albeit an excellent
literary translation — is not quite detailed enough for a
closer examination of individual words and half-lines.

   Poem IV. This poem is particularly interesting because
it is extremely regular in its syllable count. It has only
four syllables per half-line, meaning that whether the
syllable count or the "beat" is pertinent, there is little
room for error.

IV
[BT 58]

	Eg gorffowys	can rychedwys
	parch a chynnwys.	a med meuedwys.
	Meuedwys med	y oruoled
	a chein tired	imi yn ryfed.
5	A ryfed mawr	ac eur ac awr.
	Ac awr a chet	a chyfriuet
	a cyfriuyant.	A rodi chwant.
	chwant oe rodi	yr vy llochi.
	Yt lad yt gryc	yt vac yt vyc.
10	yt vyc yt vac	yt lad yn rac.
	racwed rothit	y veird y byt.
	Byt yn geugant	itti yt wedant
	wrth dy ewyllis.	Duw ryth peris
	rieu ygnis	rac ofyn dybris.
15	Annogyat kat	diffreidyat gwlat.
	gwlat diffreidyat	kat annogyat.
	gnawt amdant	twrwf pystylat.
	Pystalat twrwf	ac yuet cwrwf.
	kwrwf oe yfet	a chein trefret
20	a chein tudet	imi ryanllofet.
	Llwyfenyd van.	ac eirch achlan
	yn vn trygan	mawr a bychan
	taliessin gan	tidi ae didan.
	ys tidi goreu	or a gigleu
25	y wrdlideu.	Molaf inheu
	dy weithredeu.	

Ac yny vallwyf hen
ym dygyn agheu aghen.
ny bydif ymdirwen
30   na molwyf vryen.

URIEN AT HOME

In the hall of the men of Rheged
there is every
esteem and welcome,
offerings of wine
for jubilation,
fair lands
for me as riches;
riches a-plenty
and gold, gold;
gold and gift,
esteem. -
And estimation:
to give my wish
and wish to give,
for my comfort.

He kills,
he hangs,
he nurtures
he dispenses;
dispenses
and nurtures,
he kills
in the front line.

To be sure,
they bow down to you,
according to your desire,
that,
for you,
has God ordained.
Kings bellow
for fear of your onrush:
battle's goader,
country's defender,
defender of country,
goader in battle.
Constantly around you
is the pounding of horses,
horses pounding,

and the quaffing of beer,
beer to be quaffed:
and lovely homesteads,
lovely apparel
was handed out to me.
Comely Llwyfenydd
And the whole of Eirch
all and sundry,
big and small,
the song of Taliesin,
you entertain them.

You are the best
for reason of your virtues,
Urien,
I praise your deeds.

And until I am old and ailing
in the dire necessity of death
I shall not be in my element
if I don't praise Urien.

While several half-lines appear to the non-Welsh speaker to have too many syllables (notably IV.13.a, IV.14.b, IV.19.a, and VI.19.b), they are actually the right length. The apparent discrepancies are due to certain rules spelled out by the Medieval grammarians — rules such as "epenthesis" that are still found in standard literary Modern Welsh.

A regular exception can be found in certain pronouns. These are fuller, "doubled" (reduplicative) forms such as *imi* 'to me' in IV.4.b and *itti* 'to thee' in IV.12.b, *tidi* 'thou' in IV.23.b and IV.24.a. Evidently, the original poet had only the shorter, one-syllable (monosyllabic) forms in his vocabulary. By removing the syllables added by some later scribe (and which subsequently became the norm) and making other adjustments to reconstruct the original, we reduce the lines to the proper syllable count.

The only remaining irregular line in the poem is IV.2.b. This has every appearance of being mesotomic: *a med meuedwys* 'and mead he prized (bestowed as a prize)'. The word *meuedwys* 'he prized' maintains identical vowels in what would have been the pretonic syllables in Old Welsh. However, the same word is found in the next line IV.3.a, and it is clearly not a case of mesotomy: *Meuedwys med* 'he prized (bestowed as a prize) mead'. Either the first line is correct, and the poem is an Old Welsh composition; or the second line is correct, and the poem is a Middle Welsh composition. Ifor Williams has suggested that *a med* 'and mead' should be shortened to *med* 'mead' for the sake of the meter, but he was writing before the discovery of mesotomy.

Our answer to this riddle is found later in the poem. In line IV.17.a the word *amdanat* 'concerning it' is a clear candidate for mesotomy, but counting the syllables mesotomically would violate the meter. This is also the case with the word *pystylat* 'stamping, trampling' in line IV.7.b. Obviously, Williams' solution is the correct one, and there are no mesotomic syllables in poem IV.

Making the above adjustments, we are left with a very regular poem with relatively short lines. Moreover, the scribe clearly demonstrated that he was not concerned with maintaining the regularity of the lines — he was a scribe, not a poet (fortunately for us). The poet who actually composed this poem was not of the Old Welsh period, but wrote rather in Middle Welsh. The poem is frankly too regular and too devoid of Old Welsh transmission errors to be anything but a relatively recent composition.

Moreover, at least one of the redactor of this poem was somewhat idiosyncratic in his reliance upon those doubled pronouns. They occur rarely in the collection, never more than one per poem. Here, however, there are five, indicating a transmission history different from the other poems and doubtless from a different source. When we add this fact to the fact that this is our only poem with such a regular count of four syllables per half-line, we are left to conclude that this poem must indeed be set aside as unique.

Yet, the poet identifies himself as Taliesin.

Poem IX. Far more evident of mesotomy and of an Old Welsh date of composition is poem IX. It maintains five syllables per half-line; and where there is a deviation in one half-line, the same deviation is seen in the other.

IX

DADOLWCH VRYEN

[BT 65]

	Lleuuyd echassaf	mi nyw dirmygaf.
	vryen a gyrchaf.	Jdaw yt ganaf.
	pan del vygwaessaf.	kynnwys a gaffaf.
	Ar parth goreuhaf	ydan eilassaf.
5	Ny mawr ym dawr byth	gweheleith a welaf.
	Nyt af attadunt	ganthunt ny bydaf.
	ny chyrchaf i gogled	ar meiteyrned.
	kyn pei am lawered	y gwnelwn gyghwystled.
	Nyt reit am hoffed.	Vryen nym gomed.
10	Lloyfenyd tired	ys meu eu reufed.
	Ys meu y gwyled.	ys meu y llared.
	ys mae y delideu	ae gorefrasseu
	med o uualeu	a da dieisseu
	gan teyrn goreu.	haelaf rygigleu.
15	Teyrned pop ieith	it oll yd ynt geith.
	Ragot yt gwynir	ys dir dy oleith.
	kyt ef mynasswn	gweyhelu henwn.
	Nyt oed well a gerwn.	kyn ys gwybydwn.
	weithon y gwelaf	y meint a gaffaf.
20	Namyn y duw vchaf	nys dioferaf.
	Dy teyrn veibon	haelaf dynedon.
	wy kanan eu hyscyrron	yn tired eu galon.

Ac yny vallwyf i hen
ym dygyn agheu aghen
ny bydaf yn dirwen
na molwyfi vryen.

THE CONCILIATION OF URIEN

I shall not cast aside
the bravest leader,
I'll go to Urien,
to him I'll sing.
When my guarantor comes,

I get a welcome.
And the very best place to be
is under this chieftain.

I don't greatly care ever
what progeny I see,
I'll not go to them,
I'll never be with them.
I'll not go to the north and the half-kings.

Even though I'd give a lot
to make peace with you,
no need for me to boast
my gifts,
Urien will not refuse me.

Mine are the riches
of the lands of Llwyfenydd,
mine their bounty,
mine their kindliness,
mine their cloth,
their victuals,
mead from horns,
goodies galore,
and the hand of the best of kings,
the most generous
that I've heard tell.
The kings of every people are all
bound over to you.
There's lamentation before you,
it's difficult to give you the slip.
Even though I wanted him,
there's the throwing of twigs
at an old man.
There would be no-one
that I would love more;
ignorant though I was,
I see now the extent of what I have:
except to the highest God
I'll not give him up.
Your regal sons,
the most generous of men,
from now on
their twigs will be whistling
towards the land
of their enemy.

> And until I am old and ailing
> in the dire necessity of death
> I shall not be in my element
> If I don't praise Urien.

Line IX.5.b appears to have a discrepancy with six syllables, but *gweheleith* 'princes' is obviously mesotomic, reducing the half-line to the proper five syllables. In line IX.7.a we find *ny chyrchaf* 'I shall not go (to)' which is counted as one word and can be seen as mesotomic, and its reduction restores the half-line to the proper five syllables. The word *delideu* 'merits, rewards; feasts' in IX.12.a is either disyllabic (having two syllables) in its own right as a variant of *dlideu* or it is disyllabic due to mesotomy from the older *dilideu*, in which case the prefix would indeed indicate an earlier, Old Welsh form and would help identify the poem as genuinely Old Welsh. Line IX.22.a should have six syllables to match the six in the second half-line, and this number is recovered with the mesotomic syllable in *hyscyrron* 'branches, songs'. This longer line may signal the end of the poem — the coda having been added to the poems later (which we see by the mismatching of mesotomy in codas and poems).

Line IX.6 has two mesotomics in each half-line that would appear to reduce both half-lines to a short four syllables each, with *attadunt* 'to them' in the first half-line and *ny bydaf* 'I shall not be' in the second. It is significant that the only short line has mesotomics in both half-lines and that both half-lines are thus maintained as equal. While the device may have been invisible to the Middle Welsh scribe, it was quite visible to the Old Welsh poet. Once again, this would indicate an Old Welsh date of composition (and not an Old Welsh redaction of a Brythonic or Early Welsh composition).

Line IX.18.a has an extra syllable due to a routine scribal error. As for *gwybydwn* 'I knew' in the second half-line, the *wy* would have been perceived differently than the *y* and would not have been subject to mesotomy.

The only other discrepancies are in IX.8 and IX.20.

In the former, the six syllables per half-line are equal as is, but the scribal changes discussed by Ifor Williams would reduce these to five syllables each, neatly restricting the use of the long line to the end. As for IX.20.a, *namyn* 'except' is quite normally one syllable.

Thus, poem IX is highly regular in its application of mesotomy. Moreover, some of the devices used appear to indicate that the poet knew how to use the device and that the composition thus took place in Old Welsh — not in Middle Welsh and not in Brythonic. The regularity of the representation further indicates that this poem probably did not pass through many scribes between its composition and its final redaction.

This Taliesin, then, is quite different from that of poem IV. This Taliesin's poem is undoubtably Old Welsh and transmitted fairly directly to the scribe of the Peniarth manuscript.

Poem V. That being the case, the person who composed poem V was a different Taliesin altogether, for the poem passed through a different route between poet and ultimate scribe. That a single collection would have split up, been transmitted through Old Welsh and into Middle Welsh in separate collections, and then have been rejoined in the Middle Welsh manuscript is more fortuitous than we could reasonably expect.

V

[BT 59]

	Ar vn blyned	vn yn darwed
	gwin a mall a med.	A gwrhyt diassed
	Ac eilewyd gorot.	a heit am vereu
	ae pen ffuneu	Ae tec gwyduaeu
5	ei pawb oe wyt	dyfynt ymplymnwyt.
	Ae varch ydanaw	yg godeu gweith mynaw.
	a chwanec anaw	bud am li amlaw.
	wyth vgein vn lliw	o loi a biw.
	biw blith ac ychen	a phop kein agen
10	Ny bydwn lawen	bei lleas vryen.

ys cu kyn eithyd
A briger wen olchet
a gran gwyarllet
A gwr bwrr bythic.
15   Am ys gwin ffeleic.
Am sorth am porth am
        pen
tauaw gwas yr drws
ae dayar a gryn
dygwynyc ychyngar
20   Ossit vch ymryn
Ossit vch ym pant
Ossit vch ymynyd.
Ossit vch yn riw
Ossit vch yg clawd.
25   Vch hynt vch as
Nac vn trew na deu
Ny bydei ar newyn
Gorgoryawc gorlassawc
eil agheu oed y par.

y eis kygryn kygryt.
    ac elor y dyget
am waet gwyr gonodet.
A uei wedw y wreic.
Am ys gwin mynyc gyltwn.
ky naphar kyfwyrein.
        kymaran
gwarandaw py trwst
ae mor adugyn.
wrth y pedyt.
neut vryen ae gryn.
neut vryen ae gwant.
neut vryen a oruyd.
neut vryen ae briw.
neut vryen a blawd.
vch ym pop kamas.
ny nawd yraceu.
a phreideu yn y gylchen.
gorlassar.
yn llad y escar.

Ac yny vallwyf i hen
Ym·dygyn agheu aghen.
ny bydif ym dyrwen.
na molwyf vryen.

WHAT IF URIEN WERE DEAD

For a whole year continually -
one overlowing
with wine and brew and mead:
here's boundless bravery incarnate.
There's crowds of poets
and a swarm around the spits,
with their head-dresses
and fine seats.
And from their food
everybody goes eagerly to battle,
his horse under him
with Manaw's battle in his sights
for more spoils
and plenty of booty besides.
A hundred and sixty calves and cows,
all of one colour,
milch cows and oxen
and many a thing of beauty as well.

I wouldn't be happy
if death came Urien's way.
(You were dear
before you went
to the clamour of hurled spears).
His white hair washed with blood,
brought back on a bier
with gory cheek
his men stained with blood;
a strong a virile man
whose wife would be a widow.
For me a chieftain's wine,
the wine of my heart's desire
from my portion
my sustenance,
my head
before the commotion of battle began.
Go to the door and look, man,
see what the noise is.
Is it the earth that shakes,
is it the surge of the sea?
No,
it's a cry coming from foot-soldiers:

   If there's an enemy on the hill,
   Urien will make him shudder.
   If there's an enemy in the hollow
   Urien will pierce him through.
   If there's an enemy on the mountain
   Urien will bruise him.
   If there's an enemy on the dyke
   Urien will strike him down.

An enemy in full flight,
an enemy on the high point,
an enemy on every bend
in the river,
not one sneeze or two
will protect them
from his grasp.
No one would starve
with spoils around him.
Will his retinue
all iron-grey, enamel-blue,
like death
was his spear

laying his enemy low.

And until I am old and ailing
in the dire necessity of death
I shall not be in my element
if I don't praise Urien.

The syllable count in poem V appears confused, having some lines with four syllables per half-line, some with five, and some with six. Thus, we must compare one half-line with the half-line in the same line or in the next to find the proper scansion and pair up half-lines with those half-lines with which they rhyme.

Even taking these precautions, however, we are faced with problems. For example, the last two lines of the poem may perhaps be rendered more precisely as follows: "Vehement with blue weapon, bright blue / like death was the spear killing the enemy." Of course, with mesotomy, the first word is still trisyllabic (three syllables). V.28.a provides us with two rhyming quarter-lines of three syllables followed by a second half-line, also with three syllables (only!). The first half-line does not rhyme with the second, but the second rhymes with the two half-lines of V.29, the first with six syllables and the second with five. This practice is idiosyncratic in the collection, making poem V unique.

Given the irregularities in the syllable count, we should expect much contradictory data concerning mesotomy. However, the device does apply with remarkable regularity if we distinguish between two types of mesotomy. In one, when a form ending in a consonant is prefixed to a word, it has a much closer bond than that resulting when a form ending in a vowel is prefixed to the word. This may appear odd to us, but given certain other developments in Welsh (known as "eclipsis"), it is really the expected thing.

For instance, mesotomy does not apply in V.10.a *ny bydwn lawen* 'I would not be happy' nor in V.27.a *Ny bydei ar newyn* 'He would not be at the point of starvation'. But it does occur in V.6.b *yg godeu gweith mynaw* 'at the battle of Mynaw'. While it apparently does not apply in V.5.b *dyfyn ymplymnwyt* 'readiness in battle', this is probably a scribal error, for the device applies V.19.a *dygwynyc ychyngar* 'a shout arising(?)' and more tellingly in V.22.a *Ossit vch ymynyd* 'If there is an enemy in a mountain' — a half-line that must be parallel with the lines above and the lines below and that maintains this parallelism only with the mesotomic syllable.

As we would expect, mesotomy within the root of a word is the most likely event, and it applies quite regularly throughout the poem: V.13.b. *gonodet* '(they) swam', V.15.a *ffeleic* 'chieftain' (disyllabic), V.28.a *Gorgoryawc gorlassawc* (cited above). The only exception appears to be in V.17.b *gwarandaw py trwst* 'listen to what the noise is', in which the verb ending could be disyllabic, especially if it is from an old form.

We can now make three observations: (1) The poet may have been writing at an early date, perhaps Late Brythonic or Early Welsh but certainly relatively early Old Welsh; (2) the poem was transmitted through the Old Welsh period, whether or not it originated in this period; (3) the poet was either more inconsistent than the rest or was following some different set of rules, or his poem was transmitted through more hands and different hands than those that copied the rest.

These observations lead us to a significant conclusion: This poem is unique in the collection — this was yet a different Taliesin.

Who Was Taliesin?

This representative sampling shows us clearly that most of the poems are in one way or another unique, with mesotomy applied in different ways and to different degrees and with syllable counts following a wide variety of practices. These poems originated at different times and made their way through different transmissions to the Peniarth manuscript. Unless he lived for several centuries, a single Taliesin could not have written them.

This observation suggests a compromise of sorts between the two extreme views presented on the one hand by J. Gwenogvryn Evans and on the other hand by Sir Ifor Williams.

According to Evans, "His [Taliesin's] allusions to historical persons and events enable us to fix dates, *before which* he had not written, for compositions do not antedate their subject, be it of battle or person, a paean or elegy. If the internal evidence, supported by linguistic and grammatical considerations, proves that our text was written in the twelfth century and after, it is sheer lunacy to claim for any part of it a sixth century origin. That Taliesin flourished in the middle of the twelfth century there can be no manner of doubt; and he was held in such high esteem that his manner, his style was imitated" (*Facsimile and Text...*, pages *ii-iii*).

Today we recognize that Evan's position was too extreme. That some poems were composed in the twelfth century does not mean that all of them were. The poems must be taken individually, for as we have seen above, even the twelve selected as the most likely candidates for a sixth-century origin were not written at the same time nor by the same author. Nonetheless, Evans is quite correct in asserting a twelfth-century date of composition (or thereabouts) for such works as poem IV.

While this position was certainly held in his selection of twelve poems of likely sixth-century origin, Ifor Williams' claim on the basis of content and faithfulness to people and events that all of these twelve poems were composed in the sixth century also needs some modification. While poem V may appear to bear the marks of a work that could have been composed in Late Brythonic, poem IX is more clearly of a later Old Welsh period, and poem IV must be Middle Welsh in origin. Nonetheless, Williams is also correct in asserting a date of composition earlier than the twelfth century for at least some of the works.

Why, then, do these twelve poems represent so closely certain historical facts from the sixth century, if they were written by many different hands over several centuries? These events were crucial in the development of the Welsh historical and literary identity, and they were told repeatedly in an unbroken oral and sporadically written transmission. It should come as no surprise that some later poets should have had the understanding of history to separate the early events from the later and represented them faithfully while some other poets mixed in more recent people and events.

So why did the later poets identify themselves as Taliesin? J. Gwenogvryn Evans suggests that his twelfth-century Taliesin was being cryptic: "Under such circumstances when the friendships of one day were the enmities of the next, a border bard like Taliesin could not, perhaps, sing with safety to himself and his patrons, except cryptically and pseudonymously" (*Facsimile and Text...*, page *xv*). Such an explanation could suffice not only for the twelfth century, but for all of history.

Another possible explanation for the identification of the poet as Taliesin and the patron as Urien may indeed derive from the very conservativeness of Welsh poetry. Well into the Middle Ages, poets were required in certain forms of poetry to call the enemy as Bernicians, centuries after the last Bernicians had disappeared.

We might suggest, however, a more far-reaching hypothesis for the use of the name Taliesin in these poems composed over several centuries by several bards. To construct this hypothesis, we must ask a different question — not *who* was Taliesin, but *what* was Taliesin.

Taliesin as Metaphor

The key to finding out what Taliesin was — what he meant to the poets who used his name — lies in the distinction between the "historical Taliesin" and the "legendary Taliesin," a distinction modern scholars have been careful to maintain (one which we ought not to confuse with the discussion of history in chapter 6). According to this approach, the historical Taliesin was quite simply the sixth-century bard who allegedly wrote the original poems. The legendary Taliesin is a more complicated matter.

The folk-tale *Hanes/Chwedl Taliesin* ('The Story/Tale of Taliesin') tells of the magical birth and life of a poet and keeper of wisdom — Taliesin, the bard of the legendary Elphin. Some poems relating to this legendary Taliesin are included in the *Book of Taliesin*, for, as Williams points out, "it is unlikely that the scribe drew a distinction between the work of the legendary Taliesin, Elphin's bard, and the work of the historic Taliesin, Urien's bard . . ." (*The Poems of Taliesin*, page xix).

Perhaps the scribe did not draw a distinction between the two figures for a reason. Perhaps the two figures were far more intermingled than our modern literary scholarship would like to admit, a point to which we return below. What Taliesin was would thus involve not the twentieth-century scholarly penchant for isolating figures and categorizing them, but a more Medieval synthesis of them.

The synthesis of the historical and the legendary Taliesin and the answer to the question of what he was can be perceived through what is known as the "transformation." Williams records the following poem in his *The Poems of Taliesin* (page xvi — from a translation by Ifor Williams):

> I have been a blue salmon,
> I have been a dog, a stag, a roebuck on the mountain,
> A stock, a spade, and axe in the hand,
> A stallion, a bull, a buck,
> A grain which grew on a hill,
> I was reaped, and placed in an oven,
> I fell to the ground when I was being roasted
> And a hen swallowed me.
> For nine nights was I in her crop.
> I have been dead, I have been alive,

I am Taliesin.

Unfortunately, such passages have too often been taken by modern readers as referring to physical transmutations. This has lead to the misperception that Taliesin — and all such figures in Celtic literature — are magical and fantastic. Thus, Taliesin creeps into modern fantasy literature as a "shape-shifter."

J. Gwenogvryn Evans shows that this transformation was not a Welsh invention and that its use here closely parallels its use not only by the Irish Amergin, but even by Empedocles: "Whenever one of the daemons, whose portion is length of days, pollutes his hands with blood he must wander thrice ten thousand seasons from the abode of the blessed, being born throughout the time in all manner of mortal forms, changing one toilsome path of life for another. . . . I have been a youth, & a maiden, & a bush, & a bird & a gleaming fish in the sea" (Evans, *Facsimile and Text...*, page *iv*).

Empedocles was writing a religious treatise to explain his conception of the gods and daimons. As such, it is difficult for us today to say whether he viewed these transformations as physical transmutations or as spiritual experiences or as expressions of emotion. Taliesin, on the other hand, was not writing a religious doctrinal essay, but poetry; and the mark of poetry is its applicability to the reader's experience and emotion through the experience and emotion of the poet.

The literary transformation is not a literal transmutation or metamorphosis. The literary transformation is a metaphor. Taliesin was not, of course, a blue salmon; but he did go through an experience in which he was *as* a blue salmon, seeing the world and experiencing life *as does* a blue salmon in some particular way (and it is up to us, as is always the case in good poetic literature, to determine through our own life experiences what that way might have been).

Thus, when the poets over several centuries identified themselves as Taliesin, they were using a metaphor for themselves in the same way that such metaphors were used in literary transformations. The poets calling themselves Taliesin were not that particular Taliesin of the sixth century, but they did share some life experience in which they were *as* Taliesin.

In the sixth century, Taliesin was perhaps an historical figure; although he could have been a model even then — the reference in *Canu Aneirin* leaves some room for interpretation, as we shall see below. In the *Book of Taliesin*, he is clearly a metaphor.

What was Taliesin? Taliesin was the epitome of the warrior poet in the service of a mighty lord. Who was Taliesin? Taliesin was any poet who shared the attribute that made one what Taliesin was — *metaphorically*.

This observation leads to two rather important conclusions, one about the poets Taliesin and one about ourselves. First of all, the identity of the Taliesin poet was not personal but typological. To the Welsh warrior poet, identity was a matter not so much of what that poet's individual name was, but of what the poet's position in society was. Once again, *who* was not as important as *what*. Indeed, the suppression of the author's name was common throughout Europe during this period for a number of reasons.

As for ourselves, we have a fundamental problem in dealing with this early medieval concept. For us, "scientific" history is a literal recitation of facts. If someone who calls himself Taliesin claims to have been a blue salmon, our twentieth-century literalist minds insist that this must be taken as fact or as fiction.

For our minds to comprehend what the poet is saying, we must recast the poet's words: "I am a poet *as* Taliesin, and I have been *as* a blue salmon." Our modern concern for scientific historical "accuracy" requires us to state things as facts. The scholar must reduce poetic, dynamic metaphor to prosaic, anemic simile.

What we must appreciate in Medieval Welsh poetry is that the poet's world is not so neatly divided into fact and fiction. Metaphor bridges the gap between fact and fiction and allows the poet to deal with his own complexity as a person with knowledge and perception, thoughts and feelings. Taliesin was just such a complex of fact, of fiction, and above all of metaphor.

The Name Taliesin

Now finally we can proceed to the heart of the matter. Just who was this sixth-century Taliesin mentioned by Aneirin in his elegies to the Gododdin, and what did his name mean? To answer the first part of the question, though, we must begin with the second.

To determine the meaning of his name, it may be useful to see what the earliest writers thought his name meant. Here we turn again to *Hanes/Chwedl Taliesin* ('The Story/Tale of Taliesin') — the legendary Taliesin. According to this tale, Cyrridwen (the wife of Tegid — a Welsh form of Tacitus) prepared a potion for her son Afagddu, to make him the wisest sage in the world and thus to off-set his extreme ugliness. As the lad Gwion Bach was stirring the potion, he accidentally swallowed the three drops that contained all wisdom. Cyrridwen pursued Gwion, with both undergoing a series of transformations — here physical transmutations. When Gwion finally changed himself into a grain of wheat, Cyrridwen turned into a hen and ate him. As a result, the bard Taliesin was born (Williams, *The Poems of Taliesin*, pages xvii-xviii):

> Nine months later she was delivered of him, and because of his beauty she could not bear to kill him herself. So, she put the babe in a skin bag and threw him into the sea. This bag was found in a weir by a certain young princed named Elphin, who picked him up, and with great gentleness carried him home. Because of his lovely forehead (*tal*), he called him *Taliesin*, "beautiful brow," and was astounded when the beautiful browed infant began to talk with the wisdom of a patriarch, not only in prose, but in flowing rhyme as well. Poems streamed out of his mouth. Gwyddno, Elphin's father, when he

came in, asked about the catch at the weir. "I got something better than fish," his son replied. "What was that?" "A poet." "Alas," said the father, "what is a thing like that worth?" — using another Welsh word *tal*, meaning worth, value. The child immediately answered back. "He is worth more than you ever got out of the weir," punning on *Tal-iesin*, as if it meant "fine value."

Thus, the story gives two meanings for the name *Taliesin*. The meaning of 'beautiful forehead' has traditionally been treated as the preferred, with 'fine value' merely a pun. Indeed, the meaning 'beautiful forehead' is quite transparent.

But what we have here is a fantastic story dealing with the legendary Taliesin. While the meaning may have had a great significance in the development of the fantasy, we should not lose sight of the fact that *Hanes/Chwedl Taliesin* was constructed well after the name had already been in use by "serious" poets. Surely, all of the poets using the name Taliesin did not have beautiful foreheads.

Or did they? What could make the forehead beautful? — A crown, a laurel, a coronet. What had been the traditional mark of the bard? — A crown, a laurel, a coronet.

So we are not dealing with one individual living in the sixth century and possessing an unusually good-looking forehead. What we have is a crowned bard — a poet so good that he wins the ultimate competitions and receives the mark of the best bard on his forehead.

The name Taliesin originated quite simply as the title given to the preeminent bard by virtue of the beautiful crown on his brow. While this may have represented the fount of all wisdom and may have been passed onto the legendary Taliesin in this guise, the actual unembellished meaning of the name rather neatly describes the crowned brow itself and very clumsily accounts for the sagacity.

Thus, when Aneirin states that "I, yet not I, Aneirin / (Taliesin knows it, / Skilled in expression) / Sang *Y*

Gododdin / Before the next day dawned" he may or may not be referring to one particular Taliesin. Even if it is one particular Taliesin, however, that poet is nothing more than the crowned bard of his age, for by this time Taliesin is already a metaphor, not a person — a fact evident from the use ·of what is quite clearly a title or epithet, but not a name. Indeed, by this time, our Taliesin could have received or assumed the "name" without the crown itself — the very object that would have literally made his forehead beautiful.

Who was the sixth century bard whom Aneirin knew as (the) Taliesin? Since nothing survives from the period except *Canu Aneirin*, we have no way of knowing. In fact, we do not even know how many Taliesins may have been crowned by how many different rulers (?) at the time of Aneirin. Nor do we know if the title had become so metaphorical by this time that Aneirin's Taliesin may have simply assumed it himself.

Even in the case of the Taliesin of the Gododdin, then, just *who* he was is not the important issue. The issue for Aneirin is *what* he was — the crowned bard, the warrior poet, so good at his craft that it was not he who wrote the verse, but the Muse — the *Awen*.

This insight into the "name" Taliesin will prove extremely important in our examination of the other names as well. We are dealing with a period in history which recognized people not as individuals by some name arbitrarily or hopefully attached to them at birth by their parents. People in the Dark Ages of Britain received their historical names — the names by which we remember them — on the basis of what they themselves accomplished in their life and in their position in society.

In approaching Aneirin, Myrddin (Merlin), and Arthur then, we must bear in mind that *who* was of little consequence. The important question to ask is not *who*, but *what*. The answer to this question will tell us all the ancient Briton felt was necessary to know about the name and the person.

CHAPTER 3

ANEIRIN

Unlike Taliesin, Aneirin does have the appearance of being a personal name, rather than a metaphorical one. While Taliesin has been a name used by many poets over many centuries in an apparently uninterrupted tradition to describe the warrior poet in the service of a mighty lord and/or a crowned bard (and thus looks suspiciously like a title), the name Aneirin was not taken up by others until a considerably later period — indeed, it was not used as a name until a time when the meaning of the name had been lost. To determine why Aneirin should have been treated so differently from Taliesin, we must first try to determine who the author of the *Gododdin* might have been; and (inevitably) failing this, we must then put our efforts into figuring out what he was and what his name may have meant.

References to Aneirin

The task of discovering the poet's identity is aided little by secondary sources. The bulk of the information we have simply states that he was a great poet. For example, Nennius refers to Aneirin in the following passage from his *British History* (*Historia Britonum* — edited and translated by John Morris, pages 78 & 37):

> Tunc Outigirn in illo tempore fortiter dimicabat contra gentem Anglorum. Tunc Talhaern Tataguen in poemate claruit; et Neirin, et Taliessin, et Bluchbard, et Cian qui vocatur Gueinth Guaut, simul uno tempore in poemate Brittanico claruerunt.

45

At that time Outigern then fought bravely against the English nation. Then Talhaearn Tad Awen [T. Father of the Muse — TDG] was famed in poetry; and Aneirin and Taliesin and Bluchbard and Cian, known as Gueinth Guaut, were all simultaneously famed in British verse.

This passage, while short, may be very important for establishing the fact that Aneirin did compose *Canu Aneirin* in Brythonic shortly after the event. There is reliable evidence that Nennius was using notes for this passage written by Rhun ab Urien Rheged only about twenty-five to thirty-five years after the Battle of Catraeth, conceivably within Aneirin's lifetime and certainly within living memory of the battle. This then would indeed qualify as "factual history" in the approach discussed in chapter 6.

According to Ifor Williams the form *Neirin* used by Nennius is more reflective of the original Brythonic. If, as Williams suggests, the word derives from **naer* (cognate with Irish *nár* 'modest'), then the *A* would have been added to the name after around A.D. 1200 as one of many so-called "prosthetics" added probably for ease of pronunciation. As we shall see below, however, there is another possible derivation for the name — one that more accurately accounts for his identification.

The most provocative information about Aneirin comes from *Trioedd Ynys Prydein*, known in English as *The Welsh Triads*, edited and extensively examined and elucidated by Rachel Bromwich. Triads 33 (and 33W) and 34 are edited and translated by Bromwich (pages 70-74) as follows:

33. Teir Anvat Gyflauan Enys Prydein:
   Heidyn mab Enygan a ladavd Aneiryn Gwavtryd Mech deyrn Beird,
   a Llavgat Trvm Bargavt Eidyn a ladavd Auaon mab Talyessin,
   a Llouan Llav Diuo a ladavd Vryen mab Kynvarch.

33. Three Unfortunate Assassinations of the Island of Britain:
   Heidyn son of Enygan, who slew Aneirin of Flowing

Verse, Prince of Poets,

and Llawgad Trwm Bargod Eidyn ('Heavy Battle-Hand of the Border of Eidyn') who slew Afaon son of   Taliesin

and Llofan Llaw Ddifo ('Ll. Severing Hand') who slew Urien son of Cynfarch.

33 W. Tri Gvythvr Ynys Brydein a vnaethant y Teir Anuat Gyflauan:

Llofuan Llav Difuro a ladavd Vryen ap Kynuarch,

Llongad Grvm Uargot Eidin a ladavd Auaon ap Talyessin,

a Heiden ap Euengat a ladavd Aneirin Gvavt ryd merch teyrnbeird — y gvr a rodei gan muv pob Sadarn yg kervyn eneint yn Talhaearn — a'e trevis a bvyall gynnut yn y fen.

A honno oed a dryded vvyallavt. A'r eil, kynuttei o Aberfrav a drewis Golydan a bvyall yn a ben. A'r dryded, Iago ap Beli a drevis y vr ehun a bvyall yn y ben.

33 W. Three Savage Men of the Island of Britain, who performed the Three Unfortunate Assassinations:

Llofan Llaw Ddifro ('Ll. Exiled Hand') who slew Urien son of Cynfarch,

Llongad Grwm Fargod Eidyn ('Ll. the Bent of the Border of Eidyn') who slew Afaon son of Taliesin,

and Heiden son of Efengad who slew Aneirin of Flowing Verse, daughter of Teyrnbeirdd — the man who used to give a hundred kine every Saturday in a bath-tub to Talhaearn. And he struck her with a wood-hatchet on the head.

And that was one of the Three Hatchet-Blows.

The second (was) a woodcutter of Aberffraw who struck Golydan with a hatchet, on the head. And the third, one of his own men struck upon Iago, son of Beli, with a hatchet, on the head.

34. Teir Anvat Vwyallavt Eynys Prydein:

Bvyallavt Eidyn ym pen Aneiryn,

a'r Vwyallavt ym pen Golydan Vard,

a'r Vwyallavt ym pen Yago mab Beli.

34. Three Unfortunate Hatchet-Blows of the Island of Britain:

The Blow of Eidyn on the Head of Aneirin,

and the Blow on the Head of Golydan the Poet,

and the Blow on the head of Iago son of Beli.

The fact that Aneirin was not well-known as an individual and that this male name was not being used extensively is reflected in the errors in the W manuscript. As Bromwich points out, *mechdeyrn beirdd* 'Prince of Poets' has been corrupted to *merch teyrnbeird* 'daughter of Teyrnbeird [Lord-of-Poets]' and "Aneirin's identity so far forgotten that the Prince of Poets has become a girl, hit with a hatched on *her* head" (Bromwich, *The Welsh Triads*, page 72).

Unfortunately, there is little we can learn from these Triads on just who Aneirin was and why Heidyn would have assassinated him. Indeed, the assassin's own identity is so nebulous as to provide us with no reliable clues, but only a host of speculations that would carry us too far afield.

On the other hand, we can learn a lot from the fact that the name was not in common use. For some reason, people were not naming their sons after Aneirin, and poets were not assuming the name for themselves. If Aneirin was as important a poet as Taliesin, and if poets claimed the attributes and hence the identity of Taliesin for themselves, why was no one claiming to be (an) Aneirin soon enough after him that the meaning of his name and thus the attributes it represented could have been claimed? To answer this question, we have no source but Aneirin himself.

The Gododdin poems in *Canu Aneirin* were written by Aneirin as elegies to his friends who fell at the Battle of Catraeth around A.D. 600. He praises his friends as he laments their death in battle with a level of artistry that rightly makes him the first and foremost of the *Cynfeirdd* 'the Early Poets'. To come to some understanding of his identity then, we must ask him through his poetry where he was at the Battle of Catraeth and how it was that he managed to escape the battle with his life.

What Aneirin Was Not

One reason for supposing (as does Ifor Williams) that Aneirin's name came from a root **naer* and would mean something like 'the modest one' is the fact that in those passages in which he mentions himself, he emphatically tells us that he is not an accomplished poet, not a lord, and not a doughty warrior. It is important for us to examine these denials and to determine whether he was simply being modest or telling us something else — something far more important about who he was and what he was doing at the Battle of Catraeth.

In the passages throughout this chapter, we shall use the 1938 edition of Ifor Williams along with the modernized and harmonized 1990 edition (combining all the similar versions) of A.O.H. Jarman with his English translations. Numbers in parentheses will indicate the appropriate lines from the Williams edition for the older Welsh and from the Jarman edition for the English and Modern Welsh.

First of all, in spite of the fact that he was certainly considered one of the greatest, if not the greatest, of the Early Poets, Aneirin appears to deny that he was a poet on the level of Taliesin. This denial comes in perhaps the most crucial stanza of all — the one that also identifies Taliesin and that we examined in part in chapter 2. Let us now take a look at the entire stanza in all three versions (Williams' stanza XLVIII and Jarman's stanza 49 in English and Modern Welsh), as follows:

XLVIII

	Nyt wyf vynawc blin
	ny dialaf vy ordin.
540	ny chwardaf y chwerthin
	a dan droet ronin.
	ystynnawc vyg glin
	en ty deyeryn.
	cadwyn heyernin
545	am ben vyn deulin
	o ved o vuelin.
	o gatraeth werin.
	mi na vi aneirin.
	ys gwyr talyessin
550	ovec kywrenhin.

neu cheing e ododin
kynn gwawr dyd dilin

49

470	I am no weary lord,	Nid wyf fynog blin,
	I avenge no provocation,	Ni ddialaf orddin,
	I do not laugh	Ni chwarddaf chwerthin
	Beneath the feet of hairy slugs,	O dan droed rhonin.
	Outstretched is my knee	Estynnog fy nglin,
	In an earthy dwelling,	Yn nhŷ deyerin,
	An iron chain	Cadwyn heyernin
	Around my knees.	Am ben fy neulin.
	About mead from the drinking-horn,	O fedd o fuelin,
	About the men of Catraeth,	O Gatraeth werin,
480	I, yet not I, Aneirin	Mi na fi Neirin,
	(Taliesin knows it,	Ys gŵyr Taliesin
	Skilled in expression)	Ofeg gywrennin,
	Sang *Y Gododdin*	neu cheint *Ododdin*
	Before the next day dawned.	Cyn gwawr dydd dilin.

Here, Aneirin states that while he may have been moved to compose his poems (a point to which we return later), he is not Taliesin, who is (in contrast) skilled in expression. As we saw in the previous chapter, Taliesin could be taken as a metaphor for a warrior poet in the service of a mighty lord or as a crowned bard — though to be sure, the crowned bard would most probably have been a warrior poet to be accepted as bard and would have had to be in the service of a mighty lord to have been crowned.

At the beginning of the stanza, he asserts that he is not a weary lord, relaxing in his dungeon. Of course, this is simply an assertion that he is a prisoner, or at least that he was a prisoner when he "sang the Gododdin" (an expression that needs more careful examination below).

If he is a prisoner, then he is in need of rescue, which comes in the following stanza. There, he says that he is rescued by Cenau son of Llywarch.

Apparently then, Aneirin was captured at the Battle of Catraeth and subsequently rescued by Cenau. Such a rescue would certainly have been effected to save a valued warrior or a great lord, and it would not be an unusual course of events, if it were not for one fact: Aneirin was the only person to survive the battle.

The point that he was the sole survivor of a large, though inconsistent number is made several times throughout the elegies: *O drychant namen vn gŵr ny dyuu* (690) 'Of three hundred, save one man, none returned' (544); *Namen vn gŵr o gant ene delhet* (842) 'There would come but one man from a hundred' (661); *Tru namen vn gur nyt englyssant* (1131) 'Alas, save one man, none escaped' (870).

Indeed, at one point, Aneirin ranks himself with the two nonhumans who also survived the battle (out of three hundred sixty-three): *Ny diengis namyn tri o wrhydri ffosawt. / deu gatki aeron a chenon dayrawt, / a minheu om gwaetfreu gwerth vy gwennwawd* (240-42) 'Only three escaped through prowess in battle, / The two battle-hounds of Aeron and Cynon returned, / And I from my blood-shedding on account of my fair song' (245-47).

It would be easy for us to conjecture that Aneirin fought at the Battle of Catraeth and was so severely wounded as to be rendered unconscious from his "blood-shedding" and was thus captured, if it were not for the fact that he tells us explicitly that his wound was not what saved him. What saved him was his *gwenwawd*, which Jarman translates as 'fair song' and which we shall examine far more closely below.

If Aneirin had been a doughty warrior or a lord, it would have been a great dishonor for him to have been captured while conscious and able. Had he indeed been captured on account of his wounds (rendered unconscious or disabled), then perhaps it would not have been such a disgrace; but he admits that this was not the case. Such an admission goes far beyond the modesty that Williams attributes to his name as a derivative of **naer*. Furthermore, such a dishonor would hardly warrant his rescue by Cenau.

Indeed, Aneirin himself never admits to being a warrior at all. He sings of others as warriors, but as we see in Williams' stanza LXXXII (Jarman's stanza 80), he views the action not as a participant, but as one apart:

LXXXII

```
       Truan yw gennyf vy gwedy lludet.
       godef gloes angheu trwy angkyffret.
       ac eil trwm truan gennyf vy gwelet.
       dygwydaw an gwyr ny penn o draet.
1000   ac ucheneit hir ac eilywet;
       en ol gwyr pebyr temyr tudwet.
       ruvawn a gwgawn gwiawn a gwlyget.
       gwyr gorsaf gwryaf gwrd yg calet.
       ys deupo eu heneit wy wedy trinet.
1005   kynnwys yg wlat nef adef avneuet.
```

80

```
       Grievous for me, after toil,
       Is the suffering of death's agony in affliction,
       And again it is a heavy grief for me to see
       The headlong fall of our men,
       And long sighing and lamentation
       After the valiant warriors of our land and territory,
770    Rhyfon and Gwgon, Gwion and Gwlged,
       Bravest men in their stations, mighty in conflict.
       May there be for their souls after battle
       A welcome in the land of heaven, the home of plenty.
```

```
       Truan yw gennyf, gwedi lludded,
       Goddef gloes angau trwy anghyffred,
       Ac ail trwm truan gennyf gweled
       Dygwyddo ein gwŷr ben o draed,
       Ac uchenaid hir ac eilywed
       Yn ôl gwŷr pybyr tymyr tydwed,
770    Rhufon a Gwgon, Gwion a Gwlged,
       Gwŷr gorsaf wriaf, gwrdd yng nghaled.
       Ys deupo i'w henaid wedi trined
       Cynnwys yng nghlwlad nef, addef afneued.
```

In fact, Aneirin is not simply being modest — he was indeed not part of the Battle of Catraeth. Yet, he was there. He was captured while still conscious and able, yet

he was honorable and important enough to warrant a
rescue. He was not Taliesin, yet he was moved and "sang
the Gododdin." These apparent contradictions are
cleared up when we look at his name and at the "song"
that saved him.

Aneirin the Noncombatant

The traditional view that Aneirin's name derives from
naer and means something like 'the modest one' is
clearly on the mark in one respect: Aneirin was not the
poet's given name, but rather a descriptive epithet. This
is in the same tradition as the interpretation of Taliesin
as the crowned bard (the one with the "beautiful
forehead" — due to the poet's coronet) and the
interpretation of Myrddin's name in chapter 4 and of
Arthur's name in chapter 5. This we see also from the
facts that there is no record of an Aneirin before the
Gododdin and that the name is not used for centuries as
a given name, and then only in honor of the author of
Canu Aneirin and not for whatever the name might have
meant at the time.

Evidently, the name meant something in Brythonic
that characterized this particular individual in such a way
that others would not find it an attractive or appropriate
name for themselves or for their sons. The epithet 'the
modest one' would work only if Aneirin were an able but
modest warrior poet, for modesty was certainly a (rare)
virtue. However, we see above that if he were a warrior
poet, his own description of himself would go far beyond
mere modesty — indeed, all the way to an insinuation of
cowardice. The epithet 'the modest one' is not
appropriate for Aneirin, because he was not being
modest. Nor was he being cowardly.

Moreover, the supposed epithet 'the modest one' is
derived not from a known word in Welsh or Brythonic,
but from a reconstruction based upon a word in Irish. As
such, it is extremely tenuous. A more credible

explanation for the name must fit both the circumstances surrounding Aneirin — serving to clarify the apparent contradictions at the end of the last section — and the actual linguistic record.

First of all, the ending *-in* certainly is a noun suffix that relates an attribute to a person, and it can thus be translated as 'one connected with'. Also, as Williams quite correctly surmises, the *ei* diphthong (vowel combination) in the root of the word derives from the diphthong *ae* which has been affected by the *i* in the ending. All of this is quite normal and to be expected.

The mistake made in deriving Aneirin from **naer* comes from the supposition that since the *A* was added in the twelfth century to certain words, this *A* was thus not directly connected with the *n*, which therefore had to be interpreted as part of the root. This was a logical assumption, since both the form *Aneirin* and the form *Neirin* are found in the manuscript. There is, however, a far more credible and appropriate interpretation for the *A*, the *An*, and the *N*.

The prefix *an-* is a negative marker and is found in the vocabulary of the *Gododdin*. For example, Williams' stanza LXIII has five variants, two of which have the term *anysgocvaen* (743) or *anysgoget vaen* (754) modernized in the Jarman edition as *anysgogfaen* 'immoveable rock' (578).

The negativity of the prefix *an-*, though, comes not from the combination of letters, but from the *n*. This is common throughout Indo-European, deriving from the proto-Indo-European negative marker **ņ* and resulting in such forms as English *un-* and *non-* and in the use of the simple *n-* negative marker causing the negation of *ever* as *never*, of *one* as *none*, and of *aught* as *naught* (becoming *not*).

Even in Welsh, the *n-* has historically been the negative marker. Traditionally the verb has been preceded by negative sentence markers *ni* and *nid*, by negative clause markers *na* and *nac*. And the *n-* functions in the typical negation of common words to relate *a/ac* 'and' with *na/nac* 'nor (= and not)'.

The reason both *A-nirin* and *Neirin* are attested in the manuscript is that both begin with negative markers. The first is a "fuller" form — historically the newer innovation with the *A-* added to help in pronunciation (especially as the *n-* by itself gradually loses force as a marker). It is this form that has survived into Modern Welsh. The second maintains the bare negative marker — the one element that must be retained even if the vowel is elided or simply not produced in the first place. After all, the rhythm of the line could dictate a full syllable or not, so long as the negative marker *n* is there. Probably by the time of Aneirin himself, the latter was on the way out and would therefore not have been visible to later grammarians.

Thus, the combination of the prefix *An-* (or simply *N-*) and the suffix *-in* would give us the meaning of 'one who is not'. And it is in the root *eir* (derived from *aer*) that we find what Aneirin was not.

The final answer to this riddle can be found on the pages of *Geiriadur Prifysgol Cymru* ('Dictionary of the University of Wales', page 37), for the basic root has not changed — it is the same in Modern Welsh as it was in the earliest manuscript of *Canu Aneirin*:

aer[1] [H. Gm. *hair*, H. Lyd. *air*, Gwydd. *ár*: < **agro-*] *eb*. ll. *-au, -oedd*.

    (*a*) Rhyfel, brydr: *war, battle*.

    12-13g. C 57. 9-10. 13g. *A* 32. 6, tutvwlch treissic *aer*. 14g. *DDG* 59, Beiddiwr *aer*, bydd yr awron / Latai im at eiliw ton.

    (*b*) Cyflafan, lladfa: *slaughter*.

    10g. (*Ox* 2), *hair*, gl. *cladis*. 12-13g. C 48. 10, *Aer* o saesson, ar onn verev. 13g *T* 73. 5-6.

    (*c*) Byddin, llu: *host*.

    14g. *R* 1401. 38, hyt gaer ae *aer* ae aur mal.

Indeed, the alternation between *aer* in isolation and *eir-* preceding an ending with the vowel *i* is also attested and remains viable to this day (page 1196):

eirig [*air*[1] + *-ig*] *a.*
  (*a*) ? Rhyfelgar; llym: *warlike; sharp.*
  13g. *T* 29, 23, *eiric* y rethgren riedawc.

So what does *Aneirin* mean? It rather transparently means 'one not in the battle'. In a rather direct translation of his "name" into latinate English, Aneirin becomes the Noncombatant.

This much, Aneirin tells us himself. He was not part of the Battle of Catraeth, yet he was there — he was the Noncombatant. He was captured while still conscious and able, yet he was honorable and important enough to warrant a rescue — he was an honored Noncombatant.

(A temptingly direct etymology might derive the name from *an* + *eirin* 'without testicles' and identify the poet as a eunuch, celibate, or coward — Aneirin the Intesticulate. This would not work literally or figuratively because this particular meaning for *eirin* 'plums, berries' is not attested until the late 15th century.)

So now we have cleared up Aneirin's lack of a role in the Battle of Catraeth. He did not fight because he was the Noncombatant. Of course, his name still does not tell us what he was doing at the battle in the first place. The answer to this riddle he tells us himself: He was singing the *gwenwawd*.

Aneirin and the Gwenwawd

Now we must return to Aneirin's lament at being the only human left alive after the Battle of Catraeth: *ny diengis namyn tri o wrhydri fossawt.* / *deu gatki aeron a chenon dayrawt* / *a minheu om gwaetffreu gwerth vy gwennwawt* (240-42) 'Only three escaped through prowess in battle, / The two battle-hounds of Aeron and Cynon returned, / And I from my blood-shedding on account of my fair song' (245-47).

While Jarman translates the phrase *gwerth vy gwennwawt* (242) as 'on account of my fair song', both parts of the compound, *gwên* and *gwawd*, are considerably more complicated than simply 'fair' + 'song'.

In *Geiriadur Prifysgol Cymru* (page 1634), the word *gwên* has a crucial second meaning: 'prayer, petition, request, wish; hymn, sacred song'. These meanings are supported in the entry by an earliest reference from the 12-13th century, while the first definition of the word with meanings consistent with 'fair' also has an earliest reference from the 13th century. Thus, *gwên* carries meanings of a decidely religious and liturgical nature right from the earliest manuscripts.

As for *gwawd*, the second or root element of the compound, the following meanings are found in *Geiriadur Prifysgol Cymru* (page 1603) and are also attested in the earliest manuscripts: 'song of praise, panegyric, eulogy, verse; praise, exaltation, laudation'.

Not only are both parts of the compound religious and even liturgical in nature, but the compound itself has a religious overtone (page 1639):

gwenwawd [*gwen* + *gwawd*] *eb.* Cân foliant, mawlgerdd, cân fendigaid, cerdd ragorol: *song of praise, eulogy, blessed song, excellent song.*

It is quite clear that the compound word should not be interpreted as 'fair song', but rather as 'blessed or holy song', a possibility suggested by Ifor Williams (*Canu Aneirin*, page 138). What saved Aneirin from the enemy's sword was not the beauty of his singing, but the sung appeal for deliverance by God and/or for the souls of the departed (see below). Perhaps there were Christians among the enemy who recognized Aneirin for what he was. Or perhaps the pagan soldiers were awed by the magical incantations and were reluctant to kill someone with a diety on his side. Or perhaps they simply wanted a prisoner, and such a noncombatant was an easy capture.

In any case, the reason Aneirin was the Noncombatant was the same reason why his holy song saved his life: Aneirin was a priest.

Once we recognize Aneirin as the priest of the Gododdin, then several references he makes on his identity suddenly become clear. One such reference is found in Jarman's stanza 63, and it is evidently fairly reliable, since it exists in both the A and the more conservative B manuscripts (Williams' stanzas LXIV). According to Aneirin, *nis adraud cipno guedi kyffro cat / ceuei cimun idau ciui daeret* (788-89 — text B) 'Cibno does not tell that after the uproar of battle, though he took communion, he received his reward' (616-17). Jarman notes that similar statements are made in lines 61-63 (Jarman's 71-73) and in lines 72-73 (Jarman's 82-83), but he also points out that "D. Simon Evans, who regards all Christian references in *Y Gododdin* as late, merely notes in *Ysg. Beirn. X*, 43, that *cimun/kymun* are of doubtful meaning" (page 121).

Of course, such references would be perplexing if Aneirin were a warrior or a warrior poet who normally would not be concerned with eucharistic rites. If, however, Aneirin had been a warrior, then he would most likely have been seen as a coward who allowed himself to be captured, but who was then inexplicably given the honor of a rescue. If Aneirin was a priest, then his rescue was of paramount importance and a matter not only of honor, but of faith as well.

Of course, Professor Evans' interpretion that all Christian references in *Canu Aneirin* be later additions reflects a popular conception, in which such old literature is seen as representing a much more ancient, more pagan state of affairs. On the other hand, the battle — the actual historical event that led to the poems themselves — did take place around A.D. 600, centuries after the introduction of Christianity and indeed centuries after Celtic Britain established itself as an active area of theological controversary, particularly through Pelagius and his followers.

Another apparently troubling area cleared up in the

interpretation of Aneirin as the Noncombatant and the priest of the Gododdin is the reference made above to his activity during his captivity:

> mi na vi aneirin.
> ys gwyr talyessin
> 550 ovec kywrenhin.
> neu cheing e ododin
> kynn gwawr dyd dilin

480 I, yet not I, Aneirin   Mi na fi Neirin,
     (Taliesin knows it,   Ys gŵyr Taliesin
     Skilled in expression)   Ofeg gywrennin,
     Sang *Y Gododdin*   neu cheint *Ododdin*
     Before the next day dawned.   Cyn gwawr dydd dilin.

Of course, Aneirin would not have written *Y Gododdin* in italics (even if that printing device had been available to him), because there was neither a book nor even a set collection in an established order. Aneirin was not singing the *Gododdin*, for there was as yet no such thing (not even a concept for such a thing). What he was singing was the Gododdin — he was "singing" the fallen heroes.

As we shall we in our discussion of Myrddin in the next chapter, the *gwenwawd* was any religious or "holy" song. This would include eulogies to mark the death of individuals in a funeral (mass). By "singing the Gododdin" at the earliest possible time (while still a prisoner), the priest Aneirin was diligently performing his ecclesiastical duties.

Here we should return to the poem in stanza LXXXII cited above. After he expresses his grief at the loss of four warriors and praises their memory, Aneirin concludes: *ys deupo eu heneit wy wedy trinet. / kynnwys yg wlat nef adef avneuet* (1004-1005) 'May there be for their souls after battle / A welcome in the land of heaven, the home of plenty' (772-73). This is precisely the form of eulogy we should expect from a priest. Moreover, its structure belies the claim that such religious references were later additions. These religious references were in fact an integral and crucial part of the structure of the eulogy as delivered by a priest. If we were to remove them, we would alter the very nature of the *Gododdin*.

The final point to be cleared up is Aneirin's inspiration. He notes that "I, yet not I, Aneirin (Taliesin knows it, skilled in expression) sang..." This is interpreted by A.O.H. Jarman and also by Ifor Williams, Kenneth Jackson, and others as meaning that Aneirin was moved to sing. The epitome of the temporal poet, Taliesin, would have been well aware of what it was like to be moved to singing; but Taliesin would have been moved by the muse — the *Awen*.

Aneirin, on the other hand, claims no such talent as that of a poet who would be moved by the muse. Indeed, such apparent modesty is yet one more factor that could lead Williams to speculate that his name meant something like 'the modest one'. Rather than trying to weave interpretions around his "modest" disclaimer from being a secular poet, perhaps we should simply believe him and ask what else might have moved him to "sing" the Gododdin. Clearly, the priest Aneirin would not have claimed the ability to compose poetry or even to speak for himself in a eulogy — all would properly be attributed to the Holy Spirit working through him. As Jarman points out, "Medieval Welsh poets frequently declared that their muse derived from God or the Trinity" (page 110), and the tendency certainly would have been even pre-Medieval for a priest-poet such as Aneirin.

Conclusion

As in the case of Taliesin, we once again see that the name is not personal, but descriptive (if not metaphorical). When we eschew stretched etymologies and appeals to reconstructions from Irish Gaelic and simply take the poet at his word, the identity and position of the writer become quite clear. We are no longer faced with perplexing dilemmas such as that between dishonorable capture and honorable rescue.

Rather, in seeking a more straightforward meaning for the name, we find that Aneirin's words are quite consistent with his actions (or lack of actions) and with the actions of those around him. As the priest, he would necessarily have been the Noncombatant. That clergy did not fight is attested in the massacre at Bangor-Is-Coed in A.D. 601 (right around the time of the Battle of Catraeth), in which 1100 of 1200 monks were killed without a fight when they assembled to pray for a British victory over the Germanic host.

As a priest, he would not have suffered dishonor at being captured while conscious and able (but indeed unwilling). Moreover, as a man of God he would have been revered by his contemporaries. Thus, his rescue by Cenau son of Llywarch would have been imperative, and indeed it would have been an honor for Cenau.

Further as a priest, he would have made reference to communion and to its saving qualities — spiritually if not physically — which would have been very much out of place for a warrior poet. He would also have sung the eulogy — the *gwenwawd* 'holy song' — for the fallen heroes as an act of ecclesiastical responsibility immediately after their death, while he was still in his first night of captivity or even while he was still in the field. And certainly he would have blessed them and prayed for the salvation of their souls.

In summary then, we get a far more consistent picture of Aneirin if we view him as a Christian priest and chaplain of the Gododdin, rather than as a warrior poet. Moreover, as a priest, his name *Aneirin* 'the Noncombatant' makes perfect sense in the attested forms we have from the earliest periods, and his actions and those of the people around him achieve the same level of consistency and common sense.

CHAPTER 4

MYRDDIN/MERLIN

Before we can address who Myrddin/Merlin may have been and what his name may have meant, we must wade through some rather tricky water left in the wake of Geoffrey of Monmouth's *History of the Kings of Britain* (*Historia Regum Britanniae*).

The first thing we can dispense with is Geoffrey's use of the name Merlin, which is unfortunately the only name we are likely to encounter in English. Of the many variants of the name (which will be discussed below), Geoffrey was evidently using *Merdin*, which would have been pronounced something like a Modern Welsh *Merddin* [merðin]. But Geoffrey of Monmouth was a Cambro-Norman, and he was writing in Latin for a largely (Norman) French-speaking audience, and the form which he would have written (and assuming quite safely that the bulk of his audience would not have been aware of the Welsh pronunciation) would have been *Merdinus* 'one connected with excrement' (compare French *merde*). Obviously, this would not do.

Thus, Geoffrey had to change the name. As it were, the closest sound to this [ð] in Geoffrey's Welsh was the [l]. When we look at the technical specifications of the two sounds, this substitution was rather obvious: The [ð] was a voiced dental fricative "susurrata" — a sound like the *th* in English *though*, made with the tongue between or behind the teeth, with the breath creating friction but not obscuring the vowel, and very weakly articulated; and the [l] was a voiced dental/lateral susurrata — a sound like the *l* in English *low*, made with the tongue behind

62

the teeth and touching the side of the teeth, with the breath creating friction but not obscuring the vowel, and very weakly articulated.

The name Merlin, then, was a linguistically sound invention by Geoffrey of Monmouth to avoid a scatological reference in his work and doubtless to avoid the merciless ridicule that would certainly have ensued had the name Merdin been used. For historical purposes, we can thus dispose of Merlin and proceed to Myrddin.

Unfortunately, we cannot yet leave Geoffrey, for he has left his mark not only on the name, but also on the legendary figure himself. Of course, it is quite correct to point out that Geoffrey was using written sources that are not available to us today. What he and/or his sources did with Myrddin has had a profound influence on the development of the legends surrounding Arthur.

The Legends of Myrddin

While the name Myrddin first appears in the *Gododdin* (see below), he is much more extensively treated in some of the poems in the *Red Book of Hergest* and especially in the *Black Book of Carmarthen*. These sources follow a tradition in which Myrddin was a poet and prophet — a tradition that is evidently quite old. In fact, we find the name in *Armes Prydein*, which, as we have seen in chapter 2, is definitely of Old Welsh origin.

Examining passages dealing with the prophet's life, Rachel Bromwich (*Trioedd Ynys Prydein*, pages 470-71) has reconstructed the following details concerning the life of the original Myrddin:

> According to the story which can be reconstructed from these allusions, Myrddin was a north-British warrior who fought at the battle of *Arfderydd* in Cumberland ..., at which battle his lord Gwenddoleu ... was slain .... Myrddin became insane as a result of this battle, and for many years afterwards lived a wild life in the forest of *Celyddon* (situated somewhere in the western lowlands of Scotland). Here he lived in terror of Rhydderch Hael .... One poem, the *Cyvoesi* ..., is in the form

of a dialogue between Myrddin and a certain *Gwendydd*, who
is here represented as his sister, but elsewhere is apparently
his mistress.

This, then, is the original Myrddin — a warrior who went
insane (actually showing classic symptoms of Post-
traumatic Stress Disorder) after a battle fought around
A.D. 573 (according to the *Welsh Annals* — *Annales
Cambriae*) and fled into the wilderness.

Of particular importance in this oldest tradition of
Myrddin is the series of prophecies and discussions in the
Black Book of Carmarthen. This source is particularly
important because it is generally regarded as the oldest
manuscript in the Welsh language, and a version of it
may well have been known to Giraldus Cambrensis in the
twelfth century. In the following discussion, the 1989
edition of Meirion Pennar will be used, in which the
Welsh is copied from the diplomatic text of J.
Gwenogvryn Evans and the translations are those of
Pennar (who of course translates Myrddin as Merlin for
the English reader).

In a famous poem in the *Black Book*, Myrddin
converses with Taliesin about the battle that triggered
Myrddin's insanity. While Myrddin never acknowledges
anything he did in the battle, he vividly recalls the actions
of others, friend and foe. It is quite odd though, that
Myrddin and Taliesin are quite obviously discussing
different battles, for Taliesin's battle involved Maelgwn
(Maglocanus), a late contemporary of Arthur who would
have been much too old to have taken part in any battle
by the time of Myrddin — if in fact he had not died of
the plague around A.D. 547 (according to the traditional
story of his death, which helps to place the latest possible
date for Gildas' *The Ruin of Britain*, which we treat in
detail in the following chapter).

What is occurring in this conversation is that Taliesin
and Myrddin are comparing their own separate traumatic
battles. Evidently Taliesin had prophesied defeat in or
after his battle, as Myrddin did in or after his, for

Myrddin ends the conversation: *Can ẏs mi mẏ mẏrtin guẏdi. taliessin. bithaud. kẏffredin. vẏ darogan* 'For I, / Merlin, / as Taliesin before me, / shall see my prophesy / go far and wide' (pages 39 & 42).

(Indeed, the Taliesin of Myrddin would have come a generation before Myrddin's battle, and the Taliesin of Aneirin would have come a generation after it. Once again, as in chapter 2, we see that Taliesin was not one particular poet, but a metaphorical designation for the warrior poet or the title of the crowned bard.)

In two other groups of poems in which Myrddin speaks, he addresses nonhumans. In one group he addresses a piglet in what is known as the "Oh's of Myrddin." It is from this poem that most of the conclusions about Myrddin's life can be drawn.

The other group of poems is more important from the standpoint of Arthurian legend. In this lengthy and prophetic poem, Myrddin talks both to the piglet and to the apple trees in what is clearly a cultivated orchard (pages 67 & 71):

Afallen pen p ẏ chageu. puwaur maur weri rauc enwauc in vev.
A mi disgoganave rac pchen machrev. Jn diffrin machavuẏ
merchẏrdit crev. go2uolet ẏ loegẏr go2goch lawnev. Oian a
parchellan dẏ dau dẏwiev. go2volet ẏ gimrẏ go2uaur gadv. ...

> Sweet apple-tree
> with branches sweet,
> fruit-bearin
> much valued
> famed
> my very own,
> before the owner of Machrau
> I prophesy
> in the valley of Machafwy
> on bloody Wednesday
> tirumph for the English
> with their all too red blades.
> Ah, little piglet,
> come Thursday
> there'll be triumph
> for the Welsh ...

The word for 'apple tree' is *afallen* or *awallen* and would have been pronounced [avalen]. It takes no imagination at all to see the connection between *afallen* and the legendary place Avalon. Perhaps this *afallen* gave rise (or helped to give rise) to the legend of Avalon; or perhaps Avalon already existed in legend and influenced the source of the *Black Book*. In either case, though, it is highly significant that the *ll* combination would have been pronounced [l] only until the tenth century, when this combination changed into a voiceless aspirated lateral fricative [ɬ] (a sound made by placing the tip of the tongue against the upper front teeth, one side of the tongue along the teeth on the side, and in effect blowing). For the connection to have been made between *afallen* and Avalon, the source of the poem must have preceded the tenth century, lending a considerable amount of credibility to the claim that these poems were indeed composed by the historical Myrddin or within his memory, or at least that they were early enough to be somewhat immune from the legendary Myrddin/Merlin.

Thus we come once again to the second Myrddin — the Merlin of Geoffrey of Monmouth. Certainly for our purposes of trying to gain an understanding of these four famous names from the dawn of British legend, this Myrddin is the "false Myrddin."

Geoffrey draws on different sources to construct this legendary figure, an amalgam of previous legends. For example, there is the famous story about Vortigern summoning Myrddin to explain a commotion in the ground. Myrddin identifies the commotion as coming from two dragons — one red and one white — fighting beneath the ground, and he issues a prophecy regarding the dragons and the fate of Britain and of Vortigern. As we see in Nennius' *British History*, this story was originally attributed not to Myrddin, but to Ambrosius Aurelianus (whom we shall meet in chapter 5), a figure who somehow becomes associated with Myrddin (as pointed out by Giraldus Cambrensis). Thus, Geoffrey takes a figure from a generation after Arthur, combines him with legends connected with a leader from a generation before Arthur, and places his new construct Merlin squarely in the "court" of Arthur. As he elevates Arthur to the rank of king, he transfigures Merlin into a sorcerer.

The Merlin of Geoffrey of Monmouth was centuries in the making (with undoubtedly a good deal of invention from Geoffrey himself), and the legends of King Arthur and his sorcerer Merlin make excellent fantastic legend. If we are to understand the beginnings of this legend and the figures named in *Canu Aneirin*, however, we must dismiss this false Myrddin.

Aneirin would have known no other Myrddin than the one who went insane from the Battle of Arfderydd around A.D. 573. That battle was, after all, a scant quarter of a century — one generation — before the Battle of Catraeth, in which Aneirin in his turn got to see the warriors of his generation fall in slaughter. Aneirin would not have known any legendary Myrddin, but only the Myrddin who was still discussed in living memory, if indeed he was not a contemporary.

Myrddin and the Gwenwawd

What Aneirin says about Myrddin would necessarily be the most reliable information available. Gildas wrote before Myrddin became known as a poet and prophet. In fact, if Gildas died around A.D. 570, and Myrddin was unknown before the battle in A.D. 573, there is no way Gildas could have had any knowledge of him (at least, in the capacity that made him noteworthy). On the other hand, Aneirin wrote about a battle a quarter century after Myrddin's battle (which he too survived, living for some time afterward), and as we see in chapter 1, Aneirin's poem was composed before the Old Welsh period. Thus, Aneirin becomes the first writer we know of who could historically have been in a position to mention Myrddin.

While it is always tempting to claim that the reference to Myrddin or to any other name that ultimately figures into Arthurian legend is the addition of a later copiest, the form of the name in the *Gododdin* does reflect an archaic, pre-Old Welsh orthography — *Mirdyn* (suggesting a yet older *Mirdin*, as Ifor Williams points out in his edition of *Canu Aneirin*, page 188).

We shall delve more deeply into the form of the name and its possible meaning in the next section. For now, let us bear in mind that such claims that the name was a later insertion stem from nothing but unsubstantiated guess. If we were to eliminate names from *Canu Aneirin* simply because they appear only once or they figure prominently in later legends or we simply have no other reference to them, then there would be very little left. As it stands, the name does in fact appear, and it appears in an archaic spelling and with a reference that indeed corroborates the authenticity of the name in the context of Aneirin's song of the Gododdin — his liturgical eulogy, or *gwenwawd*.

Let us examine the three-line context of Myrddin's reference in the *Gododdin* according to the 1938 edition of Ifor Williams (lines 465-67) and the English translation and Modern Welsh rendition in the 1990 edition of A.O.H. Jarman (lines 444-46):

> amuc moryen
> gwenwawt mirdyn. a chyvrannv penn
> prif eg weryt. ac an nerth ac am hen;

> Morien defended
> The fair song of Myrddin and laid the head
> Of a chief in the earth, with support and sanction.

> Amug Morien
> Gwenwawd Myrddin a chyfrannu pen
> Prif yng ngweryd â channerth a chamen.

The passage is problematic from beginning to end, and Jarman is by his own admission uncertain of this translation. Of course, this is one good reason for treating it as part of the original composition, for a later poet would have been using less obscure language to make his point (whatever precisely it may be!), and the language would have had fewer opportunities for such muddling in what must have been numerous transmissions.

Whatever this passage means, whatever Morien's actions precisely were, and whatever they had to do with the memory of Myrddin, one thing is clear: Myrddin, like Aneirin, composed a *gwenwawd* — a liturgical eulogy for his fallen comrades.

Of course, this should come as no surprise. After all, Myrddin survived the Battle of Arfderydd, which in the view of Aneirin was a precursor for the Battle of Catraeth both from its disasterous outcome militarily and from its impact on the survivor spiritually. Both Myrddin and Aneirin were devastated by the defeat — the former enough so to be driven to insanity.

It is no wonder that the Aneirin who identifies himself as the one who sang the *gwenwawd* for the fallen heroes of Catraeth also identifies Myrddin as the one who sang the *gwenwawd* before him, doubtless for the fallen heroes of Arfderydd. Aneirin was an accomplished composer of poetry, the first and perhaps the greatest of the Early Poets, and such a parallel in composition would certainly not have been beyond him.

In this vein, it is highly significant that Aneirin mentions the *gwenwawd* only twice: Once to identify himself as the composer of the eulogy for those who died at Catraeth; and once to identify Myrddin as the composer of a similar eulogy, probably for those who died at Arfderydd and who were at least momentarily avenged by Morien.

Unlike Aneirin, however, Myrddin was certainly not the chaplain of the army that fell at Arfderydd. We do not have a similar story of Myrddin's capture and rescue as a priest, and Aneirin would not have let the opportunity afforded by such a parallel slip by him. What we do have is the story of Myrddin's flight into the wilderness in apparent madness after the battle.

The conclusion that can be drawn from this on the

identify of Myrddin rests at least partially on the reliability of the *Black Book of Carmarthen*. Of course, such reliance is weakened by the proliferation of legends; but it is strengthened by the apparent age of the book, by the archaic spelling of Myrddin in it (as we shall see in the next section), and by the pronunciation of *afallen* with [l] rather than with [ɬ] (as discussed above). According to the *Black Book*, the "wilderness" into which Myrddin fled was stocked with pigs and boasted an apple orchard.

From the description, it is evident that Myrddin fled to a monastery. Here he would have gained the knowledge and the authority to pronounce the *gwenwawd* for his fallen comrades. Here, too, he could hide from the world and from those (perhaps Rhydderch Hael) who would try to bring him back into military service or punish him for fleeing. He was not, after all, a noncombatant at the time of the battle.

Myrddin the Waterman

The Myrddin who went insane at the Battle of Arfderydd, who shut himself away in a monastery, and who composed the *gwenwawd* for his fallen comrades was not the same man who rode into battle as a warrior. We know nothing of the warrior before the battle, not even his name. In the monastery, he would have taken a new name, one with religious significance; and it is that religious name alone — Myrddin — that comes down to us.

There are many variants in the manuscript for the name we spell in standard Modern Welsh as Myrddin. In the *Black Book* he is *Mirtin* and in *Canu Aneirin* he is *Mirdyn*, both very conservative (= old) spellings. In other manuscripts he appears as *Myrdin* or other variants. In all of these, the *m*, *r*, and *n*, are constant and apparently well established in the tradition. As for the dental consonant in the middle, the *t* would have been pronounced as a *d* [d] in the context, and the *d* is the forerunner of Welsh *dd* [ð]. By taking into account predictable sound changes and orthographic practices before and after the time in question, we are left with the *d* [d] as the appropriate form of the consonant for the time.

As for the vowels, this is a bit more complicated. As noted above, the use of *i* for *y* in the *Black Book* and in the *Gododdin* is often seen as a mark of an archaic spelling. In the Middle Welsh orthography of the final scribes, the two letters were often written for one another, but the *y* was pronounced closer to the *i* in the last syllable (the ultima) and closer to *e* in the next-to-last syllable (the penult). Thus, Geoffrey of Monmouth's problem with *Merdin* derived from the spelling of *y* as *e* in the penult, and Aneirin's spelling of *Mirdyn* was quite conservative, since the *y* was closer to the *i* in the penult (reflecting an earlier state). The vowel in the ultima, however, would have been close to *i* or *y*, however it may have originated.

What we end up with, then, is four possibilities for the original or at least for oldest possible form of the name: *Mirdin*, *Myrdin*, *Mirdyn*, and *Myrdyn* (the realization with *e* would not be an issue in this case, given the antiquity of the name). So to determine what the word might have meant, we must examine both syllables in both possibilities, each in context with the other. And we must use a modicum of common sense as to what an individual might have been named.

In the scholarly literature, there is no doubt but that the first syllable was derived from a word in Celtic reconstructed as *more 'sea' or the plural *mori 'seas' (where the star designates a reconstructed word). These are realized in later forms of Welsh as *môr* and *mŷr*. Making this choice also necessary is the fact that there was no *mir opposed to *mŷr*, anyway (where the star designates an unattested or hypothetical form — a confusing ambiguity in linguistic notation).

Either the singular or the plural could have supplied the appropriate form, since both yield *myr-* in the compound. The plural is naturally realized in this way due to the vowels in the Celtic form (the *i* changes the *o* to *y* in a process known as vowel affection, or umlaut), and the singular would have come to be realized in this way due to the very same effect of the vowel in the following syllable of the compound.

As for *din/dyn*, here we indeed have a choice. Most scholars opt for *din* and derive the name from the Celtic **dūnom* 'fort', realized in Welsh as *din* (whence *dinas* 'city'). This etymology receives support from a folk etymology of the Middle Ages (reported by Giraldus Cambrensis) that claimed that Myrddin must have come from the city of Caerfyrrdin (Carmarthen in English), since the name could be read as the *caer* 'fortress/camp' (< Latin *castra* 'camp') of *Myrddin* (realized in the second part of a compound as *Fyrddin*). Thus, the folk etymology goes, Caerfyrddin must be named for Myrddin — from the sea fortress. Such Medieval legends, however, are always suspect, for their main purpose was to prove something significant about the city and thus boost its prestige. In the name Caerfyrddin, *myrddin* certainly means 'sea fortress', since that is what it is and this is the definition that makes sense *in this context*.

With regard to the person Myrddin, however, this derivation does not make sense. This Myrddin was a person, not a fortress; and he had no reliable connection with Caerfyrddin (in fact, he would have come from the North and not from Wales at all). We should thus choose the alternative form *dyn* deriving from Celtic **donios* 'man' and realized in Welsh as *dyn* (*dŷn*).

Indeed, *dyn* is the form of the word for 'man' that the scribe of *Canu Aneirin* would have known and recognized and which he did spell as *Mirdyn* after all. This derivation not only makes sense to the scribe and to us, but it makes far more sense in general to propose a personal name that recognizes the person as a person rather than as a fortress. In any other context and given any other tradition of folk etymology and scholarly research,

certainly 'man' would win out over 'fortress'; and so it is
proposed here.

Moreover, the personal ending *-din/-dyn* is far more
consistent with the northern British *Canu Aneirin*, in
which the names Aneirin and Gododdin both sport an
ending *-in*, which relates to a person or people. Indeed,
the latter ends in the syllable *ddin*, an appropriate form
of *din* in a compound, with a vowel that is once again
close to and often interchangeable with the *y* in *dyn*
'man'.

For reasons both of common sense (people are not
fortresses) and of consistence with the *Gododdin* (and
with the Gododdin), let us define Myrddin's name
tentatively as 'seaman'. Certainly, Seaman is an
appropriate name or epithet for an individual. There is,
however, a problem: If Myrddin fled to a monastery, or
if he simply fled into the wilderness, or even if he did
nothing at all but wander about in a state of insanity, why
would he be called the Seaman?

There are two possibilities for naming Myrddin the
Seaman. The most obvious is that he might have taken to
the sea after the slaughter at Arfderydd drove him
insane. Given this possibility, he might have adopted the
life of the sea, he might have committed suicide in the
sea, or he might have sailed to a refuge over the sea. The
first two variants are unlikely if he did sing of/for the
fallen heroes of the battle. The third variant is entirely
plausible and would not necessarily conflict with the
second possibility. (Indeed, the notion that the *afallen*
would be on an island of some sort would certainly
support later legends.)

The second possibility deals with contemporary
tradition and supports the interpretation that Myrddin
sang a *gwenwawd* for his fallen comrades, as Aneirin does
tell us after all in the earliest reference in all of the
literature (and hence the most reliable of all references).
In this possibility, *myr-* could have either of two
meanings, or indeed it could have both meanings
combined in a pun — an extremely popular device in the

literature.

First of all, monastic life in early Britain consisted of individuals and groups living within the walls of a monastery and also leaving the monastery as necessary to minister to the community and to perform missionary activities. These missionaries followed established sea routes and were thus very closely associated with the sea. For such a missionary to be called Seaman as an epithet was by no means unreasonable. Furthermore, a monk in a monastery that was especially linked with these sea routes could very well receive the epithet from former military colleagues who would tend to lump all of the monks into the same boat.

Alternatively and perhaps even more likely, we should recognize that *mŷr*, which could be an affected form of the singular *môr* or simply the plural *mŷr* (as noted above), could be 'sea' or 'seas'. In either case, it could well be that we are not speaking of a particular sea or seas, but of the substance of the sea(s): water. In this interpretation, Myrddin would be the Waterman.

Water, however, also carries a profoundly religious significance in the context of early British Christianity on at least two counts. First, British ecclesiastics were especially associated with the rite of Baptism, to the point that their emphasis on the method of Baptism was viewed by Rome as a point of contention in the early church, leading even to accusations of heresy. Second, the pagan sacred wells had by no means died out with the Druids, and they were now maintained as holy sites by the early British Christians (for example, St. Seiriol's Well in Môn). Furthermore, pagan rituals and beliefs regarding these wells were incorporated into Christian Welsh folklore, surviving until very recently.

Perhaps most importantly, the identification of the cleric with the epithet Waterman is attested in one of the Briton's chief saints — Saint Dubricius. The Latin ending *-icius* means 'one connected with', and the Brythonic root *Dubr-* means 'water'. This assumed compound name among churchmen was fairly common, reflecting the importance placed on Baptism and the crucial role in this rite played by the cleric.

Thus, Myrddin was simply a variant of Dubricius. Of course, this is not to claim that the Myrddin who fled the Battle of Arfderydd in a state of insanity was one in the same with the chief Saint Dubricius. Saint Dubricius — the one known today in Welsh as Dyfrig — lived and died long before the time of Myrddin. Perhaps, however, the connection between the names gave rise to the legend that a "Myrddin/Merlin" was a chief miracle-worker at the time of Arthur, with whom Saint Dubricius would indeed have been contemporary. Such is certainly the stuff of which legends are made, but we must be careful to keep legend separate from history (or virtual history from factual history — see chapter 6).

Nor was Dubricius the only known form of Waterman in the British church. Saint David also had the epithets Dyrwr and Aquaticus. The root of the former *dyr* derives from *dyfr* (compare the Welsh form of Dyfrig for Saint Dubricius), which is a well-known variant of *dwfr* 'water' (the direct descendant of *dubr-* in Saint Dubricius), found in such word pairs as *dwfrgi/dyfrgi* 'otter' (literally 'water dog'). In *dwfr* the *f* [v] also undergoes a very common weakening (lenition) to null that is attested in the word itself through the word pair *dwfr/dŵr* 'water'. Moreover, this use of *dyr* goes far beyond the meaning of water in a container (be it a cup or a baptismal font) to include the waters of the seas (as in the word for 'otter'). The ending *-wr* simply means 'one connected with' and is treated in detail in chapter 5. Thus, the Welsh epithet would be the Waterman.

As for Aquaticus, the Latin epithet is quite transparent: Latin *aqua* 'water' + the adjectivising ending *-tic-* 'connected with' + the masculine singular nominative ending *-us* 'man, one'. Thus, Aquaticus is simply a repetition of the Welsh epithet meaning Waterman. Furthermore, the root *aquatic-* can be seen to refer not primarily to water in a container, but to the water of the seas.

In the Brythonic epithet that was the name Dubricius and in the Welsh and the Latin epithets for Saint David, we have variants of the same epithet that we find in Myrddin. Brythonic *dubr-*, Welsh *dyfr/dyr-* (in compounds), and Latin *aqua* all mean 'water' and all can refer not only to the water of the font, but also to the water of the sea or seas — *môr* or *mŷr*. Thus, we have *myr/mir* as just another variant. Now we can see more clearly that the second element *din/dyn* cannot mean 'fortress', but must mean 'man'. The name is an epithet: Myrddin the Waterman. And the Waterman was not a sailor nor an abstainer from alcohol nor a taker of baths (the latter two arising in traditional folk etymology for Saint David's epithets). The Waterman was a holy man in the British church — a priest and baptizer.

So Myrddin, like Saint Dubricius, Saint David, and a host of others during that period in the history of the British church, was the Waterman. This gave him the liturgical right and responsibility to compose a *gwenwawd* for his fallen comrades.

Conclusion

Thus we see that the Myrddin to whom Aneirin makes reference in his *gwenwawd* — his liturgical eulogy — for the fallen at the Battle of Catraeth was the very clergyman who pronounced his *gwenwawd* for the fallen at the Battle of Arfderydd. While Aneirin was the priest chaplain for the army of the Gododdin and composed his *gwenwawd* immediately (as was proper) in prison or even still while in the field, Myrddin became a cleric later, fleeing into the monastery after being driven insane by the trauma of battle. He could not pronounce his *gwenwawd* until he held the proper office and communed with the dead Taliesin (received instruction in poetry at the monastery?). Indeed, if he actually wrote his eulogistic poems down, he would probably have had to join the monastery to learn to write first.

Compared with the traditional arguments, this interpretation of Myrddin is far more consistent with the oldest (pre-Geoffrey) Myrddin legends, with Aneirin's considerable poetic artistry (prominently including parallelism), with the relative timing of Myrddin and Aneirin, with the reasonable definition of the name, and with the known practices of the early British church.

Once again we see that the names of key figures from the dawn of British legend were chosen, not given at birth. This stands to reason, for these individuals lived in tradition not for what their parents had named them, but for what they did themselves. In essence, they earned the names that have been passed on through history and legend.

Taliesin earned his name by earning the laurel coronet of the poet. And his many "progeny" Taliesins assumed the name (arguably rightly or wrongly) for their skill as warrior poets in the service of a mighty lord. Aneirin earned his name for refraining from fighting at the Battle of Catraeth — an act that would have violated his priestly functions. Myrddin became a cleric in a monastery associated with the missionary sea roots, with an island, and/or with the energetic exercise of the rite of Baptism.

Now, finally, we can turn our attention to the name from the dawn of British legend that doubtless interests us the most: Arthur. As with the others, we may expect that this name was not given, but taken as a descriptive epithet for what he was and what he did.

CHAPTER 5

ARTHUR

Now we can at last address the identity of Arthur himself. The first mention of Arthur's name anywhere in the literature is found in the *Gododdin*, stanza CII (following as always the 1938 Williams edition with the English translation and modernized Welsh in stanza 99 of the 1990 Jarman edition), as follows:

CII

Er guant tratrigant echassaf
ef ladhei auet ac eithaf
oid guiu e mlaen llu llarahaf
1240   godolei o heit meirch e gayaf
gochore brein du ar uur
caer ceni bei ef arthur
rug ciuin uerthi ig disur
ig kynnor guernor guaur*dur*

99

He charged before three hundred of the finest,
He cut down both centre and wing,
He excelled in the forefront of the noblest host,
970   He gave gifts of horses from the herd in winter.
He fed black ravens on the rampart of a fortress
    Though he was no Arthur.
Among the powerful ones in battle,
In the front rank, Gwawrddur was a palisade.

Ef gwant tra thrichant echasaf,
Ef lladdai a pherfedd ac eithaf,
Oedd gwiw ym mlaen llu llariaf,
970   Goddolai o haid meirch y gaeaf.
Gochorai brain du ar fur caer.

Cyn ni bai ef Arthur.
Rhwng cyfnerthi yng nghlysur,
Yng nghynnor, gwernor Gwawrddur.

There has been much discussion on whether this passage existed in the original composition or it was added later, after the name of Arthur was well established in legend. The language certainly shows that it was not added in the final redactions, and the *-ur* was definitely Brythonic (as we shall see below). Nevertheless, some scholars have argued that the name had been slipped in sometime during the transmission.

No evidence has ever been presented though to demonstrate conclusively that this should be treated as a later addition to the composition. The arguments all seem to assume that Arthur was nothing more than legend to begin with, so therefore this must have been added. After all, the argument goes, *Canu Aneirin* was composed around A.D. 600 or shortly thereafter, and Arthur would have been in the memory of some of the oldest in the audience; and since he never really existed, the author would not have used his name.

Of course, such an argument begs the question. If we trust the manuscript, then the use of Arthur's name this soon after his life should provide striking evidence for his existence, not against it. Once again, there is no evidence that this is a later addition and there is no reason not to trust Aneirin in this regard (and if we toss out the reference to Arthur, why should we keep any of the rest?).

Of course, the best argument that there was a very prominent military leader named Arthur at that particular time is the fact that in the next generation there are no less than four prominent military leaders who assumed the name. No doubt, there were even more Arthurs in the next and subsequent generations who simply did not make it into the manuscripts. It would be very difficult indeed to explain this sudden popularity of the name without a very important military predecessor right at that particular point in history.

On the other hand, there is an earlier writer — one who would have been alive at the time of Arthur. This was Saint Gildas, who wrote *The Ruin of Britain* (*De Excidio Britanniae*) which seems to chronicle the very events taking place at the time. Arthur died around A.D. 537-542; Gildas wrote his work (often called the Complaining Book) around A.D. 540-545, and he died around A.D. 570. So he was writing around the time of Arthur's death, and the Battle of Catraeth was about three decades after Gildas' death. Yet, Gildas makes no mention at all of Arthur.

Thus, there are two issues that must be resolved: What is the nature and meaning of the name Arthur that does appear in the *Gododdin*, and why was Arthur not mentioned by his own contemporary? To resolve these questions, let us treat each in its own major section (in effect, its own chapter) and draw the two issues together at the end.

I. ARTHUR'S NAME

Of the many theories that have come in and out of fashion on the origin or etymology of the name Arthur, borne by the defender of Britain in the sixth century, the most popular and widespread notion is that his name is derived from that of an ancient Celtic god. In spite of its popularity and its mention in encyclopedias, this notion is untenable for two reasons.

Firstly, Arthur would have been a Christian — or at the very least he would have needed Christian support — and would not have used a pagan name, especially in his struggle against pagans. The most effective evidence that Arthur was a Christian has been rather insightfully made (indirectly) by Geoffrey Ashe in his *Kings and Queens of Early Britain*. Ashe notes that Gildas, whom we meet in the next major section of this chapter, denounces all of his contemporaries as "bad" Christians; but he makes absolutely no mention of any British leader not being a Christian in the first place. Certainly, if Arthur had been a leader of the Britons and had been a pagan, Gildas would have mentioned his name — at great length.

Secondly (as mentioned above), the name itself is nowhere to be found up until Arthur's time. After his death, however, it immediately becomes a common and widespread name, especially among the command caste. We are in fact not dealing with a name established before Arthur's time, but with a title or epithet first used as an appellation by Arthur himself and imitated after him out of reverence for his memory.

Among scholars perhaps the most widely accepted (or least questioned) etymology derives the name from Latin *artōrius* 'plowman', apparently independently of the Celtic god hypothesis. To call Arthur a plowman, however, is less than transparently descriptive (even in its astrological aspect — see below), and an obvious meaning would have been necessary given Arthur's position. Indeed, an obvious meaning would have been the name's very *raison d'être* — a rallying cry for the Britons and Romano-Britons in their resistance to the Anglo-Saxon domination.

Whatever it meant, the epithet must have been recognizable both to Britons and to Romano-Britons. Let us begin then with the word *Arthur* and see where the form of the word itself leads us in Latin and in Brythonic. To accomplish this, we must start not with preconceived notions of what the name could have meant, but rather with the more mundane art of historical linguistics: Given the phonological shape of the name (the sounds in their combinations), what could have preceded it?

In approaching the problem in this more pedestrian manner, we will not arrive at anything that has not (at least in isolation) been suggested before at least in passing (and often in dismissal). By proceeding methodically from known linguistic fact in both Latin and Brythonic together, however, we might achieve a more credible conclusion.

The Latin Etymology

Let us begin, then, with the form *Arthur* as it is first attested in the *Gododdin*. As it is, this form is unacceptable for Latin. For one thing, the *-ur* ending is not a Latin termination for a masculine noun, particularly one adapted as the name of an individual. The normal ending *-us* (second declension masculine nominative singular) would have been necessary and was indeed often added to non-Latin names to give them a Latin appearance and to provide them with a basis for Latin case endings. This would lead us to **Arthurus* (again, with the star designating a form that is not attested anywhere in writing).

Our next problem is with the *-th-*, which is not Latin at all. In fact, it would not even have been acceptable in the Brythonic contemporary with Arthur's early sixth century (a point to which we return in the next section). In between the time of Arthur and the composition of the *Gododdin*, however, the *-th-* representing the fricative [θ] developed from one of two sources: (1) the geminate *-tt-* as in Brythonic **cattos* 'cat' and resulting in the fricative *-th-* as in Welsh *cath* 'cat'; and (2) the combination -rt- as in the Latin root *part-* 'part' and resulting in the combination *-rth-* as in Welsh *parth* 'part'. We can thus extend **Arthurus* back to **Artturus* or far more likely back to *Arturus*.

In fact, the form *Arturus* is what is found in the earliest Latin reference of Nennius and the *Welsh Annals*. With either form though, we already have a word that would have been recognized by any of Arthur's Latin-speaking contemporaries in beleaguered Britain. Of course, this was not the Classical Latin of Cicero (both had been dead for centuries), but the Late Latin of the sixth century. For at least a hundred years, the pertinent changes had already been attested in writing. On the one hand, the usual source for an innovative -tt- (one not present in Ciceronian Latin) was the -ct- [kt] cluster (series of consonants); and on the other hand, a -c- [k] in the middle of a three-member cluster was dropped. Either way we choose to proceed takes us inexorably to the Classical Latin *Arcturus* — a form which, of course, Arthur and his contemporaries would not have heard, but which is needed to reveal the meaning of *Arturus* to us.

With *Arturus* < *Arcturus* we have not only a word with the appropriate second declension masculine nominative ending, but we have a name with significant meaning, as in the following entry from the *Oxford English Dictionary* (compact edition, page 109):

> Arcturus (ālktiū°rūs). *Astr.* Also ₄ arthurus, arturis; arture, ariture, arctour. [L. *arctūrus* a Gr. ἀρκτοῦρος, f. ἄρκτος the Bear + οὖρος guardian, ward (from its situation at the tail of the Bear); the forms *arture*, etc. were from Fr.] The brightest star in the constellation Bootes; formerly, also, the whole constellation, and sometimes the Great Bear itself.

As we see in the variant forms given in the *Oxford English Dictionary* the same sound changes took place in English — at least until English speakers relatinized the word as they fitfully attempted to latinize the language.

If *Arthur* could be derived from *artōrius* 'the plowman' with reference to the Great Bear itself (rather than through the Celtic god hypothesis), then he would be connected with the plowman of the Wain and his name would be tied together with the star Arcturus, the Late Latin *Arturus*. While such references are indeed found in the literature, they point not to the Latin word for the plowman, but to the name of the prominent star in Bootes, as we see in the following entry under *wain* in the *Oxford English Dictionary* (compact edition, page 3668):

2. The group of seven bright stars in the constellation called
the Great Bear: more fully CHARLES'S WAIN. *Lesser Wain*:
the similarly shaped group of seven stars in the Little Bear.
    OE. had *wænes þísl* or *þísla*, 'pole or poles of the wain'.
With Scotts 'Arthur's slow wain' cf. 'Arthouris Plowe', Lydg.
Chron. Troy 1.682; Arthur here represents Arcturus, regarded
as the teamster or wagoner of the plow or wain.

As we shall see below, it is significant that Arcturus
is the brightest star in a constellation closely connected
with the Great Bear and that this star is regarded as the
leader (the teamster or wagoner) of the rest. It will also
prove significant that the name *Arcturus* means the
'guardian of the bear'.

At this point though, we cannot overemphasize the
fact that the oldest attested Latin form of the name is
indeed *Arturus*. Had any Romano-Briton of the period
been asked *Quid est Arturus?* 'What is Arturus?' before
there was the personal name, he would have answered
"The bright star in Bootes, beyond the tail of the Great
Bear." Moreover, given the widespread knowledge of
astrology at the time, he would probably have been able
to identify it as the guardian of the bear and would gladly
have so informed anyone who did not know. *Arturus*
would have been as obvious to the Romano-Briton as
Polaris and the Big Dipper are to us.

Thus, deriving this meaning from this word is not a
matter of stretching etymology. It is nothing more than
supplying the well-known meaning for a well-known
word. If a general today were to take on the name
Taurus, we would know the word, the meaning of 'the
Bull', the fact that it is a constellation and sign of the
zodiac, and the attributes the general was claiming
(bravery, stubbornness, etc.). The military leader in sixth-
century Britain took on the name *Arturus* precisely for its
clarity — its obvious meaning to all.

Such a straightforward word-meaning relationship
would have been an essential element of the British
strategy of defense. In spite of the brilliant derivations

and arguments presented by scholars, the fact remains that people do not rally behind names of obscure etymology.

Brythonic Etymology

Before becoming embroiled in the semantic significance of the word, let us remember that not everyone in non-Anglo-Saxon controlled Britain spoke Latin. In order to gain as much support as possible, the leader would have to have had a name that would rally the rest of the British throughout the island.

Given the form *Arthur* as it first appears in the Brythonic/Welsh *Gododdin*, we are faced with the same problem we found in Latin: The ending *-ur* does not occur elsewhere, in spite of arguments from the speculated name of a god **Artor*. Nor can we simply add a Brythonic ending and solve the problem.

The solution comes from the fact that *-ur* is not an ending. If not an ending, then it must be a word in a compound. As in the derivation of *Arturus* from **Arthurus* in the Latin, there are two possibilities by which we may account for this word; and both bring us inexorably to the same form. On the one hand, the form *-ur* could be a rather straightforward representation of the Brythonic word for 'man', reconstructed for Late Brythonic as **uur*.

On the other hand, it is more likely that the [u̯] had already become [gw], which would have yielded **gwur* or **guur* had the glide not disappeared whenever it occurred before a rounded vowel (a vowel produced with pursing of the lips). The word for 'man', then would have been *gur*, realized in later Welsh spelling as *gwr*. In fact, the word *gur* itself does occur in the more conservative stanzas (the B text) in the *Gododdin*.

The realization of *gur* as *-ur* is quite normal and predictable. By the time the British leader had taken the epithet, a number of changes collectively termed "mutations" had affected the language. Among the mutations in place by around A.D. 500 was a change from initial *g-* (perhaps through an intermediate fricative [γ]) to null. This mutation would have occurred in the second element of a compound. Thus, the compounded element *-ur* would have meant 'man'.

From precisely the same source comes the Middle and Modern Welsh compounding form *-wr*. This form means 'one who does, one connected with' and can be found in numerous words such as *ffermwr* 'farmer' (literally 'one connected with a farm'). Since such words refer to a man connected with the previous element in the compound, the meaning is transparent — as indeed it would have been in the Brythonic use of *-ur*.

(Of course, the name Arthur was never modernized to **Arthwr* in Welsh. As a name, it stayed in its Brythonic form in spelling. Indeed, it had to maintain the archaic *-ur* to be parallel with the Latin *Arturus*, as the name changed from oral rallying cry to written form in history and legend.)

So what was it that the man Arthur would have been connected with? The first part of the compound is *arth*, for which the following entry is found in *Geiriadur Prifysgol Cymru* ('Dictionary of the University of Wales' — page 212):

> **arth** [H.Grn. *ors*, Gwydd. *art*: < Clt. **artos* < IE **r̥kþos*, Llad. *ursus*, Gr. ἄρκτος] *eg.b.* ll. *eirth, arthod, eirthod* ... *bear, often fig. of a rough, unmannerly or fierce person.*

In Arthur's Brythonic, the form would have been *art-* (as shown above in connection with the Latin etymology), possibly with an ending *-os* (masculine nominative singular) that would have dropped out in a compound. *Art + ur* would thus have meant 'one connected with a/the bear'. This could have referred to a bear or to a human with bear-like attributes. In addition, for those versed in the Roman interpretation of constellations, the word could also have referred to the constellation the Great Bear; although this reference would not have been necessary from the British perspective.

The compound word *Artur*(-) thus takes on a significant meaning. To the Brythonic ear, this word would have referred to the 'man of the bear'. And in the parlance of the budding feudalism of the day, the 'man of the bear' would have been the 'soldier or guardian of the bear'.

Here again, we must bear in mind the fact that this derivation of the name is no more a case of stretching etymology than is the Latin *Arturus*. Any Briton hearing the word *Artur* (or possibly *Arturos* with a nominative masculine ending) would have heard someone saying the equivalent of English *Bear-man*. If we were told that we must rally for defense around the famous *Bear-man*, we would immediately assume that this is a person with bear-like attributes that make him particularly effective as a leader in our defense. Indeed, if there had been no Arthur and the Welsh today were rallying behind a leader they called in Modern Welsh the *Arthwr*, they would hear it in exactly this way — the Bear-man. And this is just how they did hear it in the early sixth century.

Once again, people do not rally behind names of obscure etymology. This straightforward word-meaning relationship would have been just as essential to the British strategy of defense in Brythonic as it was in Latin.

The Latin/Brythonic Arthur

By using the epithet *Arturus* or *Artur*(-), the British military leader would thus have had a rallying cry that could have been heard and immediately understood both by those who spoke Latin and by those who spoke Brythonic. Not only would the word have sounded alike in both languages (especially if the Latin *-us* and the Brythonic *-os* endings were realized as the unstressed, centralized [əs]), but it would have meant the same thing: 'the guardian of the bear'.

This title or epithet would have held great

significance in the context of the early sixth century. Arthur was *dux bellorum*, the military commander-in-chief, as our earliest Latin reference calls him (Nennius, *British History*..., page 76), to whom both Briton and Romano-Briton rallied in defense against the Germanic domination. The overriding attribute he had to show was a fierce tenacity — the quality of holding one's ground. This fierce tenacity is the basic image of the bear in the ancient world, as attested in the Book of Daniel (7:4-6), in which the image is used for Persia (compare also Revelation 13:2). More pointedly for the defense of Britain, this fierce tenacity is traditionally seen in the context of protecting one's ward, as in 2 Samuel 17:8, Proverbs 17:12, and Hosea 13:8, in which the bear is portrayed as a fierce defender of her cubs. Not only would the image have been firmly established by time, but its Biblical references would have been highly appropriate for use by Christians fighting pagans.

Returning to the star Arcturus, which would have been heard by the Romano-British as *Arturus* and would have been associated in the Brythonic tongue with *Artur*(-) both in sound and in meaning, we find a rather transparent significance. As the *dux bellorum*, commander-in-chief of all leaders, Arthur would have been visualized as the most prominent star in a pair of constellations and the guardian of them all. The fact that the constellations were both northern (for Britain) and included a bear (for fierce tenacity) would have solidified the image needed for the rallying cry of British resistance.

Moreover, the frequent appearance of the bright and easily recognized star crossing the night sky would certainly have served as a reminder of Arthur faithfully riding across the island. Indeed, it is through just such an image that symbol becomes legend and legend becomes myth.

Why was there no Arthur before Arthur? Obviously, the name of the star bore no particular significance for anyone before one leader among Britons and Romano-

Britons was needed to draw together the other leaders in tenacious defense. There have been many other images that could be used for a leader in times of beleaguerment, but none that would combine the linguistic elements so that one epithet could be understood in the languages of these two peoples.

Why were there many Arthurs after Arthur? Just as obviously, the epithet of the valiant leader would have become a name in precisely the same tradition in which Augustus had become a name. One need not even know that the name refers to the 'guardian of the bear' to respect what that one guardian accomplished and to name one's son after him in the hope that the son might turn out to have the attributes of Arthur. The fact that the name does appear in the very next generation in connection with four prominent British leaders demonstrates the immediacy of this effect and the fact that it had not been a name either of a person or of a god before.

So what was Arthur's given name? This we are not to know. With the Brythonic speakers in the country and the Latin speakers in the city each probably doubtful of the other, Arthur's given name would best have been kept secret. After all, the epithet would have appealed to both groups, but a given name would have to have been one or the other; and such a choice would have been politically dangerous. Perhaps this fortunate (but quite deliberate) bilingualism also helps to account for the popularity of the new name among the command caste just one generation later.

Nor are we to know where he came from (later legends involving Tintagel, Glastonbury, etc. notwithstanding). As commander-in-chief of both the Britons and the Romano-Britons, he could not have afforded an association with one area or another. He must indeed have been, then, a military *imperator* in the oldest Roman tradition — not the king of a specific realm (compare Nennius' subsequent reference to him as *miles*

'soldier' — *British History...*, page 83). In all things, Arthur
could be neither Briton nor Romano-Briton; rather, he
and his name had ever to be both.

II. GILDAS AND ARTHUR

One of the more perplexing problems in determining
the identity of Arthur is the fact that Gildas, the one
historically reliable writer of the period, does not
mention him. When we consider his silence in light of the
fact that Gildas does go into detail on several other
British leaders, we may come away with doubts as to
whether Arthur ever indeed existed outside the realm of
legend.

In a later *Life of Saint Gildas*, the omission is
explained by a story in which Arthur kills Gildas' brother.
In vengeance, Gildas takes all references to Arthur out
of his book. Such an explanation is clumsy at best and
obviously simply a story created to explain the omission.

As we shall see below, however, there was good
reason for Gildas to avoid any direct mention of Arthur's
name. Moreover, given the meaning of the name as
determined above, we can see that Gildas probably did
make an oblique reference to the *dux bellorum*, as he
criticized another of his contemporaries.

Gildas the Prophet

In *The Ruin of Britain* (*De Excidio Britanniae*), Saint
Gildas points out that he was born in the same year as
the Battle of Badon Hill but makes no mention of the
fact that this was one of Arthur's twelve victories
(according to Nennius). This battle was fought between
about A.D. 495 and A.D. 516 (the latest date, though
doubtful, given by the *Welsh Annals*). If, as the *Welsh
Annals* (*Annales Cambriae*) suggest, Arthur died at the
Battle of Camlan between A.D. 537 and A.D. 542, then

the British leader should have had some influence on Gildas during much or most of the cleric's life (he died around A.D. 570). Indeed, if Gildas wrote his work around A.D. 540, then Arthur could have been alive during part of its composition (although he was surely dead by the time Gildas wrote of Cunaglasus — see below). While he does praise the British leader Ambrosius Aurelianus from two generations before his own, Gildas makes no direct mention of his contemporary Arthur. Why?

To escape this rather perplexing dilemma, we should ask just who Gildas was and, more importantly, how he viewed himself. Reference works typically identify Saint Gildas simply as the British monk who wrote his Complaining Book in Latin. A Breton legend also has him coming to Britanny and founding a monastery there.

For insights into how Gildas viewed himself though, we must consult his works, especially *The Ruin of Britain*. When we read such passages as the following, it is quite clear that Gildas viewed himself as a prophet in the tradition of the Hebrew Scriptures (the edition used here and throughout is that of Michael Winterbottom — *The Ruin of Britain and Other Works* — with the translation in the text, the following from pages 99 and 29):

> Reges habet Britannia, sed tyrannos; iudices habe, sed impios; saepe praedantes et concutientes, sed innocentes; vindicantes et patrocinantes, sed reos et latrones; quam plurimas coniuges habentes, sed scortas et adulterantes; crebro iurantes, sed periurantes; voventes, sed continuo propemodum mentientes; belligerantes, set civilia et iniusta bella agentes; per patriam quidem fures magnopere insectantes, sed eos qui secum ad mensam sedent non solum amantes sed et munerantes; ...

> Britain has kings, but they are tyrants; she has judges, but they are wicked. They often plunder and terrorize — the innocent; they defend and protect — the guilty and thieving; they have many wives — whores and adulteresses; they constantly swear — false oaths; they make vows — but almost at once tell lies; they wage wars — civil and unjust; they chase

thieves energetically all over the country — but love and even
reward the thieves who sit with them at table; ...

This may be compared with the prophecy of Jeremiah
(5:24-28, citing here and throughout from the New
Revised Standard Version):

> Your iniquities have turned
>   these away,
> and your sins have deprived you
>   of good.
> For scoundrels are found among
>   my people;
> they take over the gods of
>   others.
> Like fowlers they set a trap;
>   they catch human beings.
> Like a cage full of birds,
>   their houses are full of
>   treachery;
> therefore they have become great and rich,
>   they have grown fat and sleek.
> They know no limits in deeds of wickedness;
>   they do not judge with justice
> the cause of the orphan, to make
>   it prosper,
> and they do not defend the rights of the needy.

One of the most important parallels between Saint
Gildas and the Hebrew prophets was in their view of the
destruction of their country. This was invariably due to
poor leadership, a degenerate population, and a turning
from God's will. Thus, Gildas sees the ruin of Britain as
follows (*The Ruin of Britain...*, pages 96 & 25):

> Interea volente deo purgare familiam suam et tanta
> malorum labe infectam auditu tantum tribulationis emendare,
> non ignoti rumoris penniger ceu volatus arrectas omnium
> penetrat aures iamiamque adventus veterum volentium penitus
> delere et inhabitare solito more a fine usque ad terminum
> regionem. Nequaquam tamen ob hoc proficiunt, sed comparati
> iumentis insipientibus strictis, ut dicitur, morsibus rationis
> frenum offirmantes, per latum diversorum vitiorum morti
> proclive ducentem, relicto salutari licet arto itinere,

discurrebant viam.

> God, meanwhile, wished to purge his family, and to cleanse it from such an infection of evil by the mere news of trouble. The feathered flight of a not unfamiliar rumour penetrated the pricked ears of the whole people — the imminent approach of the old enemy, bent on total destruction and (as was their wont) on settlement from one end of the country to the other. But they took no profit from the news. Like foolish beasts of burden, they held fast to the bit of reason with (as people say) clenched teeth. They left the path that is narrow yet leads to salvation, and went racing down the wide way that takes one steeply down through various vices to death.

As noted above, such a prophecy of doom at the hands of an advancing enemy and brought on by the vice of the people and their leaders and by their turning away from God closely resembles those of the Hebrew prophets, who believed the kings of Judah were leading the people away from God and ever more astray. Thus, for example, Isaiah (8:6-8) railed against Judah in the following passage:

> Because this people has refused the waters of Shiloah that flow gently, and melt in fear before Rezin and the son of Remaliah; therefore, the Lord is bringing up against it the mighty flood waters of the River, the king of Assyria and all his glory; it will rise above all its channels and overflow all its banks; it will sweep on into Judah as a flood, and, pouring over, it will reach up to the neck; and its outspread wings will fill the breadth of your land, O Immanuel.

For Gildas, there were two requisites for the salvation of Britain. The one, of course, was the adherence to God's will and the abandonment of the Britons' evil ways, particularly those of their leaders. This requisite was identical with that of the Hebrew prophets after whom he modeled his own prophecy. The second requisite was in Gildas' eyes part and parcel with the first — the return to the Roman tradition in Britain. For Gildas, Rome was not only the center of the church, but also the epitome of civilization and order.

Thus, we should expect to find praise in *The Ruin of Britain* for those who fought the invading barbarians not in the ways of the native barbarians, but in those of the Roman tradition. This is the reason for his high praise for Ambrosius Aurelianus (the Welsh Emrys), who held the military position of *dux bellorum* two generations before (Gildas, *The Ruin of Britain...*, pages 98 & 28):

> ...duce Ambrosio Aureliano viro modesto, qui solus forte Romanae gentis tantae tempestatis collisione occisis in eadem parentibus purpura nimirum indutis superfuerat, cuius nunc temporibus nostris suboles magnopere avita bonitate degeneravit, vires capessunt, victores provocantes ad proelium: quis victoria domino annuente cessit.

> Their leader was Ambrosius Aurelianus, a gentleman who, perhaps alone of the Romans, had survived the shock of this notable storm: certainly his parents, who had worn the purple, were slain in it. His descendants in our day have become greatly inferior to their grandfather's excellence. Under him our people regained their strength, and challenged the victors to battle. The Lord assented, and the battle went their way.

The outspoken Romanophile Gildas praised Ambrosius Aurelianus for having established himself not as a British king, but as an old Roman *dux bellorum* or military *imperator*. Gildas considered Ambrosius Aurelianus' Roman attitude as the only way that Britain could be saved both from the Germanic domination and from the baseness of the British moral decay.

But this attitude should have justified some mention of the more recent and even contemporary *dux bellorum* Arthur. Arthur was following in the footsteps of Ambrosius Aurelianus and should have been praised by Gildas. Had he lapsed, he most certainly would have been mercilessly attacked by the British prophet. Why is there no mention of the name Arthur in the works of Gildas?

To answer this question, we should look to the Hebrew prophet Zephaniah, whom Gildas extensively quoted and who certainly formed part of the image embraced by the British prophet. In the superscript to the Book of the Prophet Zephaniah, a scribe identifies him as follows: "The word of the LORD that came to Zephaniah son of Cushi son of Gedaliah son of Amariah son of Hezekiah, in the days of King Josiah son of Amon of Judah" (Zephaniah 1:1).

So Zephaniah lived at the same time as King Josiah. According to the Hebrew Scriptures, Josiah was one of the few kings who "did what was right in the sight of the LORD, and walked in all the way of his father David; he did not turn aside to the right or to the left" (2 Kings 22:2). When the book of the law Deuteronomy was found during his reign, the king tore his clothes and set about instituting the Deuteronomic reforms with vigor and piety.

Since Josiah strove to do the Lord's will and instituted the Deuteronomic reforms that were so important to the religious establishment of Judah, we should expect extensive references to him in the recorded testament of the prophet. However, aside from the superscript added by a later scribe, there is not one single mention of Josiah's name in the entire book. It is as though he had never existed!

Nevertheless, Zephaniah (2:5) does rail against his other contemporaries in bitter passages such as the following:

> Ah, inhabitants of the seacost,
>   you nation of the Cherethites!
> The word of the LORD is
>   against you,
> O Canaan, land of the
>   Philistines;
> and I will destroy you until no
>   inhabitant is left.

Now there is no question that King Josiah existed — we know his dates and his achievements from the Hebrew Scriptures, supported by archaeological evidence.

Why then did Zephaniah mention others but not Josiah?

The Hebrew prophets saw themselves as the spokesmen for God against a people and peoples who had gone astray. Indeed, most prophecies were written to explain that previous disasters had happened as just retribution by God against those who had broken their covenant. Thus, for example, most of the prophecies on the fall of Jerusalem and the Babylonian Captivity in the Book of the Prophet Isaiah were written during the Captivity itself as a means of instructing the people in the importance of following God's will and in the disaster that occurred whenever their ancestors had strayed.

It is therefore totally out of character for a Hebrew prophet to praise a reigning or even a recent king. Even King David was severely criticized by Nathan (2 Samuel 12) for sins not at all unlike those attributed by Gildas to such leaders as Maglocunus (the Welsh Maelgwn). In fact, the prophets never accepted the authority of a king over God's people in the first place, and they were thus loath to give any support to a living or even to a recent king.

Returning to Saint Gildas, we find a Dark Ages British cleric who viewed himself as a prophet in this Hebrew tradition. The disasters that were occurring in Britain were attributable to the sins of the leaders and the moral decadence of the population. Gildas could look back to Roman rule and Romano-British leaders such as Ambrosius Aurelianus as to a golden age of order and obedience to the will of God and to the reason of (Roman) civilization. To account for the current calamities, however, he had to attribute the withdrawal of God's support to the rejection of God and of God's ways by the Britons. As such, he was prophesying precisely within the tradition of the Hebrew prophets whom he so extensively quoted.

On the other hand, how could he praise Arthur for being just what he believed was needed for the salvation of Britain? Clearly, he could not — just as Zephaniah could not praise Josiah for adhering to the will of God.

To both the British prophet and the Hebrew prophet, the doom of an advancing army of overwhelming strength had to be justified in the only way a prophet could possibly conceive — through the lapses of the leaders and the decadence of the people. Neither a valiant Roman-styled *dux bellorum* like Arthur nor a pious reformer like Josiah could even be mentioned at such a time.

Thus, given the manner in which Gildas viewed himself as a prophet of the Hebrew tradition in his times (and this is quite clear in his frequent references to them), we should not be surprised to find no direct mention of Arthur. But is there any indirect mention?

Gildas on the Bear

One very typical mark of Saint Gildas' writing is the reference to a person as an animal or other being, a characteristic that was probably widespread at the time (and that certainly had a more positive application in the naming traditions). Thus, four of the five tyrants of Britain are described as follows: Constantine as a tyrant whelp of a filthy lioness, Aurelius Caninus also as a lion whelp, Vortipor as a leopard spotted with wickedness, and Maglocunus (Maelgwn) as a dragon of the island

As for Cuneglasus (the Welsh Cynlas), however, Gildas carries his metaphor a bit further and makes a rather cryptic comment, which has traditionally been linked with Arthur (*The Ruin of Britain...*, page 31):

> Why have *you* been rolling in the filth of your past wickedness ever since your youth, you bear, rider of many and driver of the chariot of the Bear's Stronghold, despiser of God and oppressor of his lot, Cuneglasus, in Latin 'red butcher'?

This passage is even more obscure in the Latin, as follows with the problematic passage underlined (Gildas, *The Ruin of Britain...*, page 101):

> Ut quid in nequitiae tuae volveris vetusta faece et tu ab adolescentiae annis, urse. multorum sessor aurigaque currus

receptaculi ursi, dei contemptor sortisque eius depressor,
Cuneglase, Romana lingua lanio fulve?

In order to understand this reference, we must carefully
analyze it.

Gildas addresses Cuneglasus as *ursus* 'bear' (*urse* in
the vocative case). This appellation is clearly designed to
be an insult, conjuring up the explicit image of the bear
rolling in its own excrement. As noted in the first section
of this chapter, the Welsh *arth* 'bear' is used to designate
a 'rough, unmannerly, or fierce person', and the Briton
Gildas could certainly be using it in this way.

The word *multorum* is in the genitive case and can be
used possessively as 'of many' or partitively as 'among
many'. *Sessor* does not normally mean 'rider' *per se*, but
anyone who sits on or over something. It is only the
following words that evoke the translation 'rider of
many'. Indeed, it could as well mean 'ruler of many' or
'ruler among many', or it could be 'inhabitant of many
[lands]' or 'inhabitant among many [leaders]'. Given the
general negative tenor of Gildas' comments, it is likely
that the prophet is denegrating the king either by direct
insult or by a set-up. As we see next, Gildas was using
the genitive partitively and was clearly intending a set-up.

It is true that *auriga* (the *que* is simply a postposed
conjunction 'and') does mean 'driver' and is appropriate
for the driver of a chariot. However, there are other,
clearer words for 'driver' as well, and *auriga* does carry
with it a much more specialized meaning — one that has
been borrowed into English as in the following entry in
the *Oxford English Dictionary* (compact edition, page
142): **Auriga** (ǭrəi·gă) [L] A charioteer. **a.** *fig.* Leader
(*obs.*). **b.** *Astr.* One of the northern constellations, the
Waggoner...

This is a clear reference to the constellation *Ursa
Maior* 'the Great Bear' with its guardian/leader star in
Bootes known in the Late Latin of Gildas' time as
Arturus (Classical Latin *Arcturus*). As noted in the first

section of this chapter, this was the Latin name for Arthur.

In this context, *currus* is not 'chariot' as we think of it in military terms. In warfare, the chariot, which had been used by the Britons in conjunction with the infantry at the time of Julius Caesar, had long-since given way to the mounted cavalry. Speaking in the context of Arthur and his predecessors, Henry Marsh notes that "by the fourth century and by the period of the Barbarian Alliance, the cavalryman was well established" (*Arthur: Roman Britain's Last Champion*, page 41).

Even in the classical period, *currus* had been used in a more specialized sense for a victory chariot or for the victory itself (thus used as early as Cicero). While it is tempting to place some importance on the fact that the term could also refer to a plough with wheels and would thus associate the *auriga* more closely with the Wain or Plow (that is, the Great Bear) and hence to Arthur, the Latin word for this version of the constellation was not *currus*, but *plaustrum*.

Nevertheless, we have in *auriga* and in *currus* a reference to something that would have been clear to anyone versed in astrology at the time (and that would have been many, and by no means limited to the most educated or superstitious): Gildas was drawing a connection among Arthur, Cuneglasus, and the victory chariot — victorious leadership in war. To understand how this connection was intended, we must draw in the other necessary element in leaders and leadership — who it was that was being led.

The one being led was the *receptaculum ursi* 'the stronghold or refuge of the bear'. In his edition, Michael Winterbottom makes the following note (Gildas, *The Ruin of Britain...*, page 152):

BEAR'S STRONGHOLD. Gildas' Latin literally translates 'Din Eirth'. Of several strongholds so named, the best known is Dinarth near Llandudno, three miles from Deganwy, traditionally Maelgwn's fortress. If this place were meant,

Cuneglasus at one time mastered much of Maelgwn's land.

Actually, in the phrase *receptaculum ursi* the 'bear' is singular (as Winterbottom does translate it into English). As such, it would not be *Din Eirth* 'stronghold of the bears', but *Din Arth* 'stronghold of the bear'. Whether the widespread use of this designation preceded Arthur and supported his name or followed Arthur and was thus supported by his name is unclear and quite frankly unimportant. With Arthur as the *Bear-man* well established in the minds of his readers, Gildas could use this term with the confidence that his readers would indeed make the connection with Arthur. After all, *ursus* is masculine (as opposed to the feminine *ursa* which gives its name to the constellation), and the word for 'he-bear' would be appropriate for 'bear-man' as well.

But why, we may ask, did Saint Gildas not use the more transparent *artos* for 'bear', in its Late Latin form (Classical Latin *arctos*)? As we see from the Greek ending, this was a much more specialized word in Latin, used in the mythological contexts surrounding the Bear. Moreover, Gildas wished to draw a parallel between Cuneglasus the unmannerly bear and Arthur the bear with the stronghold or refuge (probably referring to undominated Britain). While mixing *ursus* and *artos* may have been more explicit, it would have been poor style and, more importantly to the British prophet, it would have been much less virulent and sarcastic. (The use of *artos*, by the way, would also have been confusing and inappropriate. After all, that was the Brythonic form of the word, too, and its use would have suggested simply a gloss of Latin *ursus*.)

Gildas' virulent sarcasm is also blatant at the end of the passage, where he says that Cuneglasus' name in Latin means 'yellow butcher' (translated by Winterbottom as 'red butcher'). The name actually means 'blue dog' — a fact that could hardly have escaped the Romano-British prophet. By changing 'dog' to 'butcher', Gildas discards the established image of loyalty and nobility connected with the dog in naming in favor of the far less palatable image of the dog as a ripper of meat; by changing 'blue' to 'yellow', he replaces a noble color with its opposite.

From this obvious sarcasm and the awkwardness of the passage if taken at face value, we can conclude that Gildas' use of language here was indeed cryptic. So what was Gildas saying in this cryptic and apparently awkward passage? This nebulous phrasing becomes quite clear when we take the position that Gildas was making a veiled reference to Arthur — veiled enough to make the point against Cuneglasus without the prophet's having to praise a recent leader and thus soften his calumny against the Britons. What Gildas was saying can be illuminated as follows, spelling out the full impact of his sarcasm:

> You unmannerly and filthy bear, only one among many yet [fashioning yourself as the new Arthur] taking credit for being the victorious leader of the stronghold of the Bear [the British refuge of Arthur].

Such an interpretation is fully in keeping with the Latin of Gildas and far more in keeping with the general tenor of his criticism. In this manner, he could use Arthur's well-known success in battle and his adherence to Roman tradition to put down a contemporary barbarian without having to interrupt his criticism with uncomfortable praise for a recent leader who appealed to the rustic barbarian Britons as well as to the civilized Romano-Britons.

Of course, this interpretation is conjectural. Nonetheless, the passage is awkward and cryptic enough to require interpretation. And this interpretation credits Gildas with consistence both in his Latin and in his prophesying.

Conclusion

This interpretation of Saint Gildas' comments on

Cuneglasus thus sheds light on one of the great mysteries of the age of Arthur: Why did the most reliable historian of the time not mention Arthur's name?

On the one hand, he could not have made reference outright to someone who would have contradicted his basic premise and the entire character of his prophecy in the tradition of the Hebrew Scriptures. Just as it would have been impossible for Zephaniah to mention Josiah, so it was impossible for Gildas to mention Arthur.

Yet Arthur did present a tempting foil to the degeneracy of his contemporary Britons, a foil more effective and more recent than Ambrosius Aurelianus. This temptation makes the above interpretation of Gildas' comments on Cuneglasus (by no means a new one) all the more convincing. Nevertheless, he had to be circumspect in his reference, allowing the reader to draw conclusions from his obviously cryptic passage. In this way, the sarcastic criticism against Cuneglasus was perhaps even more effective, for it forced the reader into the position of applying the judgment of the virtuous and victorious Arthur against the vile and pretentious Cuneglasus.

III. CONCLUSION: ARTHUR AS ARTHUR

So Arthur was the *dux bellorum* — the military *imperator* — of a combined army from several regions of unknown size, but certainly including rural Britons and urban Romano-Britons. The fact that he is mentioned by Aneirin well within a century and within the living memory of Aneirin's elders indicates that he must have been a rather impressive figure — not the mere leader of a war band, as he is sometimes portrayed by those who would go to extremes to counter the legend of his having been King of the Britons.

As for the great and mighty king who invaded Gaul

to fight his Germanic enemies and to pursue or protect the emperor of Rome (depending upon the version), this was not Arthur; but it may have been someone a century before him by the name or title of Riothamus, derived from Brythonic *rigotamos* 'high king'. In this respect, Geoffrey Ashe raises some interested hypotheses in his *Kings and Queens of Early Britain* (a book which is well worth reading).

Following Ashe's argument, according to Jordanes in his *Gothic History*, Riot(h)amus the High King of the Britons [or Bretons] invaded Gaul around A.D. 467 to support Rome against the Visigoths. Near Bituriges he was attacked by the Visigothic King Euric, and he fled to Burgundy. There, according also to Gregory of Tours, he was decisively defeated and disappeared, probably being killed. It is this Riothamus that Ashe claims to have been Arthur. This claim is supposedly corroborated in the Breton *Legend of Saint Goeznovius* by an author known simply as William. William recounts the exploits of Riothamus, with the high king identified by the name Arthur.

There are some problems with the Riothamus hypothesis, however. William was writing legend in the eleventh century and was striving to relate the Britons with the Bretons. His account can therefore not be considered terribly more reliable than that of Geoffrey of Monmouth.

The legend is further complicated by the fact that one hundred years before Riothamus, a Spanish Roman claimant to the imperial throne, Magnus Clemens Maximus, invaded Europe from Britain in an attempt to seize full power. His exploits and his ultimate fate vaguely resembled those of Riothamus (William's Arthur), further muddling the picture. Moreover, the Welsh seized upon Maximus' British connection, weaving the *Dream of Macsen Wledig* in the Medieval collection of the *Mabinogion* out of it and giving him definite Arthurian attributes.

On the other hand, both Jordanes and Gregory were

writing in the sixth century. Although they were contemporary with Arthur, they made no such connection, allowing for the conclusion that Arthur did not really exist in the sixth century. However, their concern was not with the internal situation among the Britons, but with the Goths and Franks.

The story of Riothamus as it appears in *The Legend of Saint Goeznovius* and the history and legends of Maximus in the *Dream of Macsen Wledig* are obvious sources for Arthur's continental exploits in Geoffrey of Monmouth's *History of the Kings of Britain* (*Historia Regum Britanniae*). What we must be very careful to keep from doing, though, is to claim that Riothamus or any other such source *was* Arthur. Riothamus was not Arthur for Aneirin, nor for the author of the *Welsh Annals*, nor for Nennius. It was not until William and Geoffrey (as far as we know) that the two figures were merged into one legend.

Here let us recall what Geoffrey did with Myrddin in turning him into Merlin. The legend that Myrddin confronted Vortigern and prophesied about the dragons battling under the ground was originally attributed to Ambrosius Aurelianus in the generation before Arthur. The real, historical Myrddin did not make his appearance until a generation after Arthur. While it is often convenient to refer to the first "Myrddin" (the false Myrddin, or Merlin) in Welsh as *Myrddin Emrys* 'Ambrosius Myrddin' and to the second as *Myrddin Wyllt* 'Wild Myrddin' (or in Latin as *Myrddin Silvestris* 'Myrddin of the Forest'), the fact is that historically only the second Myrddin was Myrddin — the first "Myrddin" was (the legendary) Ambrosius Aurelianus.

In our treatments of history and even in our scholarly examinations of legend, we make an attempt to keep the two Myrddin figures separate. Ambrosius Aurelianus was Ambrosius Aurelianus, not Myrddin. We never refer to Ambrosius Aurelianus as an insane, albeit reputedly excellent poet and prophet; nor do we refer to Myrddin as a mighty *dux bellorum*. When Geoffrey (on his own or influenced by earlier works) combined the two into the fanciful Merlin figure who was told to have lived between the two actual figures, he did so for the sake of literary legend, not of historical understanding. And we appreciate this.

Now, let us approach Arthur in the same way. Riothamus was Riothamus, not Arthur. We ought not to refer to Riothamus as a *dux bellorum* at the Battle of Mount Badon in the sixth century; nor ought we to refer to Arthur as a high king who invaded Gaul. That Geoffrey combined the two (and more) into one monumental giant of legend should be recognized as a device of semihistorical fictional literature, not as historical fact.

The fact is that our Arthur — and Aneirin's Arthur, and the *Welsh Annals'* Arthur, and Nennius' Arthur — lived in the early sixth century, was a great military leader, and gave rise to legends of his own before his legends were combined with those of Riothamus, Maximus, and others. In all of this, then, we need to distinguish among three types of history — actual history, factual history, and virtual history.

CHAPTER 6

HISTORY:
ACTUAL, FACTUAL, VIRTUAL

The relationship between Arthur, Riothamus, and Maximus provides us with a valuable insight into the nature of history. At some time there is a person who performs some action. Those who are eye-witnesses to the person and to the action have a unique and privileged position in history, for they have witnessed the part of history that involves the deed or act. We can call this facet of history *actual history*.

Once the witnesses attempt to relate the actual event, however, the entire nature of history changes. They cannot relate all that they have seen; nor can they relate all aspects of the action, for they themselves were limited in their view of events (they did not see everything). Moreover they interpret the action in the light of their own experiences and attitudes, further limiting what they report to what they feel is important (and not personally embarrassing). Thus, when the witnesses relate a story or when later compilers simply relay it, they make the action into a comprehended and comprehensible form. We can call this "made" history *factual history*.

When factual accounts are passed on though, the nature of history may change once again. Later commentators have their own agenda quite apart from those of the writers of factual history. Rather than relating the history, they may simply use the history to serve these agenda — to comment not on the events as they were perceived to have occurred in the past, but as they reflect on contemporary issues. This is history that must be believed to be counted as history at all, and we can thus call it *virtual history*.

The Actual History

The actual history of Arthur and of his contemporaries is, of course, lost to us forever, for there is no way that we can witness the actions that took place in the sixth century and form our own ideas about what happened. Outside of factual history, the closest we can come to the action is in examining the "actual" remains — the artifacts.

This is what archaeologists attempt to do when they probe sites connected with historical figures. Needless to say, archaeologists also must rely upon written records — upon factual or even virtual history — to determine where to look and what to expect. With no guidance whatsoever, they would have to comb the entire island for artifacts. And once they found a sword or a shield that could have belonged to Arthur, they would have no particular reason for assuming that it did in fact belong to Arthur — or to that Arthur in whom they are interested. The Medieval experience with religious relics has convinced most of us not to place great faith in local traditions or even in affidavits of authenticity in determining the historical validity of an artifact.

The next best "physical" evidence we have is something we do not, as creatures of the late twentieth century, generally acknowledge as concrete (although, to be sure, earlier cultures have viewed it so). This evidence is the name itself. If the name is recorded within living memory, it becomes as reliable as the physical evidence is for the archaeologist. Certainly, we are not always sure that the name fits the person being described (as Geoffrey of Monmouth's stories so aptly demonstrate). Furthermore, the form of the name may have changed even in a brief period. But then, the archaeologist's physical evidence undergoes change from the moment of manufacture.

In treating names as actual historical evidence then, we must be extremely careful to keep our vision as limited and as focused as possible. There are indeed scholars who would attribute characteristics of the fictional sorcerer named Merlin to the poet named Myrddin on the basis of whatever meanings a word like *merlin* might have had, in spite of the fact that the name never coincided with the individual. This would be tantamount to an archaeologist's claiming "New Age" philosophical and psychic attributes for Stonehenge.

The name can only mean what it could have meant to those who witnessed the actual history. This is why in this study we have taken pains to see what Arthur's name would have meant neither to Geoffrey of Monmouth nor to Cicero, but only to those inhabitants of Britain who spoke Brythonic and/or Late Latin in the early sixth century.

In the case of the Dark-Age Arthur and the others discussed in the previous chapters, the name as it appears in *Canu Aneirin* is the only piece of actual historical evidence we have. No other physical evidence can be so closely linked so early in history with the figures themselves. Certainly the traditional stories cannot, for they have already passed out of the realm of actual history and into (or through) factual, recounted history.

The Factual History

As for Arthur himself, depending upon how stringent we wish to be, we can admit little reliable factual history aside from the mention in *Canu Aneirin* — at least little direct factual history. This is certainly not to say that the writings attributed to Nennius and to the author(s) of the *Welsh Annals* were derived only from sources of legend — from virtual history. It is most likely that the names and dates associated with Arthur were available to these writers, and the simple relaying of such factual history certainly qualifies as factual history itself. But the evidence is very scanty, and the authors were far enough removed from the action and certainly exposed to enough stories (as the plethora of Arthurs in the next generation suggests), that these historians had to make a conscious decision on what to believe and what not to believe. Of course, since they were attempting to write as reliable a history as possible rather than legend or virtual history (as opposed to Geoffrey of Monmouth who freely added and blended to make his own, contemporary points), they certainly ought not to be dismissed. After all, even factual history as such involves a great element of belief and intentional inclusion and exclusion.

An example of intentional exclusion in factual history is certainly to be found in Gildas' *The Ruin of Britain*. That there should have been no "good" Christian in the estimation of the saint among all the inhabitants of Britain within an entire generation is totally preposterous. Gildas, in keeping with his self-image as the modern British Hebrew prophet of God, could not bring himself to admit anything in his Britain save sin, treachery, and iniquity.

Yet, Saint Gildas was there, and the history he produced was indeed factual history. In this regard, we must be careful in defining the word *factual* very precisely. A fact is not the action itself; but rather, it is something that has been made. As noted by the great German philosopher, author, and scientist Johann Wolfgang von Goethe, there are no facts independent of theory — they are all created and perceived by people with particular understandings (and agenda!).

The single most reliable bit of factual history regarding the names from the dawn of British legend is found in Aneirin's eulogies. Of course, there may have been changes made to the poems between the seventh and thirteenth centuries apart from simple modernizations of the orthography. But since they demonstrate through the lack of mesotomy (which would have been invisible and therefore inalterable in transmission) that they do indeed originate in Late

Brythonic, the burden of proof must lie with those who would claim that certain passages were added later. In the case of Arthur, Myrddin, and Taliesin, no such proof has been forthcoming.

Of the names under study, the evidence to support the name Aneirin is certainly the most extensive insofar as the factual history of *Canu Aneirin* is concerned. Obviously, Aneirin was giving his account of his own participation in events and was therefore working from a definite and definable point of view — he had his own agenda. Nonetheless, he has provided us with enough factual history to determine the crucial bit of actual history: the meaning of his name.

Through this factual history, we gain insights into another piece of actual history: the meaning of Myrddin's name. To support this, however, we must rely upon yet more references — references in the *Black Book of Carmarthen*. Here again, we find ourselves in the same position as with Arthur and Nennius, and we drift dangerously close to virtual history. However, the single reference for Myrddin in the *Gododdin* provides us with the limitation of vision we need to deduce *plausible* actual history from factual history (of course, "real" actual history is quite beyond our grasp). Those references in the later work that support the interpretation of Aneirin, who was a contemporary of Myrddin after all, can be examined.

As for Taliesin, the factual evidence abounds, for we have writings by people claiming to be Taliesin(s) throughout the early centuries of Welsh literature. What we can deduce from their writings — from their factual histories (at least their histories of themselves) — fully supports the context in which Aneirin uses the name/epithet/metaphor. The identity of any one of them as an individual with his own name, of course, is a bit of actual history we can never attain, and it will not even enter into history at all until some reliable manuscript is discovered with an individual name. As we have seen in chapter 2, however, such a discovery is unlikely, since *who* was not as important as *what* to the Medieval poet.

All the rest of what we know about Taliesin, Aneirin, Myrddin (Merlin), and Arthur comes not from factual history but from virtual history. At this point then, we must leave the safe but terribly limited realm of factual history that has been the underpinning of this work and comment about the vast expanse of virtual history that has developed and is still developing in the guise of modern fantasy literature directly and (usually) indirectly from the written facts.

The Virtual History

Virtual history is the most difficult form of history for the late twentieth-century mind to comprehend, at least from the standpoint of "history *per se*" (which, as we see even in factual history, is a rather elusive concept in itself). To us, the very idea of embellishing facts with one's own beliefs simply does not qualify as history.

Concerns about "rewriting history" though, are only a very recent development among "scientific historians." To historians in ages past, history was simply a vehicle for getting beyond the facts and to the broader human truths. Thus, for example, the first historian Thucydides in his account of the Peloponnesian War could manufacture a speech by Pericles without worrying whether those exact words were used or even if a speech had been given at all. The speech was merely a vehicle for Thucydides to illustrate the attitudes and the broader issues and events of the time.

This is history in its original form — a story about humans. Whether the details of the story are used to make an attempt at recreating the action (which, of course, is technically impossible) or they are used or even manufactured just to tell us something about the human condition is a matter of outlook for the historian — what it is about humanity that the historian is trying to convey.

This is the aspect of humanity that we today relegate to the historical novel (a word betraying its very recent development) — an aspect that previous generations counted in the domain of history itself.

The fact is that "scientific history" (as we think we know it) is of no avail when we must delve into past histories of Arthur. Geoffrey of Monmouth's *History of the Kings of Britain* is indeed history. But it is not what actually happened — it is not actual history (which, again, it cannot be); nor is it an eye-witness account or an account relaying eye-witness testimony or records — it is not factual history. What it is is virtual history.

When we speak of virtual history in the Arthurian tradition, we are speaking of *legend* in the most technical sense: virtual history centered upon a human. Like *myth*, which in its technical and theological sense is virtual history relating humans with the divine, it is not "false," but it is by its very nature concerned with "truth," regardless of the "facts." As such, it must be believed in order to be history — hence the term *virtual* history.

In this sense, Geoffrey of Monmouth and the other Medieval "story tellers" (historians) were most assuredly writing history. But theirs was history written to pass on the truths in which they believed — truths about human nature, truths about the feelings of the Britons, truths about their aspirations and indeed about the aspirations of humanity in general. So long as we read these histories as statements of truth, then they are history; and so long as we believe these statements, to be reliable vehicles of truth (at least for the historians who wrote them), then they are accurate history.

This is a far different thing from accepting these histories as statements of fact — as factual history. They were never intended to be factual history, for such a pedestrial approach to truth was frankly beneath the dignity of the Medieval historian. To us today, such a practice would be considered a "lowering of standards" by a modern historian, and it would surely amount to academic purgery.

Now that we have placed Geoffrey of Monmouth into proper perspective as an historian, let us return to the present to recognize that although he was an historian appropriate to his time, he would not be an historian appropriate to ours. Our goal in history — what we mean by the very word history today — is not virtual history or legend (or myth, which unfortunately carries with it today a connotation of falseness, alien to its very nature), but a reconstruction of a possible and appropriate factual history — the reconstruction of events as they could conceivably have been reported by an eye-witness.

When it comes to virtual history within the context of modern historical research, we must be very careful to keep explicit both the various types of history and our purposes in studying them. If we are tracing events in virtual history, we must always keep the fact before us that we are dealing with people's beliefs and values as applied to a story, not with events as they occurred in actual history and as they were reported in factual history. The virtual historian will use factual history only as a starting point to make a contemporary statement, much as the writer of fantasy literature today will use a fanciful Medieval world to make a statement about the society of the writer — not about that of the hypothetical world and certainly not about some real "historical" Medieval society.

When we fail to keep virtual and factual history separate, we run the risk of making conclusions about actual history that have no basis in events, but only in virtual history itself. For example, the works of Norma Lorre Goodrich are often dismissed in scholarly circles for falling into this very trap. She makes conclusions about the "historical" Arthur that are contradictory to one another and contradictory to the evidence we have of the people, places, and times. That is, the conclusions are contradictory so long as we assume that she is discussing what we call history. If, on the other hand, we recognize that she is tracing Arthur not through factual historical records to reconstruct the actual Arthur, but through virtual historical works to reconstruct the legendary types and sources, then her work becomes not only valid, but quite valuable indeed.

Unfortunately, Goodrich claims to be searching for the actual Arthur through the virtual sources. Although this route provides insights into the values and beliefs of the writers of legend, it yields little insight into the events of the sixth century. Of course, her works ought not to be abandoned, for they provide extensive probes into virtual history, which by its very nature is frought with confusions and contradictions, and we are always in need of guides. Such works simply must be placed in their proper niche and kept in perspective.

This is also not to say that there is no factual evidence in the virtual history. Indeed, there may well be some story in the legends of Arthur that reflects an actual event and that can be recognized, if we only can discover the key to recognizing it. We will not find a reliable key in the virtual histories themselves, however, for we do not know what we can trust.

To find reliable information in the legends of Arthur, we must probe in the other direction. We must begin with the actual historical residue — the names and archaeological evidence — and justify it in the factual historical records written about Arthur or at least revealing the situation at his time. Only then can we examine the virtual historical legends to see what might possibly be reliable. Of course, working in this direction provides very little information, but what information it provides is the most trustworthy information we can find.

Conclusion and Beginning

This work, then, is both a conclusion about names from the dawn of British legend and a beginning of a more reliable probe into that legend. What can we conclude about those people and events of the sixth century from the actual historical names and the archaeological evidence and from the reliably factual historical written records?

We can conclude that Taliesin was not the name of one particular individual. Now at any one time, a writer could refer to Taliesin as a particular individual, and an individual could refer to himself as Taliesin, so long as the Taliesin was the epitome of the warrior poet in the service of a mighty lord and/or a crowned bard. Who was Aneirin's Taliesin? We have no idea, but we know from the very name (actual history) all that we need to know to understand what Aneirin wrote (factual history).

We can conclude that Aneirin was a very accomplished poet from the quality of his work, which is — as are all records — an artifact (actual history). We can conclude from the content of his record (his factual history) that he was present at the Battle of Catraeth, was captured, wrote a series of elegies (eulogies) for his fallen comrades (parishioners/penitents), and was rescued. We can conclude from his epithet "the Noncombatant" (actual history) within the context of the record that he was a priest, or at least some member of the clergy with the responsibility to perform the eucharist and to compose the liturgical eulogy — one form of *gwenwawd* 'holy song'.

We can conclude that Myrddin was Aneirin's predecessor in disaster. From Aneirin's record within a generation (factual history), we know he was also a member of the clergy, also with the responsibility for writing a *gwenwawd* for those who fell in the Battle of Arfderydd (factual history). This is corroborated by his name (actual history) which is firmly within the tradition of the Christian "Waterman" (factual history). More information depends upon the nature of the *Black Book of Carmarthen*, which if it indeed contains the appropriate factual history, identifies Myrddin as a warrior-turned-cleric who fled to the monastery/retreat in a state of insanity (or more precisely, showing extreme signs of Post-traumatic Stress Disorder).

Finally, we can conclude that Arthur may have been a *dux bellorum* (Nennius' conclusion from plausibly factual history) but was certainly a dreadfully effective warrior (Aneirin's factual history) who did not share in the "barbaric sins" of the Britons (Gildas' omission). Above all he was a rallying point for both the Britons and the Romano-Britons, which can be concluded from the unique construction of his name (actual history) recorded by Aneirin and evident in the written records of names in the very next generation after Arthur.

These were the people who lived in dawn of British legend — in the Dark Ages of Britain. They formed the basis for the legends we recalled at the very beginning of this book — the romantic King Arthur of the Round Table (indeed, the very word "romantic" conjures up the novel and the long tradition of virtual history). They have been merged with many other sources, each with its own actual and factual histories: Myrddin has been merged with Ambrosius Aurelianus and others to form Merlin; Arthur has been merged with Riothamus, Maximus, and others to form the High King. And, of course, the virtual historians have added and emended the record to produce their own appropriate form of history — history used not to discover earlier people and events, but to reflect upon contemporary people and events and upon the human condition in general.

Where can we find these actual people portraying themselves in the many pages of legend? That is a question far beyond this linguist tied to words and names, sound changes and etymologies. It is a question for all of us with our many different talents and views of the legend of Arthur, for we stand at the beginning of some new understanding that we all must work to achieve. Let us return to those legends we know so dearly and read them again with new insights but with the same old fascination.

SELECTED BIBLIOGRAPHY

The following selections are limited to those that have had a direct influence on this current work and to those that are referenced directly enough in the text that the reader might check this bibliography while reading some particularly provocative section in the book. Of course, since general introductions abound and are so easily found in a library card catalog, they are not included here.

I. Editions

Most of the following editions contain a wealth of information about the works, the historical and literary background, the author, and technical aspects of the literature. The editions of the Medieval Welsh texts also include detailed discussions of individual words, phrases, and passages.

Bromwich, Rachel (ed.). *Trioedd Ynys Prydein: The Welsh Triads.* 2nd ed. Cardiff: University of Wales Press, 1978.

Evans, J. Gwenogvryn (ed.). *Facsimile and Text of the Book of Taliesin.* Llanbedrog, 1910.

Ford, Patrick K. (ed.). *The Poetry of Llywarch Hen.* Berkeley: University of California Press, 1974.

Geoffrey of Monmouth. *Galfredi Monumetensis: Historia Britonum.* Ed. by J.A. Giles. Caxton Society, 1844. [Rpt. 1967. New York: Burt Franklin]

Geoffrey of Monmouth. *The History of the Kings of Britain.* Trans. by Lewis Thorpe. London: Penguin, 1966.

Gildas. *The Ruin of Britain and Other Works.* Ed. and trans. by Michael Winterbottom. London: Phillimore, 1978

Huws, Daniel (ed.). *Llyfr Aneirin: A Facsimile.* Aberystwyth: National Library of Wales, 1989.

Jackson, Kenneth H. (ed.). *The Gododdin: The Oldest Scottish Poem.* Edinburgh: Edinburgh University Press, 1969.

Jarman, A.O.H. (ed.). *Aneirin: Y Gododdin. Britain's Oldest Heroic Poem.* Llandysul: Gomer, 1990.

Jones, Gwyn, and Thomas Jones (eds.). *The Mabinogion.* London: Dent, 1966.

Nennius. *British History and The Welsh Annals,* ed by John Morris. London: Phillimore, 1980.

Pennar, Meirion (ed.). *Taliesin Poems.* Felinfach (Dyfed): Llanerch Enterprises, 1988.

Pennar, Meirion (ed.). *The Black Book of Carmarthen.* Felinfach (Dyfed): Llanerch Enterprises, 1989.

Williams, Hugh (ed.). *Two Lives of Gildas.* Felinfach (Dyfed): Llanerch Enterprises.

Williams, Ifor (ed.). *Canu Llywarch Hen.* Cardiff: University of Wales Press, 1935.

Williams, Ifor (ed.). *Canu Aneirin.* Cardiff: University of Wales Press, 1938.

Williams, Ifor (ed.). *Pedeir Keinc y Mabinogi,* 2nd ed. Cardiff: University of Wales Press, 1951.

Williams, Ifor (ed.). *Chwedl Taliesin.* Cardiff: University of Wales Press, 1957.

Williams, Ifor (ed.). *The Poems of Taliesin.* English ed. by J.E. Caerwyn Williams. Dublin: Dublin Institute for Advanced Studies, 1968.

Williams, Ifor (ed.). *Armes Prydein: The Prophecy of Britain.* English ed. by Rachel Bromwich. Dublin: Dublin Institute for Advanced Studies, 1972.

Wright, Thomas (ed.). *The Historical Works of Giraldus Cambrensis.* London: George Bell and Sons, 1881.

II. Secondary Works on Arthurian Literature and History

While there is a host of secondary literature on Arthurian legend, the following are, once again, limited to those works that have had the most direct effect on this current volume.

Ashe, Geoffrey. *Kings and Queens of Early Britain.* Chicago: Academy Chicago Publishers, 1990.

Bowen, E.G. *Saints, Seaways, and Settlements in the Celtic Lands.* Cardiff: University of Wales Press.

Chadwick, Nora K. (ed.). *Studies in the Early British Church.* Cambridge: Cambridge University Press, 1958.

Chadwick, Nora K. *Celtic Britain.* London: Thames and Hudson, 1963.

Chadwick, Nora K. *The British Heroic Age: The Welsh and the Men of the North.* Cardiff: University of Wales Press, 1976.

Chadwick, Nora K. "The British or Celtic Part in the Population of England." *Angles and Britons: O'Donnell Lectures,* 111-147. Cardiff: University of Wales Press, 1963.

Gribben, Arthur. *Holy Wells and Sacred Water Sources in Britain and Ireland: An Annotated Bibliography.* New York: Garland, 1992.

Lacy, Norris J. (ed.). *The Arthurian Encyclopedia.* New York: Peter Bedrick Books, 1986.

Laing, Lloyd, and Jennifer Laing. *Celtic Britain and Ireland: The Myth of the Dark Ages.* New York: St Martin's Press, 1990.

Marsh, Henry. 1967. *Arthur: Roman Britain's Last Champion.* Newton Abbot (Devon): David & Charles, 1967.

McNeill, John T. *The Celtic Churches: A History A.D. 200 to 1200.* Chicago, University of Chicago Press, 1974.

Rhŷs, John. *Studies in the Arthurian Legend.* Oxford: Clarendon, 1891.

Stephens, Meic (ed.). *The Oxford Companion to the Literature of Wales.* New York: Oxford University Press, 1986.

Williams, Ifor. *The Beginning of Welsh Poetry.* Ed. by Rachel Bromwich. Cardiff: University of Wales Press, 1980.

III. Linguistics and Poetics

The following selections are limited to works on the language and poetics (the rules of poetic form) that directly support this book.

Bromwich, Rachel, and R. Brinley Jones (eds.). *Astudiaeth ar yr Hengerdd: Studies in Old Welsh Poetry.* Cardiff: University of Wales Press, 1978.

Carlton, Charles Merritt. *A Linguistic Analysis of a Collection of Late Latin Documents Composed in Ravenna between A.D. 445-700: A Quantitative Approach.* The Hague: Mouton, 1973.

Evans, D. Ellis. "Rhagarweiniad i astudiaeth o fydryddiaeth Y Gododdin." In: Bromwich and Jones, *Astudiaeth ar yr Hengerdd: Studies in Old Welsh Poetry,* pages 89-122.

Evans, D. Simon. "Iaith Y Gododdin." In: Bromwich and Jones, *Astudiaeth ar yr Hengerdd: Studies in Old Welsh Poetry,* pages 72-88,

Evans, D. Simon. *A Grammar of Middle Welsh.* Dublin: Dublin Institute for Advanced Studies, 1964.

Griffen, Toby D. *Aspects of Dynamic Phonology.* Amsterdam: Benjamins, 1985.

Griffen, Toby D. "Generic Consonant Correspondences in *Canu Aneirin.*" *Journal of Celtic Linguistics* 2, 93-105, 1993.

Griffen, Toby D. (ed.). *The Linguistics of Welsh Literature*. Special issue of *Language Sciences*, vol 15, 1993

Griffen, Toby D. "Mesotomic Syllables in *Armes Prydein*." In: Griffen, *The Linguistics of Welsh Literature*, 91-106, 1993.

Jackson, Kenneth H. *Language and History in Early Britain*. Edinburgh: Edinburgh University Press, 1953.

Klar, Kathryn, Brendan O Hehir, and Eve Sweetser. "Welsh poetics in the Indo-European Tradition." *Studia Celtica* 18/19, 30-51, 1983/84.

Koch, John T. "When Was Welsh Literature First Written Down?" *Studia Celtica* 20/21, 43-66, 1985/86.

Koch, John T. "Thoughts on the Ur-*Godoδin*: Rethinking Aneirin and Mynyδawc Mwynvawr." In: Griffen, *The Linguistics of Welsh Literature*, pages 81-89.

Lewis, Henry, and Holger Pedersen. *A Concise Comparative Celtic Grammar*. 3rd ed. Göttingen: Vandenhoeck and Ruprecht, 1974.

Morris Jones, John. *A Welsh Grammar: Historical and Comparative*. Oxford: Clarendon, 1913.

Morris Jones, John. *Cerdd Dafod*. Oxford: Clarendon, 1925.

Travis, James. *Early Celtic Versecraft*, 2nd ed. Ithaca: Cornell University Press, 1973.

Watkins, T. Arwyn. *Ieithyddiaeth: Agweddau ar Astudio Iaith*. Cardiff: University of Wales Press, 1961.

Williams, G.J., and E.J. Jones. *Gramadegau'r Penceirddiaidd*. Cardiff: University of Wales Press, 1934.

IV. Dictionaries

Finally, the following two dictionaries are extensively referenced in the text. Other lexical references can be found in section III, especially Morris Jones, *A Welsh Grammar*; Jackson, *Language and History in Early Britain*; and Lewis and Pedersen, *A Concise Comparative Celtic Grammar*.

Geiriadur Prifysgol Cymru. Volumes I & II. Cardiff: University of Wales Press, 1967 & 1987.

The Compact Edition of the Oxford English Dictionary. New York: Oxford University Press, 1971.